MEMORIES

IN THE

DRIFT

ALSO BY MELISSA PAYNE

The Secrets of Lost Stones

MEMORIES

IN THE

DRIFT

A Novel

MELISSA PAYNE

LAKE UNION
PUBLISHING

Published by Lake Union Publishing, Seattle

www.apub.com

Amazon, the Amazon logo, and Lake Union Publishing are trademarks of Amazon.com, Inc., or its affiliates.

ISBN-13: 9781542004725
ISBN-10: 1542004721

Cover design by David Drummond

Printed in the United States of America

For Mom and Dad:
your love, guidance, and wisdom are a bottomless well
from which I am forever pulling.

CHAPTER ONE

Claire, thirty-six years old
Thursday, September 27

I am staring at my hands. My face is wet. For a minute, the chaos of questions inside my head is a deafening roar that drowns out the rhythm of my heartbeat. I breathe in; I breathe out, slow and controlled, letting the facts accumulate until I can put together enough pieces to understand my present situation. I wipe my face dry and sit up straight.

First fact: I'm in my apartment in front of my desk with the wide window that overlooks the harbor of the Passage Canal. I glance down at my body to find that I am dressed in jeans and my University of Alaska sweatshirt. Also, I'm wearing purple ankle socks. Second fact: I wear purple socks only on Thursday, so it must be a Thursday. The sock thing started when I was a little girl and I wanted to remember the days so I could keep track of when my father would return from his job as a long-haul trucker. Now it's a habit that comes in handy for a situation like this.

Outside, it is not dark but not bright, either, which means, in Alaska, that it's either morning or afternoon and not the dead of winter, when the light never brightens enough to be called day. I check my phone for the time. Bingo. Afternoon. I sit back in my swivel chair and survey my desk. From the looks of it, I was in the middle of recording the earlier part of my day and planning for the rest of it. My forehead wrinkles and I make a note of what I was doing inside the notebook that lies open on the desk. Something sticks out of my sweatshirt pocket, but when I reach for it, a sensation that stops my hand overwhelms me. I swallow past a stubborn lump and instead turn back to the work at hand. My notes.

Third fact (and one that doesn't surprise me): I am well known in my small Alaskan town. Not for any particular accomplishment or feat of strength or intellectual achievements, unless you count the sock thing. I am the woman with no short-term memory from the fourteenth floor. And I know this because it's written in my notebook, just above a bulleted list of To Do items I intend to complete this afternoon. Fortunately for me, the event that took my memory didn't affect my exceptional organizational skills, which helped me sail through undergrad and grad school and now, today, allow me to structure my day with confidence even when I find myself staring at my hands for no reason. I know this because it's all in my notes, and because it's a skill I've honed since I was a little girl, when my mother couldn't leave her bedroom for weeks on end, and it was garbage day or laundry day or any day where something needed to get done.

But I'm not going to think about my mother right now, because those thoughts take me down a rabbit hole where sadness sticks to the walls in hardened globs of old gum that break my fingernails when I try to scrape them off. Instead, I turn my thoughts to Dad, and already I'm breathing easier.

My father happens to be a legend here in Whittier and not just for his size; he stands well over six and a half feet tall, with shoulders nearly as broad as the hallway. But mostly for his compassion and mountain-man willingness to pull a stranger's car out of an icy ditch in the middle of the night, haul off an abusive husband, or chase away a bear from the lobby of our building. When I was a little girl, I asked him how he always seemed to be in the right place at the right time. *Learn to listen, Claire,* he'd say, and his eyes crinkled with his smile. *To this*—he'd point to my stomach—*and always to this*—he'd point to my heart. *It won't let you down.* Then he'd wrap me in his arms, and I'd lay my head against his chest, listening to the steady *thump, thump* of his heart beneath his thick plaid shirt.

I turn on a lamp by my desk—clouds have spilled over the mountains, straining the sun's already feeble light—and my apartment window creaks against an onslaught of wind. Goose bumps prick the skin on my arms and cool the warmth of the memory. Soon the last cruise ship of the season will sail out of town, the seasonal employees will pack up and leave, and the businesses that line the harbor will shutter their windows for the long, dark winter, when the rain turns to snow and the wind that buffets the window will be the Alaskan kind that can freeze a person's nose off. I turn my attention to my notebook and read an instructional line: *You are hosting dinner tonight.* I smile when I see the next line: *Recipe and ingredients in the fridge.* Good. Cooking will keep my hands busy, my mind focused. Plus, it will be good to see my friends. An uneasiness unfurls deep inside me. Today it feels like I *need* to see them. I have a feeling I can't explain, something that ripples just under my skin. Sadness. I run a hand through my short blonde hair, frustrated because I don't know why I feel this way, and it bothers me to admit that, even if it's just to myself. It's like brushing snow off the ground and discovering that I'm standing on a thin sheet of ice with nothing but a deep black emptiness beneath my feet.

Today that feeling is combined with this persistent sense that I'm sad with no idea why. But then I rest my hands across my notebook, and the heavy weight of not knowing lifts the tiniest bit. It's okay, because everything I need to know is here. From me. In my handwriting. And if I can't trust my memory, I can always trust my notes.

I flip backward through the notebook, searching for something, anything, to explain why my throat closes around a sob that I choke down. There are lines and lines of observations and information, exhaustive in detail about what I've done and who I've interacted with. I notice a few lines here and there blacked out with a thick marker, like they've been redacted. Odd. I move on. Likely it was extraneous information I removed so that it wouldn't distract me from what's important.

Reading my notes, I see that yesterday I hiked the Portage Pass Trail with Sefina, and we had good weather and even startled a bear when we reached the top. Sefina hid behind me until he was gone. That part makes me smile. Sefina is a good friend from *before* and a self-proclaimed wimp when it comes to wildlife. But spending time with her wouldn't make me feel this way, so it's not what I'm looking for. Moving on I see that yesterday was also a Wednesday, when I wash my laundry, which I like to do in the late afternoon when the kids in the building get out of school. The laundry is just down from the lobby, where the kids like to hang out, and I can listen to their talking, laughing, and goofing off while I fold warm shirts and match wool socks. I was a teacher briefly before, well, everything, and I still like to be around kids, even if I can't ever teach again and was a teacher for only—oh, there it is. Just under *laundry* but before *make dinner*. One line that gives me a pang and explains the heaviness that settles across my shoulders.

I wish I could teach again.

A thought, a wish, a yearning I had and then recorded last night before it slipped away. It's true. I do miss teaching. And the feeling that made me want it, the sadness, is what remains of that thought. There is a certain kind of relief that comes with understanding, and I breathe out, rewrite the idea along with a summary of my thoughts from today.

Satisfied, I move on to the rest of my tasks, see a line I've doodled in the margins, next to the To Do list in my notebook. *Bear that broke into building.* I chew the end of my pen, my thoughts drifting to the parts of my past that I do remember. From *before*.

Like how Dad had wanted me to leave Whittier as soon as I finished high school. Worried that if I didn't escape our remote town, which had more inches of snow and rain than people, then I would never get out, that in time I would grow to hate it just like my mother. Said he felt it in his bones. And it was the same feeling he'd had just before my mother walked out on us.

Some people in town think he's psychic. He just shakes his head with a sad wrinkle between his eyes. *Some things you just know,* he says.

Bitterness presses my lips together. Mom was a reclusive alcoholic whose depression became a heavy shroud with every dark, cold winter. Everyone knew she'd never stay in a place where the sun flirts with the farthest horizon, out of our reach for months at a time. Or in a town bounded by the cold waters of Prince William Sound and dwarfed by rock and glacier and forest that stretch for miles and miles in every other direction. My fingernails dig into my palms. And I wasn't enough to keep her sober or make her stay. Nobody had to be a psychic to see that coming.

But Dad was right about me, and now I'm Rapunzel, trapped in a tower of notebooks and calendars. I pinch the pen between my fingers until the ridges dig into the bone, try to breathe through this sudden bout of anger that slides over my scalp. It was my choice to come back to Whittier. I wanted to live here because I've always loved this close-knit community. After Mom left—after my best friend in the entire world ran off, after I lost everything—it was the people in this town and Dad who never deserted me. Whittier will always be my home. I just never thought it would be my prison too.

Rain hits the window, and I watch as it spreads down the glass in wide rivulets. I keep breathing, letting the moment thin until it trickles away, just like the rain. When I glance up from my notebook and look toward the water, I see the dark body of an orca hurl itself above the surface, twisting black and white in the air before slamming back into the water. The familiar rush of excitement floods me, and I jot a quick note:

Saw an orca breaching today. This wild beauty is just another reason I love Whittier, even if the majority of town lives entirely in one building.

Begich Towers—or BTI, as we call it—is an old military building constructed in the fifties to house officers and their families and designed to withstand earthquakes, which it has had the opportunity to do on more than one occasion. Behind its rectangle of fourteen stories loom mountains with waterfalls that cascade down the sides. Wide windows span each apartment, many of which offer stunning views of the harbor with Billings Glacier in the distance. The thousands of people who drift through our town on their way to fishing adventures or cruise ship vacations think we're crazy to live in a Cold War highrise and in weather that often forces us to live indoors for much of the year. They see the decaying and dry-docked boats, stacked and rusted storage containers, and old buildings that haven't been used in decades. I see glaciers and mountains and a community of people who make it possible for me to live here as I am.

My phone chirps and vibrates in my pocket. Across the screen is a reminder: Make a chicken Caesar salad for the dinner party. I nod—great idea. It's a family recipe that Ruth showed me how to make when I was a teenager, one with a light dressing and homemade croutons. Not that I'm related to Ruth, who believes in conspiracies and cameras capturing our every move, but when the entire town lives in a place so remote we share a two-and-a-half-mile tunnel with a train, well, even Ruth is family.

I cross-check the reminder on my phone with the written To Do list and laugh softly when I see a note about the bear that Dad scared out of our building the summer before I turned eight years old. The bear had been causing trouble that summer, trying more than once to get into BTI, scaring cruise ship passengers who wandered around our small port town, and startling local teenagers who trespassed inside the abandoned Buckner Building, another relic of Whittier's brief military occupation. And when he finally entered BTI's lobby through a door left cracked open, he filled the entire first floor with the oily stink of dead fish.

Dad got to the lobby first in nothing but his boxer shorts and wool socks, his wide, hairy chest heaving up and down, one arm slung back because he knew I was there, right behind him. Where Dad went, I went, even if he told me to stay put. "Stay behind me, Claire," he said in the same warm and gravelly tone he used to tell me to go to bed. The bear stood on his hind legs, waving his big paws in the air like a boxer. Dad mimicked his stance and straightened up to his fullest height. "Go, bear," he said, unyielding and stern. I stiffened because if I were that bear, I'd be running out the door with my tail tucked. But the bear huffed, shooting thick white flecks from his mouth. One hit my face. He stared at Dad from his good eye—the other was just an empty socket, an old scar puckered and black—with an intensity that I remember even now. Like he knew him. But Dad stood with his hands raised above his head, and his fingertips grazed the cinder-block walls, nearly touching the ceiling of our building. He is that tall.

"Go, bear!" he roared, low and guttural. He was Paul Bunyan; he was Grizzly Adams; he was Daniel Boone. The bear growled and sniffed the air once before spinning his bulk to the ground and loping out the way he'd come in.

Behind me a handful of our neighbors stood grouped together. Hank from the market nodded. "Not even bears mess with Vance."

Ruth pinched her lips together, crossed her arms. "But you were upstairs with us. How'd you know the bear got in?"

Dad placed his big palm on top of my head and looked down at me with a smile. "Well, Ruth, I could feel him enter the building. It made my bones vibrate." Then he whispered to me from the side of his mouth, "And maybe I saw him from our window, but don't tell Ruth." He winked and I covered my mouth with one hand when I giggled.

I was only seven at the time, but I remember it like it happened yesterday. I smile to myself and stare past my faint reflection in the window to the harbor. The afternoon storm has moved over the water, turning the sky a gunmetal gray, the water choppy and black and obscuring the mountains beyond in a wall of fog. My childhood memory of Dad scaring off that bear is crisp like the vibrant red of his plaid boxer shorts and pungent like the heavy musk of the bear's fur that tickles my nose even now.

I stand from my desk and turn to the kitchen, taking the notebook with me. When I flip the light switch, the murky gray light inside the apartment transforms into something warm and soft, cozy. Another chirp; I look at the screen. **Make a chicken Caesar salad for the dinner party.** On the counter by the dry-erase calendar is a portable file cabinet. First, I check the calendar, letting my eyes pass over the squares that are crossed off with a thick black line until I reach the first square without a line. Today is Thursday, September 27, and I am hosting dinner for a few friends, at—I squint at the tiny print—six this evening. From the file cabinet, I pull a folder labeled SOCIAL EVENTS CURRENT and flip it open. Written across a lavender sheet of notebook paper is the information I need. *Dinner with Ruth, Sefina, and Harriet.*

Moving on, I see that Ruth will bring dessert. I squint to make sure I read that right. Huh. Ruth never bakes. She always says she never had to learn or try because my mother was the best baker in all of Whittier. She's right. My mother had been the best, spinning magic out of dough. Even now I can taste the way she infused our small apartment with sugar and vanilla, smell the cinnamon that clung to her skin like perfume. But a sourness erupts in my mouth, erases the memory. She stopped baking when alcohol comforted her more, left me when forgetting became more important than being my mom. My eyes sting and I press a palm flat against them until it fades. Her leaving was something that even now, as an adult, I feel in the way it nips at my heart and trails me with a lasting feeling of bitter rejection.

I shake my head to dislodge the image of her, and when I return to the work of preparing for the dinner party, I relax, relieved to have something else to focus on. The next few lines in the notebook make it easy for me to move forward. *Dinner: lemon chicken Caesar with garlic bread, iced tea and water to drink. Ingredients and recipe in the fridge.* And the final line: *Review folders for guests and make a list of talking points for conversation.* My chest expands. It feels good to have a plan I can count on.

I open the refrigerator and bend my six-foot frame to see inside, where I quickly spot the romaine, Parmesan cheese, chicken breasts, a bright-yellow lemon, and a clove of garlic stacked together on the top shelf along with a lined three-by-five recipe card. Cool air from the refrigerator brushes my ankles with goose bumps and a wisp of a memory. Of Mom doing something similar and me helping, gathering the ingredients and watching her chop and mince, listening to her humming a song I didn't know, the light touch of her body beside mine, a warmth radiating from my chest.

I scrape garlic skin into the trash, and the full bin taints the air with an overripe sweetness that makes me queasy. Thinking of how Mom was, what she could have been, permeates my mood, turns it blacker than the clouds that hang heavy with rain outside my window. When I was a very little girl, before her nightmares became more than she could handle, before alcohol replaced everyone who loved her, I wanted to be just like her.

One particular memory floats to the surface. I am young, tucked under the covers, legs curled up and into my chest, pretending to be asleep. Mom leans over me; her thick dark hair swings past her shoulders, feathery across my cheek. Her breath is stale and sweet in the way that makes her eyes dull like the plastic ones on my doll. I keep my eyes squeezed shut and feel her lips brush my forehead. *It's not your fault, Claire, honey. Not your fault.* Her words come out in a slur, and it's hard to understand her. *I'msosorry, Claire bear. Sosorry.* She is crying but I don't open my eyes, I don't put my arms around her neck, because I don't make her happy. I only make her sad.

I turn to the cutting board, place my hands on either side, and breathe, ignoring how my chest aches with how much I longed for her to be better. How the feeling turns me into a little girl even now. But then Dad's face appears in my mind—thick beard, brown eyes that crinkle when he laughs. At least I have him.

CHAPTER TWO

A buzz from my phone reminds me that I'm getting dinner ready, so I reach for a green apron that hangs from a hook on the wall, and when I tie it around my waist, it barely hangs midthigh—more like a miniskirt. I snort; they don't make aprons for tall women. The rain pounds the building, heavy and loud, so I open a music app and push play, and rock music fills the apartment, mutes the noise outside. I swing my hips to the music; it's a Black Crowes tune, I think, and the rhythm of drums laced with the electric squeal of guitars soothes me with its familiar beat.

From a cabinet labeled *serving bowls, platters, and plates*, I take my favorite turquoise salad bowl and set it on the counter beside the bamboo cutting board. The salad doesn't take long to make, and I get it all on the table by 5:30. I sit and wait; fingers tap the wood surface, knee jiggles up and down. On the table in front of me is my notebook. I open it to a page in the middle with today's date and review the activities I accomplished early in the day, each one with a thick black line drawn through it: *breakfast, planning and note review for today, shower, lunch, trip to market and hydroponic gardens, planning and note review for tomorrow*. I draw a line through *make a chicken Caesar salad for the dinner party* but leave *dinner party* unmarked. It hasn't happened yet, after all.

I read through the social-event file folder again and cross off the items I've already accomplished. Based on my notes, I still need to *make a list of talking points for conversation*, so I turn to the portable file cabinet and locate and remove files for Sefina and Harriet. When I was in college, most of my classmates laughed at my old-school ways: paper planner, pens and pencils, notebooks. I guess I was behind the times in that regard, but the smooth glide of pen over paper, the satisfaction of crossing off a To Do item, the crisp pages of a new planner—well, to me, tapping on a screen or keyboard never felt as satisfying.

I read the first page in Sefina's file. Her youngest daughter, Leilani, is graduating this year. My pencil hovers and I let the shock wash over me. The passage of time is cruel and unrelenting, especially for me. Once upon a very brief period, I was a teacher at the school in Whittier, and Leilani was my student. That was *before*, though, when I was normal, and before notebooks and calendars and smartphones fully dictated my every day. Fresh out of graduate school, armed with a degree and an unexpected surprise, I was excited to start my life back in Whittier, even if it devastated Dad.

My hand rests on my flat belly, fingers pushing into softness. Dad always warned me that something bad would happen if I stayed in Whittier. I press the heel of my palm against my eyes, ignore the tightness in my limbs. There's no point in feeling sorry for myself, so I move on to my next conversation note for Sefina. When I finish with her, I start a list for Harriet, who runs the building's bed-and-breakfast.

Rain pummels the window, and the constant thrumming combined with the music causes my head to ache. I put my pen down to rub my temples and stretch my neck when a light knock on the door startles me. I check my watch. They must be early.

I remove my apron and smooth my shirt, but when I glance out the peephole, I pull back, knees weak, heart racing.

It's a face I haven't seen since the day I graduated with my master's in education. The day she ruined by showing up so drunk she stumbled and fell when she tried to leap into the aisle to hug me as I walked by, tripping me and three others. The corner of my friend's graduation cap poked me just under my eye. It left a scar.

Mom.

My fingers are already flipping through my notebook, searching for an answer to why she is here. I take another peek. She's different—older, obviously, since that day was, um, well, a long time ago, I think, even if I do remember it like it was yesterday.

"Claire?" Her voice is the same, too, but missing something. "It's Mom."

Is that a nervous lilt? I look through the peephole, see that she rubs the back of her neck, shifts her weight. Yeah, nervous. My face hardens with the memory of a different time when she stood outside the door, begging to be heard, wanting to come home.

It was the summer before I left for college. Dad had fixed dinner, setting an extra place at the table that I'd assumed was for Ruth. But the knock that came a moment later was too soft for Ruth, and I nearly cried out when I opened it to find Mom, shorter and smaller than I remembered, and so skinny she looked frail. Her skin, once smooth and flawless, was riddled with shallow lines that tracked around her eyes and forehead. And her hair—her beautiful thick brown waves—pulled into a limp ponytail. *Mom?* My arms had hung stiffly by my sides, my face a frozen mask. Inside, I remember a storm of emotions battering my heart and chest and lungs like the wind and rain that pummel our coastline.

I want to give you something.

She'd handed me a small green token. It lay in my open palm, but I didn't look down at it, because I was afraid that if I moved at all, I'd start to cry. And I didn't want to cry. *What is it?*

Dad stood behind me, a solid rock sheltering me from the elements, and I was able to breathe a little easier.

It means I've been sober for ninety days. I just want you to know that I'm trying, Claire. And—she'd gulped in air—*I'm sorry. I know it's not enough, but I will make it up to you, honey.*

My forehead touches the door. If I had been older, less wounded, perhaps I would have noticed how proud she was in the way her shoulders lifted a fraction higher. But I was raw. First she left, then Tate, and their abandonment wrapped my heart in granite. I wouldn't allow anybody to hurt me again. So I snorted at her and tossed the chip back. It hit her cloth bag and fell soundlessly to the floor, where it looked like nothing more than a small and useless token.

Ninety days? You've been gone for five years, and you think I'm going to give a fuck about ninety days? I wasn't frozen anymore; I was filled with a heated rage that had spread outward from my core, tingling my fingers and toes. All I could think about was every time she wasn't there when I'd woken from a nightmare shaking and crying, the details she'd missed, like the time I kissed Tate and threw up because he tasted like chewing tobacco, or the first time I shaved and nicked every bony part of my knees, or when Tate broke my heart, all of it adding up to a towering height that wobbled in the air between us.

Claire, Dad said in the same low warning tone he'd used for the bear he scared out of our lobby when I was seven. He was ready to welcome her with open arms. I was not. I shut my mouth and folded my arms, stared at my mom.

She'd held my gaze for a long moment, her eyes soft, but her body caved inward like I'd punched her. Then she'd bent over and picked up the token, gray hairs threaded thickly through the length of her ponytail. When she stood up she nodded, the token grasped in her hand.

Alice, Dad said from behind me, plaintive, forgiving, gentle. My spine straightened at the weakness in it, and I balled my hands into fists. She would not hurt him again. I wouldn't allow it this time.

Mom had held up her hand. *She's right, Vance. It's too soon. Claire, sweetheart, it doesn't need to be today or tomorrow or even next year. But one day I'll make it up to you. I swear I will.*

Then she'd taken in a deep breath and given me a smile that reminded me of Saturday mornings when the buttery scent of cinnamon rolls filled our apartment. I'd had to steel myself against a sudden urge to invite her inside, but I didn't relent. Her apology had come too late. I was nearly an adult, heading off to college soon, and I didn't need her anymore. *We* didn't need her anymore.

In the intervening years, Dad had tried to get me to reach out, said she was doing much better, but eventually he stopped asking. Likely because she'd slipped off the wagon, I'd guessed. And I was right, because the next time I saw her was at my graduation, when she had to be escorted out of the ceremony. But Dad had saved the token, put it into a large mason jar that he set on the kitchen counter. It sat alone in that jar for years, gathering dust, a pathetic reminder of her failed promises.

And now she's here again.

"It's Mom."

I grit my teeth, open the door a crack, and sniff the air for the familiar odor that always surrounds her, like the alcohol seeps from her pores. Instead, I smell something sweet like honey and vanilla, and a lump rises in my throat because those smells bring up unbidden memories from when she was the mom who let me lick cake batter from a spatula.

"What are you doing here?" I say through the crack.

Her eyes are soft. "I wanted to see you."

"Does Dad know you're here?" I already know the answer because if he did, he would have told me and it would be in my notes. Dad never lies to me.

Her shoulders relax with relief, maybe, or something else? I think I'm pretty good at reading body language and facial expressions. I should be because often it's all I have to go on in conversations where I can't remember who I'm speaking with or what we've been speaking about.

"Vance invited me, Claire."

My nostrils flare. Now I know she's lying—my father would never invite her to my home. And I know that the smell that infuses me with memories of the good days is nothing but a ruse, a perfume to cover the ugly truth of her addiction. When I was very little, she would cry out at night, her arms and legs thrashing around so hard that when I tried to crawl into bed to comfort her, she would elbow me. The sound still ping-pongs inside my head, brings back the coldness of the hallway on my bare feet when I ran to Ruth for help.

She holds her hand out. "Claire, wait—"

A buzz from my phone with a reminder. Make a chicken Caesar salad for the dinner party. I nod at the phone, thankful to have a job, and close the door without saying anything. Before I forget, I pick up a pad of sticky notes from the counter and write myself an important directive—*Mom is a liar*—and stick it to the refrigerator.

I back away, reading the line once more and nodding to myself. She is a liar and an addict, and she's too weak to change. I should know; I spent years thinking she could, and all it ever did was hurt.

My thoughts drift to Dad in a memory scented with fish, mud, and tears. He was my bulwark in the storm that was my mom, and as she worsened I clung to him.

I was ten and we'd been fishing all morning in our favorite cove. He was going back on the road the next day, and I knew that once he left, Mom would hide in her bedroom.

The sun had been out when we'd first arrived at our favorite spot—a lemon color that made the sky look like I'd colored it with my favorite yellow crayon. Later it hid behind clouds, taking the shine from everything and making goose bumps pop up on my skin.

Dad had thrown out a line. It plinked into the water, and tiny ripples bounced the bobber up and down.

I'd puffed out my chest, tried to feel brave. *Can I go on the road with you?* My heart beat so fast, but I kept my eyes on the water, reeled in my empty line, threw it back out, never looking at Dad while the bobber rode the waves. I sucked in my top lip and stood a little taller. *I'm good company, you know. Maybe you can even teach me how to drive a truck so I can be a truck driver like you.* I bit the inside of my cheek and tried to see him from the very corner of my eye, but he stared at the water, moving the fishing line back and forth. I gripped the rod so hard my hands turned numb. He wasn't answering and I was smart enough to guess why. My foot stomped down hard, but in the water my boot just sank into the mushy bottom. *Mom doesn't need me around be—*

Ho-ya! Dad yelled, and his bobber dipped underwater. He reeled in the line at the same time that he pulled hard on the rod. His big eyebrows looked like they'd climbed onto his forehead. He grunted and pulled harder on the rod, but whatever was on the end of his line pulled in the opposite direction strong enough to make the rod nearly bend in half.

I'd jumped up and down on my toes and clapped my hands until my palms tingled. *Wow!*

Claire! he called. *Get the net! It's a biggun!*

Got it! I'd stuck the end of my own rod into some rocks and picked up the net, running over to Dad but also trying to be careful not to fall on the sharp rocks.

He looked at me over his shoulder, lifted one corner of his mouth, then turned back to the water.

The net was heavy, so I stuck it between my arm and my side so I could jump up and down for Dad and not drop it. *Get it! Keep going, Dad!*

He pulled so hard that his muscles moved like snakes under his skin and his face turned red. I squealed when he stumbled away from the edge of the water, his rubber boots slipping on the rocks, but he didn't go down, because he'd fished his whole life. He tugged once more, and a giant fish flew out of the water, landing on the ground beside him. Dad crouched on the black rocks next to the fish, and I ran over with the net and plunked it right on top of its wiggling body, just in case it decided to grow legs and run back to the water.

That's the biggest damn salmon I've ever seen! I said and fell on my butt next to him on the ground.

Dad looked at me and started laughing so hard he didn't make much sound, and then I started laughing until my sides hurt and my cheeks felt wet. But then his whole face sagged like an old man's, and he scooped me up like I wasn't the biggest ten-year-old in Whittier, trapping me inside his tree-trunk arms and rocking me back and forth. The fish flopped on the ground beside us, and I tried to say something, except I couldn't because I wasn't laughing anymore; I was crying. Crying so hard that I was hiccuping and snot was running out of my nose and it tasted salty. He held me and hummed, and it made his chest rumble against my ear, and I cried even harder. *You are my sunshine, my only sunshine.*

I think we sat like that forever, long enough for the fish to stop flopping. It lay beside us, still. Dad's shirt was soft against my wet cheek, and I breathed in the smell of soap and water and fish. *I don't want you to leave, Daddy,* I said into his chest.

He laid his chin on top of my head; I heard him swallow.

I don't want to leave again either, Claire bear. But, hey, Ruth thinks the building manager job might open up soon, and when it does, you can bet my name will be in the hat.

I hiccuped, but I didn't cry again.

He rubbed my back, rocking me back and forth, and we sat like that until the air turned cold and I shivered.

I make Mom sad. My teeth chattered when I spoke.

He squeezed me in his arms, and I heard him sigh. *Never, Claire. Mom's sad for reasons that have nothing to do with you. You make her happy, sweetheart. You've always made her happy.*

Then why does she sleep so much? And how come she hardly ever leaves our apartment anymore or bakes or does anything like she used to? And do you know what's in her water bottle? Tate does. He says it's booze, and that's what makes his dad so mean. I snuggled deeper into his arms. *Mom's not mean, but she cries a lot.*

17

Dad didn't speak, and I burrowed my head against his chest, sure that I'd said something wrong. Eventually, when the silence was too much, I pushed out of his arms to see his face, and when I did, I wished I hadn't looked. His eyes were so wet they were shiny, like he was crying, except Dad was too big and strong to cry.

Oh, Claire, no, honey. Alice, she just . . . oh. He looked up at the sky as if he thought the answer was up there. But all I saw were thick gray clouds that hung down so low I thought I could stick my fingers into them like Play-Doh. His breath was a gentle wave that pushed my head up and down. *Mom will get better, Claire, I just know it. All she needs is some time, okay?* He looked down at me. *I can't think of anything I'd love more than you as my driving partner, but you need to stay in school, not drive trucks with me. I can't make things different for your mom right now, sweetheart, so I drive trucks to make things different for you. Okay? And your job is to stay in school and learn everything you can and then go out there*—he pointed in the direction of the tunnel—*and share it with the rest of the world.*

My phone buzzes with a reminder. Make a chicken Caesar salad for the dinner party. On the kitchen table is my turquoise salad bowl filled with Parmesan-dusted romaine lettuce along with glasses of tea, with ice cubes melting on top, and a basket of bread that gives the air a bite of garlic. Dinner is ready. I swipe left and the reminder disappears.

CHAPTER THREE

When my clock reads 6:05, I open the door and stick my head into the hallway just as Harriet steps around the corner from the elevator with Sefina, who waves and smiles. Sefina moved here when we were both nineteen, but I was in college and she was a single mom of two young girls. Despite our differences, a friendship grew over visits home and summer breaks, a shared scorn for men, and a similar determination to be in control of our own lives. Even now, when everyone I knew from college has stopped calling, Sefina is still my friend. It's all in my notes.

"Hi, Claire! Oooh, that smells good," Sefina says. "Must be your lemon-pepper chicken, hey?" Her smile is wide, teeth white against her smooth, dark skin. One dark winter night, Dad hauled away her abusive asshole of a husband. But that was a long time ago, at least for her.

Behind me I hear a door open, and when I turn, Ruth is stepping out of her apartment, holding a cellophane-wrapped tray with a tub of ice cream balanced on top.

"You made dessert?" I ask.

Her forehead creases. "Oh, um, no, I didn't." She stands with her lips pressed firmly together. My mouth quirks up. Ruth's not a soft person, but she's a good one. She stepped in when my mother turned to vodka, and well, truth is, at this point I'm probably more than she bargained for, but she doesn't let on, at least not according to my notes. Her eyes travel over my shoulder and harden.

I turn and see nothing but my refrigerator covered in sticky notes. Some have directives like *check expiration date on milk*; others are observations: *you hate broccoli*. That one makes me laugh softly. No, I don't. I've always loved it. Must be some kind of mistake—maybe I was thinking about someone else. I've just reached up to take it off when Harriet speaks from behind me. "Don't take that one off, Claire, it's true. You really, really hate broccoli now. Believe me; I forgot and served it the last time I hosted, and it made you gag."

"Oh," I say, and leave the note in place, a prickling frustration raking across my skin at the idea that I lose far more than I record. Wishing for all the world that I could just know and feeling the exhaustion of trying to exist as a normal person pooling in my pores. I am tired and, at the moment, feeling sorry for myself. Tears collect in my eyelashes, and I swipe at them, angry for this surge of weakness. It's why I write everything down—so I can avoid this situation. I roll my shoulders, make a note about broccoli in the notebook, and turn back with a smile, hope they didn't notice my emotional slip. "Guess I've changed my ways. No more broccoli, then."

Ruth reaches past me, points to a note that says *Mom is a liar*. "Everyone can change, Claire, even your mom."

I fold my arms, ignore her sentiment about my mother because Ruth will always have a soft spot for Alice. I touch the mark under my eye from where the graduation cap gouged into my skin. It was the last time I saw her. In some ways, I'm grateful for the physical scar she left then. It's a reminder to me of how scarred I am on the inside. Ruth stares at me. At one point she and Mom were close, and despite everything, Ruth is the kind of person to see the good in everyone. I should know. She's always managed to find the good in me, even when I was a teenage girl who thought smoking pot and picking fights would fill the sinkhole my mother left behind.

I take the tray from her hands, inhaling a rich chocolate scent that makes my mouth water. "Smells amazing. Thanks for baking."

Ruth snorts, lifts one side of her mouth in a half smile that doesn't reach her eyes. There's something different about her. I tilt my head. She looks pale, and her back, normally straight up and down like she's preparing to have her height measured, rounds just the slightest bit. "Everything okay, Ruth?"

She holds my gaze, then says, "I don't know, Claire; do you think everything is okay?"

Her words aren't heavy with sarcasm or clipped with rudeness; it just comes across as a question, so I don't take offense to the oddness of it. I am very good at figuring situations out, so maybe Ruth is just testing my honed skills. I study her: red-rimmed eyes, the skin around her nostrils flaky with dryness, her cheeks slightly pale. "Looks like you don't feel well. A cold? It's okay if you're not up for joining us for dinner tonight," I say. "I can make up a plate and bring it over for you if you'd rather rest at home."

She blinks, shakes her head, and taps my hand, wordless. The contact startles me. Ruth is not a touchy kind of person. "I could use some company tonight, Claire," she says. "Let's go, or Harriet will eat all of that garlic bread I smell before we get a chance to sit down."

From the table, Harriet barks a hoarse cigarette laugh and says, "She's not wrong!"

Later, with the garlic bread gone, a few stragglers of soggy romaine stuck to the sides of the empty salad bowl, and Ruth's surprisingly exquisite brownies drowning in vanilla bean ice cream on a plate in front of me, I slide the SOCIAL EVENTS CURRENT folder from the file storage by my feet and open it on my lap. I scan the conversation plan quickly. "So, Harriet, I heard you had an interesting pair of renters last week. Sefina said something about witches?"

Sefina laughs and it's such a clear and bright sound that I can almost forget the person my friend was when she first moved here. The one with the hollowness in her eyes and the yellowing edges of a bruise forming a half moon on her cheek. "They told Harriet they were green witches," she says. Her black hair swings around her face, and her peace-fulness is at odds with the other memory that rises—the one of Dad, his eyes narrowed and fist tight, standing over a man sprawled on the floor with a bleeding and broken nose. And Sefina, holding her little girls close to her sides, her face streaked in tears. That was years ago, but to me it feels recent because it's part of the memories I retrieve quickly, the ones that stuck because they are from *before*. I don't remember the—my eyes drift to my notebook . . . there it is, at the top of each page. Ten *years* since it happened. I don't remember the days and months that made Sefina into the woman she is today. I blink against a wetness in my eyes. I can't lie. It sucks to be me.

Their chatter moves around me, but I can't recall the conversation. My gut twists and I shake my head, feel the fuzziness that muddles the present. This is why I take notes; this is why I'm organized, so they can't see the real me, the woman who can't remember shit. I'm breath-ing a little too rapidly, so I scan the notebook to anchor myself. *Dinner Party. Harriet and renters.* "So you had renters at the B & B?" I shake my head. No, that's not a worthy conversation point. Of course Harriet had renters. I bite a nail, flip through my notes, which are extensive. I try to get everything I can down, so sifting through it to root myself in a conversation takes all my focus. They wait until I find what I'm looking for, and when I do, I say, "You had renters who were witches?"

Harriet nods. "They said they came to Whittier to worship nature in all her glory."

"The witches?" I ask.

"That's what they wanted to believe," she says. "They were here to see the Buckner. Called it the building that had become one with nature." Her eyes roll. "Their words, not mine."

The Buckner Building once housed nearly a thousand military per-sonnel, and much like BTI, it was a self-contained city under one roof. Now it's just a decomposing building up on the hill that looks like something out of an apocalypse movie.

"They said they wanted to commune with the spirits." Sefina laughs so hard her eyes close. "Then they pulled out a joint and asked Harriet for a light."

Harriet takes a bite of the brownie, licks the vanilla ice cream from her lips. She's a quirky woman but with a head for business and a bed-and-breakfast that attracts all kinds. She and her husband, Pete, were nomads who traveled from one outsized adventure to the next. They came to Whittier in the eighties, intending to stay for one summer of fishing before heading off to some other destination. Harriet says that once they made it through a winter here, they decided they were tough enough to survive a few more. So they never left. "Which is why," she continues, "income be damned, I told them to leave. They broke my no-weed rule, *and* they're stupid." She blows air through her lips. "Witches. Silliest thing I ever heard. Didn't even know a single spell either." Pete owns the only bar and restaurant that stays open in the winter, the one I can see from my apartment window. For a shared glass of wine, Harriet will let anyone use a pair of binoculars to check whether a spouse has left the bar. It's good to know in case they stumble into a bear or lose their way in the fog. Harriet pushes the empty plate away from her. "Melt in your mouth. I'll have to give my compliments to the baker. But something was different from her last batch. Can't quite put my finger on it."

Sefina nods. "A little spicy. Cinnamon, maybe?"

"I'll be damned," Harriet says. "She's just as creative as she's always been."

"Who?" I ask.

The table goes quiet, punctured by Ruth's fork clattering heavily onto her plate. "Alice," she says. "She said she was going to stop by this afternoon. Did she?"

My grip on the fork tightens, sends the tines skittering through melted ice cream. My mother is in Whittier? I can feel their eyes on me, expectant—probably waiting for my reaction. I breathe in and out, try to untangle the knot in my stomach and focus on the tender crumbs of brownie drowning in the ice cream. Do I know she's back? I try to act like the news hasn't skyrocketed my pulse, try to casually flip through my notebook. No notes about Mom, and I can only imagine how it's affecting Dad. I look up, shrug. "Nope, she didn't."

Ruth's gaze flickers and she wipes her mouth. Something is off about her, and it pricks at my skin. I turn back to my notebook, flip through pages and pages of my writing, desperate to find some hint of why a room of my friends is subdued, different in some important way that I can't see. But another conversation has started around me, and in the din of voices my thoughts scatter like dandelion fuzz, drifting until they catch on something substantial. There in my notes from this morning, doodled in the margins. Dad and the bear. It makes me smile. "Remember that bear that Dad thought followed him around? The one he chased out of our building when I was seven?"

"Before my time," Sefina says. "But I've heard the story from you and all the old-timers here."

"Hey!" says Ruth, and Sefina laughs.

But Harriet is nodding. "Vance said he'd catch sight of it for years afterward. Said they had a connection."

"Like his spirit animal?" Sefina says.

"Or just a pesky bear who'd gotten used to scavenging dumpsters for human food," Ruth says. "But Vance has such a soft spot for animals. It wouldn't surprise me if that bear had taken to him in some way."

I smile. "Of course he did. Everyone loves Dad."

"Bigger than life," Sefina adds. "And a psychic to boot."

Harriet grunts. "Or the man just listens to his gut," she says. "That's an Alaskan quality, if you ask me."

I'm half listening now because when I think of Dad and that bear, my thoughts drift to Tate Dunn. We were both seven years old with larger-than-life fathers. His was a fisherman, gone for long stretches of time in the summer, hardly leaving BTI for longer stretches in the winter.

Tate and his dad had been in Whittier only a few weeks, and I was curious about the scabby-kneed boy with long black hair who never spoke. That night in the lobby, after the bear was gone and Dad had slung me over his shoulder to take me back to bed, I saw Tate, curled into a tiny ball outside the laundry room, asleep. I'd tapped Dad on the shoulder and pointed. He'd made a noise in his throat, walked down the hall, and without putting me down, picked Tate up in his other arm. I remember thinking my dad was stronger than any other dad, stronger even than that bear. Tate's eyes had fluttered open, and with our heads hanging over Dad's shoulders, we stared at each other across his broad back. I smiled; he didn't smile back, but our eyes stayed locked all the way up to his floor. When we got to his apartment, I was sleepy, trying to keep my lids from sticking together, and when Tate slid off Dad's shoulder, I let them close all the way. Dad's voice vibrated softly against his collarbone. *Found him in the lobby.* A woman responded, her tone low but brittle: *You were supposed to be in bed, Tate.* Later I learned she wasn't his mom, just the first in a string of women his father rotated through.

It was later discovered that the bear had found his way in through a lobby door that someone had left propped open, and what followed were signs posted on every exterior door and papering the insides of the elevators, warning all residents to CLOSE THE DOOR TO KEEP WILDLIFE OUTSIDE.

"Claire?" Sefina's voice, soft and calm but laced with something else. Concern?

I doodle across the page while I wait for the burning in my cheeks to fade. I've forgotten something. I don't know what. Could be a question someone asked me, or maybe I'd been talking and stopped mid-sentence, but all I know is that I do not want to meet their eyes. I can already sense their pity; it slides across the table like a gelatinous glob, and when it touches me, I am reminded that this is all a charade, an act that they put on to help me feel like the normal twenty, no—I check my notes—thirty-six-year-old woman I am not. I love them for it, but the reality is that I am anything but normal, anything but the Claire I used to be. I take a deep breath and lift my eyes because self-pity is a luxury I don't rest in for more than a second.

I give Ruth a smile with a confidence that I feel only in the lift of my shoulders. "Let me guess. Another *Groundhog Day* moment?" I say lightly.

Ruth laughs, seems relieved. "What a great movie."

"Yeah, but as Bill Murray movies go, he could never top *Caddyshack*," Harriet adds.

Ruth sits back in her chair. "I'm a *Ghostbusters* fan myself."

Sefina, who grew up in a tiny Alaskan town without cable or, at times, running water, draws her eyebrows together. "Who's Bob Murray?"

And everyone, including me, laughs, my forgotten moment a thing of their past as well. This is why I love them.

Ruth claps her hands and reaches for the brownie-crusted spatula. "Another round?" she asks, and we all push our plates toward the center of the table.

My fork sinks into chocolate gooeyness, and I swirl it around the ice cream before sliding it into my mouth and tasting the explosion of sugar and vanilla, the coolness of the ice cream mixed with the slight bitterness of chocolate. "Wow, this is so good. Who made it?"

There's a beat, a pause, a lingering in their gazes; then Ruth finishes chewing her brownie, smiles. "I did."

The air around the table lightens with their laughter, and while I know that in some way I've let my mask slip, shown the real me, I shake it off. Sometimes there's only so much pretending I can do.

CHAPTER FOUR

Friday, September 28

"It's really nothing like *Groundhog Day*, you know?"

"What do you mean?" Kate crosses her legs. She wears navy-blue hiking pants, the kind with thin material that dries in an instant, and worn-in hiking shoes. She's a good therapist, I think. She's calm, patient, and honest, and when I get off course, she gently guides me back to whatever conversation we were having that I've forgotten about. I used to see Kate when I was a teenager, after Mom left. It was Dad's idea. Kate lived in Whittier then, before she started her own practice here in Anchorage, so I remember her from *before*. I don't know if therapy makes any difference for me, but talking with her calms me and helps me to stay focused. This information is all in the file that I keep on her, so I know it to be fact.

"Bill Murray's character knew he was living the same day over and over again," I say. "I don't feel that way. I mean, I guess in some ways I am, but I'm not frustrated about it the way he was. I'm just"—I shrug—"existing."

Kate leans forward. "Do you ever feel like that's not enough?"

Her question is personal in a really intrusive way, even for a therapist, but especially for Kate, who should know better than to ask me something that's literally impossible. It's almost cruel of her. "It has to be enough, Kate. What other options do I have?"

Instead of answering, because it was rhetorical anyway, she slides on a pair of reading glasses and opens a blue file folder. "You were talking about Tate earlier."

"I was?"

She nods. "Yes, about your feelings when he left Whittier."

"Oh, right. Well, it hurt like hell." I stop, hating the bitterness that punctuates my words. Tate understood something early on that I didn't get until much later: we couldn't heal each other, no matter how much love there was between us. He tried to tell me that he was leaving, I think, but we were teenagers, and I was too embroiled in the storm of my own thoughts to understand what he was trying to say. It was a late-October evening, and Tate and I sat in the bed of his pickup truck at the head of the bay, a six-pack of beer between us, our middle fingers raised to each car headed out of town.

We were happy, I thought, content with the universe of our friendship—at least I was. It was Tate's eighteenth birthday, and I'd just finished putting the last candle into my impromptu cake of Twinkies and Ho Hos. *Make a wish,* I'd said.

We sat with our legs crisscrossed, our knees touching, and Tate looked at me with his green eyes that nearly always took my breath away.

I love you, he said.

It wasn't the first time. We'd been telling each other for as long as I could remember. With him, it was simply a feeling that had always existed. But this time when he said it, the hairs on the back of my neck stood on end because I thought he was trying to tell me something more, and I didn't understand. I ignored the feeling and kissed him— light, probing, sweetened by packaged sugar and cream filling. Soon his hands roamed, leaving heated trails down my back. This wasn't new, either, but when he lay on top of me, it felt like he savored me in a different way, and it left me with an empty yearning.

Afterward, we'd settled back onto the truck bed, lain next to each other, and watched the stars pop out one by one. The length of his body warmed my side, simultaneously familiar and intoxicating. I was happy, satiated, sure that this was something that would never change.

I can't s . . . s-tay here, Claire.

I'd sat up so fast my vision blackened. *What?*

His eyes stayed on the sky. *My dad will never leave, you know that, r . . . r-ight?*

So? I'd said and drawn my knees up, wrapped my arms around my shins, suddenly cold, shivering. I'd had it all planned out. We'd go to college; I already knew I wanted to be a teacher by then, and Tate, well, Tate could do whatever he wanted. Grow pot and sell it for all I cared, as long as we were together. *This is our home.* My voice had pitched higher, and the last word came out as a whisper.

He had an arm across his forehead, and it shaded his eyes so when he turned his head to look up at me, I couldn't see what he was thinking. *I'm n . . . n-ot strong like you, Claire.*

I'd almost laughed. *You broke your dad's nose last week, remember?* He'd grown taller than his father. *He didn't even punch you back. I bet it's because he's scared of you now. I bet he knows you're stronger than him.* My mind scrambled for other examples. *And that tourist? Remember the one who grabbed my ass two summers ago? He was like an adult, right? And you pushed him so hard he fell into that pile of reindeer poop.* Now I was laughing.

But Tate hadn't raised his arm from his eyes, didn't laugh with me. *That's not what I'm t . . . t-alking about.*

My voice had been small, nearly absorbed by the train going by. *Then what are you talking about?*

The train passed and the silence that followed was too loud.

When he finally spoke, his words were what I wanted to hear. *F . . . f-orget I said anything, okay?*

And I did because I knew that Tate would never leave me. Ever. Until he did.

"I saved the note he left me," I say to Kate. He had left it taped to my apartment door. *I'm sorry. I love you.*

"Why is that?" she says.

"To remind me that I was better off." His leaving felt like an earthquake, left the ground shaking under my feet, and at first I wasn't sure if I could keep from falling. But I did and somehow I was stronger, more motivated than ever. I quit smoking, stopped acting like a spoiled kid, and decided I could have any future I wanted because I was the one in control of it. My hands trace a circle in my notebook, and I look up, my mind holding on to the image of Tate, unsure of how or why it's there. "Um, oh, sorry . . ." I busy myself with my notes, desperately searching for a conversation thread that I can make sense of.

Kate clears her throat. "Last time, you brought up the fight you had with your dad when you were pregnant. Did you want to talk about that today?"

My hands go limp in my lap. "Oh, well, okay." I bite my lip, can see the sad squint of my father's eyes when he looked at me, the grip of his hands around my journal. "He shouldn't have read it," I say. "But I know why he did."

"And why was that?"

"He was worried about me." I look down. "I'd been having dreams about becoming just like her."

"Like your mother?"

I shoot her a look. "Of course. But I hadn't realized how badly I wanted to be a mother until I saw those two pink lines. I was scared because nothing about it was ideal. No father to help, about to start my first job out of college. Of course I was having nightmares, you know?"

She nods. "But your dad was worried?"

I fiddle with the pages of my notebook because I don't need my notes for this moment. It's branded in my head. And surely I've spoken of this with Kate. Probably a dozen times.

She seems to anticipate my question. "This is something you are still working through, Claire. But, if it helps, each time you seem to gain perspective."

I nod and write that bit down because it does help to hear that, even if I'm not sure how it affects me when I can't remember it, but knowing that in this moment, it feels good to talk about it, nice to have someone listen even if it doesn't change the past.

"Why did he read your journal?"

I sigh. "I'd told him the baby's dad was this egocentric grad student who didn't want to tie his boat to a girl from Whittier."

"But he was worried," Kate says.

"Yes, very. I can't blame him. I was twenty-six and about to have a baby on my own. It was scary." The pain from that night is vivid and bright. I'd woken up with a headache, and it didn't matter anymore what he'd read in my journal because the pain was so bad I couldn't see. I'd fumbled for the phone. He was there in minutes. "He picked me up and carried me to his car." I look at her with my hands spread out on either side of me. "Can you even picture that? I'm six foot *and* I was nearly nine months pregnant. It would have been like picking up a small truck." I remember lying across the back seat, the tunnel lights flying by, and thinking Dad was driving too fast and it was too late to be in the tunnel and—"Nothing."

Kate leans forward. "What's that?"

"I don't remember what happened after that, except what everyone has told me. But I do remember one thought."

Kate nods and I deflate because she's heard this, of course, probably more times than she can count.

I carry on regardless. "That I was going to lose the baby." I remember cradling my stomach and the fear that crawled over my skin, the tears spreading down my cheeks.

Kate nods again, prodding me to continue. It's annoying, like having my hand held by a teacher. I don't remember being an overly emotional person from before, but now my skin spreads thin, my emotions delicate butterflies that easily whip themselves into a frenzy.

"Dad was right to be scared for me." I shake my notebook in the air. "But it's all for the best anyway. What kind of a mother would I have made like this?" Tears sting my eyes, curl my hands into fists that I pound on my thighs. I remember with painful clarity the itchy stretch of skin, taut over my rounded belly. The fullness of my breasts, the rib kicks that woke me every morning. Even now, there is a hollowness inside me that grows when my hand involuntarily moves to touch my stomach, flat and deflated. I inhale, exhale, and read from my notebook to remind myself that ten years ago, I had a seizure when I was pregnant that left me with anterograde amnesia and took my baby girl.

Tears run down my face, the pain I feel as real, as present as if it had just happened. Kate hands me a tissue and waits until my face is dry. "You had eclampsia, Claire. There was nothing you could have done, and you're lucky to be alive."

"Am I?"

"Yes. And for the record, I think you would have been a wonderful mother, even like this."

I meet her gaze, strong and unwavering, and I can see that she means what she says. I give her a small smile, grateful for the sentiment. "Not very professional of you, though. Seems like you've gone off script, Kate."

Kate laughs, leans back in her chair. "I'm always off script when it comes to you."

Before the moment disappears into the muck inside my head, I record the last few minutes, even my tears. Then I pick up the file folder labeled THERAPIST SESSION CURRENT, and air rushes from my lungs in a relieved whoosh at the organized thoughts and talking points I've assembled in the file. There's a line from my notebook that I'd copied into the file: *I wish I could teach again.* It's the reason I think I feel sad. A piece of paper drops from the file, and when I see it, my lips flatten. It's a flyer with a sticky note on top. *Give guitar lessons??* I look at the flyer.

INTERESTED IN BEGINNER GUITAR LESSONS? CONTACT CLAIRE HINES, APARTMENT 1407

"What's that?"

I hold it out to Kate. "Apparently I want to give guitar lessons." I drop my eyes to my notebook, embarrassed by the idea. What in the world put that into my head? How can I teach when I can't recall what I had for breakfast? I run the tip of my pen over a line, keep tracing it until the line is thick and black and imprinted onto the page below it.

"Does that upset you?" When I look up I find her looking at the angry line in my notebook, eyebrows raised. "This is a new idea." There's excitement in her voice.

I put a hand to my chest and say jokingly, "My God, Kate, have we actually reached new territory?"

She laughs. "Always the funny one, but yes, you haven't tried something like this before, and I think it would be fun for you." Her forehead wrinkles. "When did you learn?"

"My mom taught me when I was a little girl. Well, she was teaching herself and wanted me to learn, so . . ." I blow air into my cheeks, try to hold on to an attitude of *I'm too old to be hurt by memories of my mother* but find it difficult when this particular memory is spiced with warmth and sweetened by chocolate. *We'll learn together, Claire bear.* I was six, in the years when she read me a story every night, snuggled beside me on my small bed, my head resting in the crook of her arm.

The years when her laugh was clear and free and I was enough to keep her nightmares at bay.

I start to tear at the page. "It was stupid of me to think this was possible. I wouldn't even know where to start."

Mom's voice fills my head: *It says here to start with these eight chords.* She'd read from a booklet she'd found at a used bookstore in Anchorage, the one that said BEGINNER GUITAR in white block letters across the front. I sat beside her on the couch, our legs touching, my feet swinging above the floor, and she looked at me with a smile that touched the blue green of her eyes.

I close the notebook. "Not possible."

Kate tilts her head. "You're allowed to have dreams, Claire," she says softly, and points to my notebook. "Look at what you've done already with your notes and calendars. It's remarkable and truly impressive how you've taught yourself to remember in this way. But maybe this would give you something more."

I stiffen. "More than what?"

"More than just trying to remember," she says softly. "An experience that you would enjoy."

"An experience?" I say, rolling my shoulders, suddenly annoyed. "Only if I can keep my notes organized enough so I can read about it later." I shake my head. How could I do something like this without messing up? Without exposing the real me? I feel the blood pulsing under my skin. "Yeah, that seems like a pretty stupid idea."

There's a long silence, and then Kate shifts in her seat, closes her file folder, and crosses her legs at the ankles. "But how will you know if you don't try it?"

I give her a look. "I can't remember a damn thing, Kate. How will I know either way?" My words come out biting, rude, and I suck in my bottom lip, ashamed. Kate's only trying to help.

She shrugs, seems unfazed. "True, true. But still."

I read once more—*I wish I could teach again*—and straighten up in my chair. A tingling sensation fingers into the muscles of my back. Maybe she has a point. I pull a black felt-tip pen from my bag, underline the sentence, flip forward, and jot it under today's date. Then I pull out my folder labeled "THERAPIST SESSION CURRENT," record *I wish I could teach again*, followed by, *teach guitar?* But when I read it over, my pen freezes above the page and I have to fight the urge to rip the paper out. What makes me think I could ever do something like this? It's an impossible dream. I cross it out once, then twice more. I'm not the kind of person who can dream.

My phone dings and I glance at the screen. Session is over. Drive home to Whittier. Text Ruth that you're leaving and will make 1:30 tunnel. "Time's up," I say. I open my text messages and send a quick message to Ruth before sliding my notebook and file folder into my bag. The one-lane tunnel switches directions every fifteen minutes, which isn't too bad unless a train comes through, and that will have me waiting longer than normal. When I stand I sling the strap over my head, letting it rest across my shoulder. "Thanks, Kate. I think this was a good session today."

She smiles, stands. "I agree."

~

My car idles at the signal outside the tunnel. A vehicle is allowed in every fifteen seconds, so I watch as the taillights of the sedan ahead of me glow red in the dark tunnel, wait for the signal to turn green. My voice floats from the car speakers, giving me a repeating loop of instructions: *You are driving home to Whittier from Anchorage after seeing Therapist Kate. You are driving home to Whittier from Anchorage after seeing Therapist Kate.*

It might seem impossible that someone like me could ever drive again. I know Ruth thought it was. Something I don't have to remember because I simply know her well enough to guess the worried slant of her eyes, the thin line of her lips. I'm sure my driving worries her, but for me it's the most normal thing I do. To keep from getting lost or confused, I stick to dependable routes, like the one from Whittier to Anchorage and back again, which I had traveled often *before*. But just in case, I play the audio file for each trip so that I don't forget and accidentally end up in Seward.

The signal turns green, and I accelerate into the tunnel, letting the rocky mouth swallow me whole. Overhead lights blink past in a familiar rhythm. The walls are rough with blasted rock hewn into a narrow but tall interior. I was a teenager when the tunnel opened up to cars. Before then the only way we could get into or out of Whittier was by train, plane, or boat. Dad always said the tunnel came too late for Mom. But I know that nothing would have made her stay.

My hands grip the wheel until the flesh over my knuckles whitens. I don't remember much after my headache overwhelmed me, but I can recall Dad's truck sailing through this narrow tube, the red swaths of light that painted the walls and his face, worry lines deeply embedded into his forehead. *It's okay, you're going to be okay, Claire bear, it's all going to be okay.*

Ahead is a small semicircle of light that brightens and grows with each rotation of my tires. And just like that, the tunnel spits me out and I emerge on the other side of the mountain. Muddled light sifts through bottom-heavy clouds, clinging to the tops of mountains and brushing over gray water. I don't look in the rearview mirror at the yawning black hole behind me, don't want to think any more about the tunnel that stole my memory and squirreled it away into its dark, damp, and unreachable recesses.

When the road opens into Whittier, a heaviness lifts from my chest and my breathing flows unhindered. The entire town encompasses something like twelve square miles. A small U-shaped plot of land bounded on one side by the deep waters of the Passage Canal. Begich

Towers sits toward the backside of town, a blocky, yellow monolith that is at odds with the wild Alaskan landscape surrounding it.

I breathe out a smile. I don't care what it looks like. It's my home.

But as I turn down Glacier Avenue, my voice still looping from the speakers, perhaps unnecessarily by now—*you are driving home to Whittier from Anchorage after seeing Therapist Kate*—a big black body, its thick fur glistening wet, lopes across the road in front of me. Heart pounding, I slam on the brakes; Ruth's ancient Jeep is no match for a bear. Instead of running off, the bear stops and turns its huge round head toward me. It's a big bear, easily the biggest one I've ever seen here, but when he looks my way, I don't feel scared. Instead, I'm back in the lobby of BTI, seven years old and standing behind a man who can take on a bear, probably a wolf if he had to—anything to protect me. The bear turns and runs down the road, his rounded backside quickly retreating, then disappearing into the park.

A smile stretches the corners of my mouth, and when I park the Jeep at BTI, I write down about the bear I saw and how it reminded me of Dad.

CHAPTER FIVE

When I get back—from my visit with Therapist Kate, my notes remind me—I sit down at my desk to review what we talked about. I see the flyer I made about guitar lessons and the jagged lines that cross the idea out in my notes, along with a note that says, *Impossible.* I nod, agreeing with myself, yet I hesitate when I start to throw the flyer into the recycling bin, feel a pang at the thought of letting this idea slip away. Instead, I toss it into the wire basket on my desk, but when I do I notice a newspaper clipping crumpled underneath.

I lay it flat on the table, turn on my desk lamp to see it better because the rain clouds have gathered in a thick gray mass outside my window. It's dated February of last year with a short article highlighted in yellow.

> The body of William Dunn, 60, of Whittier, Alaska, was discovered by a local couple snowshoeing Shotgun Cove Road. Authorities believe that he lost his way home early Tuesday morning and fell into a snowbank. Foul play is not suspected.

In shock, I let the article fall back to the desk. Tate's father is dead. A flicker of sadness passes through me at the idea of anyone dying, but when it comes to Bill Dunn, my heart is hardened winter earth, and the news of his death a blunt spade.

The very first time I saw Bill was outside BTI. He was standing beside a dented and rusted pickup truck, setting a case of beer into the waiting arms of seven-year-old Tate. There were few kids in our town, so I'd tried to make friends with the new boy, but he hardly looked up from his shoes, leaving school as soon as it was over, sometimes not even showing up for days. I was curious about the boy who still hadn't spoken to me since moving to Whittier a few months before, and I'd followed him outside, hoping he'd want to make a snow fort with me.

His father's voice shot across the parking lot, and I'd hesitated by the door, unsure. Bill Dunn was not a tall man like my own dad, but he was an angry one, and I remember how it shot off him like porcupine quills, sharp and needlelike and mostly directed at his small, stuttering dark-haired son. Tate wore a T-shirt, and his skinny arms had trembled with the weight and the cold, tightening around the case of beer that was slipping from his grip. When his father set a pair of work boots on top, the box fell from his arms, and Tate cried out. It thumped to the ground, breaking a bottle, which stained the snow at his feet a dark brown.

Goddamn you, Tate!

Tate's whole body shook with the effort to respond. *S . . . s . . . s . . . s—*

It was all he could get out, and I remember how my eyes burned from his struggle. Then his father did something that made my seven-year-old self so angry I pounded my small fists into the metal stair railing. My hands hurt for days afterward.

He mocked him. *S . . . s-orry, D . . . D-ad.*

Tate's head hung so low I wondered how he could breathe all crunched up like that. Then his father slapped him upside the head, and Tate tumbled backward, falling onto his bottom. I bit my bottom lip because I was crying and mad and filled with something I didn't understand. Rage.

But I did understand rocks. So I picked one up, packed it in fresh, powdery snow, then crept across the lot until I was only a few feet away from the two of them. His dad's back was to me, but still my heart galloped in my chest, and I was breathing hard and fast. Up close, Tate's dad looked scary. Like a giant about to eat a whole village of children. From the ground, Tate met my eyes and shook his head once. But I ignored him because my dad had taught me that what's right is right, and this seemed like the rightest thing I could do. So I lifted up my fist that had gone cold holding the snow-covered rock, and I pulled it behind my head, and I closed one eye and stuck out my tongue so I could aim better, and then I let the snowball fly. When it sailed through the air, the snow flicked off in a spiral so that when it landed exactly where I had aimed—smack-dab in the middle of his big, fat head—the sharp part of the rock bit right into his skull. I knew this because he said, *Ow, goddamn it,* and bent over like I'd shot him.

I grabbed Tate by the hand, yanked him to his feet, and ran inside BTI and into the laundry room, where we hid between a vending machine and the wall. My heart thumped so hard I felt it in my temples, and beside me Tate's breath was ragged and hot in the small space. I felt his body jerk, and when I looked at him, his mouth was open like he was going to talk, but nothing came out. I was still holding his hand from before and I didn't let go, waiting until he spoke. *He m . . . m-ight k . . . k . . . k-ill you.*

I shook my head, squeezed his hand. *I don't think he saw me, and besides, my dad won't let him.*

Afterward, I hid under my covers, suddenly unsure and scared. Would he come after me? When Dad came home later, I told him everything, and he pulled me into his lap and rocked me, his soft laughter vibrating against my ear. *You're the bravest girl I know, Claire. But maybe next time leave the monsters to me.*

And now Bill's dead. I can't help but think about Tate. He left Whittier because he couldn't bear to live anywhere near his father, was scared of becoming just like him. He never would have; I'd always known that, but Tate hadn't. He thought leaving was his only choice. I look at the article. Would this change anything? My fingers tap the desk. Of course not. And it wouldn't matter if it did, because I am a ghost of the person he once knew. I rub my arms against the cold truth. By now, he's likely built a Whittier-free life somewhere in the lower forty-eight with his wife. My cheeks burn at the thought of him ever knowing me like I am now. I pin the article to a bulletin board I keep beside my desk. I want to remember that Bill Dunn is gone, if only for Tate.

I push "Favorites" on my phone, click on Dad's name.

"You've reached Vance, building manager. Leave a message."

"Hey, Dad, it's Claire." I pause, cradle the phone against my shoulder, scratch the skin on the top of my hand until I've left red lines. An uneasiness wriggles in my gut, but I can't place why or what could be causing it. I glance at the article. "Did you know that Bill Dunn died? I wonder if Tate knows." The clipping is wrinkled and worn, and when I check the calendar, a burn spreads across my cheeks. He died a year ago. Of course Tate knows, and Dad, and everyone else. Silence from the other end; that's right, because I'm—I check my notes—leaving a message. There's a line highlighted and circled with *Tell Dad!* written beside it. "This bear ran in front of my car today, and it reminded me of the bear you scared out of the lobby when I was seven. Do you remember that?" I smile, the memory rich in detail, comforting in its clarity. "Okay, I'd better go. I love you. Talk soon, Dad."

I head to the kitchen to make something to eat, but a nervous energy worms through my leg muscles, and I have a sudden desire to see Ruth, share my day with her. It's a habit I developed when I was nine and my mother began sleeping most of the time. At first it was only a morning here, an afternoon nap there. I thought Mom was tired, so I didn't think too much of it, until I'd come home from school to find her still in bed, blinds drawn, the air that drifted from the room smelling like unwashed hair and sweat mingling with the musk of alcohol. Things started to pile up around the apartment: dishes, laundry, garbage. And when she did emerge from her room, she couldn't meet my eyes. Like she'd given up. I missed her sitting with me at the kitchen table after school, a plate of cookies between us, her head cocked to the side as she listened to me talk about my day, my homework, my friend troubles, anything and everything. I missed the feel of her lips on my forehead, kissing me good night. Her soft voice, humming gently while she measured and stirred, the sweetness of her creations clinging to her skin, a perfect perfume. She was disappearing, pieces of her falling off like discarded clothing, bit by bit, until one day I realized the mom I loved was gone.

It takes me only a few seconds to get to Ruth's door. I knock, but there's no answer. I knock again. From inside I hear a shuffling, then what sounds like muffled voices, more than one. I put my ear close to the door. "Ruth?"

"Hang on," comes her voice. The door opens a crack, and Ruth pokes her wiry gray head out. "Game night doesn't start until seven thirty."

My notebook shakes in my hands when I blurt out, "Did you know that Bill Dunn died?" I flip pages. "And that I thought I could give guitar lessons?" I snort. "Isn't that the most ridiculous idea?"

Ruth's apartment has always been a refuge for me. To some she might come off as unfeeling, like she's made of steel, because she keeps her emotions on a tight leash. But I know a different side of her. I know the woman who let me sleep on her sofa after my mom left, whenever Dad was on the road and I didn't want to be alone because I was having nightmares. Who rested a cool cloth across my forehead when I had the flu. Who made tea and drank it with me while I cried over my heart, which Tate had shattered when he left Whittier. And I know the woman whose husband went through the tunnel with Becky from the second floor and never came back. Ruth may not show her feelings, but they're there; they just run so deep they're cool.

Still, Ruth doesn't invite me in, and drifting out from behind her in a mouthwatering breeze is the aroma of oranges and cinnamon.

"Were you baking?" I ask doubtfully. The air is rich with buttery dough, and my stomach responds with a quiet growl. "It smells amazing, Ruth. When did you—" Movement from behind her, and then a cough or a sneeze brings my eyebrows together. "Is someone here?"

Ruth sighs and pushes the door all the way open. "It's Alice, Claire. She's here and I know she'd love to talk to you."

Her name hits me like the cold winter wind that sweeps up from the harbor, and for a second I can't get my breath.

Ruth's eyes soften. "Come in."

My mother appears from behind Ruth, the same and yet so different from how I remember her last—stumbling down a row of folding chairs, her eyes glazed and too bright, tripping, falling, grasping for anything to keep herself upright. Her words smushed together in a long slur. *ImsoproudofyouClaire.*

"I've moved back to Whittier, Claire."

I cross my arms against the painful beating of my heart. "Why?"

She doesn't answer, wringing her hands like she's unsure of herself. "I would like very much to be part of your life, if you'll have me." Her shoulders rise when she takes in a long breath. Like she's preparing for battle. I feel my face harden. If she wants forgiveness, that is not something I can give, nor is it something I think she has the right to ask. Not after all the pain she's caused me and Dad, even Ruth, who stands there likes she's forgotten it all. My lips press into a firm line. I remember for all of us.

"I haven't been back long, but I don't believe you've written it down yet." She smiles, and lines fan out from her eyes. "That's okay—when you're ready."

The words collect in my throat, a logjam of biting and perfectly timed responses expressing the years of sadness and disappointment that are a callus around my heart. That can describe this everlasting feeling of not being good enough for her, for Tate, for anyone. And now . . . my thoughts trail away because now, I knit my eyebrows together, turn to my notebook. Now it is ten years later, and she is back in Whittier. I picture the look of horror on Dad's face when he saw Mom at graduation, lurching toward me. Saw him lift his bulk from the seat, stretch his arms out even though he was too far away, the lines of sadness that had carved a path in his face. He's never said it, but I know he's never given up hope that she'd come home. Never stopped believing she'd get better. And hurting him, even more than the pain of leaving me, is what I can't forgive her for.

I swallow and all the words disappear. "I don't want to see you." I am thirteen and she is the mother who left me. My fingernails bite into my palms, and I use that little bit of pain to keep from crying.

Mom gives Ruth a sideways glance. "I understand, Claire. But I've been sober for nearly ten years now, sweetheart, and I know it doesn't seem that way to you, but I am stronger now, and the things that made me drink don't hurt me in the same way. I want to be here for you now." She chews on her bottom lip. "Vance thought it was time for us to be together."

Anger rocks me, starts in my fingers, moves up my arms, and I'm speaking through my teeth. "Dad doesn't want you here, Mom. I just talked to him—" I stop because I'm not sure that's true, yet just because I can't remember doesn't make it untrue either. I start to flip through my notebook, looking for an interaction with Dad that might indicate he knew she was back, because he would have told me.

"It's true, Claire."

Ruth's voice shocks me, brings me out of my notebook that is full of teaching aspirations, bears, but nothing about Mom, not a mention that she's living back in Whittier. I look up. "True?"

"Alice has moved home. She and Vance want to help you—"

I hold up my notebook as if it's a shield that can deflect her words. A part of me understands that my reaction is juvenile, but I can't help feeling as though everyone I thought I could trust is keeping me in the dark. It's a terrible feeling, but that's why I have my notebook; that's why I write everything down.

So I don't forget.

I turn away from them, my chest hurting with the effort to keep from crying, and hurry back to my apartment, write everything down I can remember. *Mom lives in Whittier, and Ruth knows but didn't tell me. They say Dad knows but it's not true. He's never told me and I know this for a fact. Don't believe them.*

Once it's all down, I can breathe out. I sit back and let my pen fall to the desk. I rub my hand; it aches. The corners of my mouth are weighted into a frown, and I can't lift out of the fog that surrounds me. I read the lines that explain this clinging sadness. *Mom lives in Whittier, and Ruth knows but didn't tell me.*

I sit at my desk and stare out the window. A cruise ship is docked in the port, its length and height dwarfing the smaller boats that fill the slips in the harbor. Cars and trucks dominate the parking lots. In September, Whittier is still bustling with tourists and fishermen and adventure seekers, but by the end of next month, everyone will leave, taking their boats and their money and their wide-eyed enthusiasm for all things Alaska, and give us back our town.

A buzz from my phone shocks me out of my thoughts and reminds me to head up to the fifteenth floor for game night. There are only fourteen floors in BTI, but the elevator numbers skip thirteen, a nod to the more superstitious among us and a laughable oddity for the rest of us. I stand and stretch, but when I sigh, it catches on a sob. I cover my hand with my palm, wait for the feeling to pass. Sad. I am sad. I start to open my notebook when my phone buzzes again with a reminder. **Game Night.** Instead, I slide my notebook into my shoulder bag and head up to the community room. I don't want to know why I'm sad. I want to see my friends and have some fun.

When I get there, Sefina, Harriet, and Kiko, who has taught the elementary-age kids for as long as I can remember, have already gathered, plus a few faces I don't recognize. There are sandwiches, salads, chips, and sodas, and I fill my plate, grateful for the food.

"How are you doing, Claire?" Kiko says.

A question like this is difficult for me. So I evaluate how I feel at this moment—surrounded by friends, my belly full—and I answer honestly, "I'm really good, Kiko. How are you?"

Kiko studies me for a moment, and I try to understand her pause. Are things not good for her? Has she been ill? Could she have a tough group of kids this year?

"I've been better." She smiles and touches my arm. "But I do have a new student, and oh my, she is a spirited one. Curious, energetic, and spicy. She reminds me of you."

I laugh. Kiko was my teacher when I went to school here and is the reason I wanted to be a teacher in the first place. "Then she's in good hands."

"You'll get a chance to meet her when you come in on Tuesday. The kids love when you volunteer."

I smile and nod, even though I have no idea what she's talking about, but as it sounds like something I would enjoy and since I've always loved being around kids, I have no doubt that it's a part of my schedule. "I can't wait!"

Sefina appears by Kiko's side, holding a bowl of small white papers. "It's celebrity charades tonight," she says and winks at me. "But only well-known people from *before* can be entered."

I duck my head when Sefina says this to hide the burning in my cheeks. She means well, I know, but the public announcement affects me regardless. I write down what Kiko said about volunteering and then try to keep on top of recording the game and who did what and who was the best guesser. I have to pause when my hand burns from writing. One minute blends into the next, and I try to relax and enjoy the game and the laughter even as it fades. Sometime later, I return home to my quiet apartment, and before I go to bed, I sit down at my desk to review and make a plan for the next day's activities, record everything on the calendar and my phone, and set out my clothes for tomorrow.

CHAPTER SIX

Monday, October 1

It's an Alaskan morning when the sun creeps slowly above the mountains, staining the sky outside a watercolor of light blues and dusty pinks. A journal lies open beside me in bed, the one with the leather cover and the pages that are going soft from the years. It's the first thing I reach for because it's where I start every morning: reading about me. On the first page is a letter I wrote to myself, dated eight years ago. One I've read every morning since I first wrote it, and I know this because I instructed myself to make a hash mark on the pages of the journal for each time I read. The marks fill pages, grouped and totaled by month and then again by year for a running total of 2,920 times that I have read this same damn letter. I read the letter even though I don't need to—years of sticking to the same routine have left an impression, if not the details. On some level I know that I'm different now.

> You were pregnant and developed eclampsia that made you have a seizure. Because of that you lost the baby and your ability to form new memories. It's hard and it sucks but it's better this way. You couldn't have been a good mother to her. Not like this. But you

have Dad and Ruth and Sefina and you are organized and detailed and you have found a way to survive this through your lists and calendars and because it's the only way you can be normal.

You lost the baby. I press a palm against my eyes to block out the truth, but the words hover in the darkness. I would have been a great mom. Loving, kind, caring, and all the things my mother couldn't be to me. I close the journal and set it on my bedside table. Mirabelle. It means marvelous and wonderful, and it's exactly what she would have been to me. I wipe at my eyes but they are dry. The information is not new; I can feel that it's not and that it's something I've mourned and grieved about and known for quite some time, even if it punches a hole in my heart every time. Something I don't have to remember to just *know*.

I inhale a ragged breath and move on to the laminated card that sits on my bedside table. There's a small clothespin clipped to the side and even with the words *Step One: Read the journal,* followed by *Step Two: Shower, Step Three: Get Dressed,* and *Step Four: Check calendar for today's schedule.* I move the clothespin even with Step Two but hesitate before standing. There is a painful stiffness, an ache that spreads from my lower back, radiates up my spine and across my shoulder blades. It rushes up like a wave, pushes into the base of my skull, runs its frothy tips around the sides of my head. I press my bare feet into the carpet, let my head hang, grip the bed with my fingers until the pain retreats into the background. I have headaches now—it's all in my notes—and I know to wait for the blur in the edges of my vision to sharpen before I push up from the bed and head for the shower.

Hot water runs down my back, at first spreading goose bumps across my skin until the heat seeps into my bones. I sigh and close my eyes, reveling in the sensation before I begin to wash my hair. Hanging beside the shampoo is a laminated card with another clothespin and a line of instructions. *Wash hair, wash body, shave under arms, shave legs, done.* I move the clothespin as I do each activity, making sure I don't end up showering until the hot water runs out.

I find a pair of athletic leggings, a sports bra, a T-shirt, and my University of Alaska sweatshirt hanging over a chair in my bedroom. A pair of tennis shoes and pink socks are on the floor under the chair. I set my clothes out when I review my schedule every evening. Must be Jazzercise day. I don't even have to remind myself to know that it's Monday. Ruth's always taught Jazzercise on Mondays. I started going to her class when I was in college and would come home for breaks and holidays. Now it's part of my routine and helps to keep me in shape. After I dress, I head out to get myself organized for the day.

The view of the harbor is clear; the clouds have thinned, and a pale-blue sky peeks out from between wisps of white and pink cotton. Steam rises from a coffee mug on my desk, infusing the air with an earthy aroma of spice and berries. I take a sip and savor the rich flavor. For a few moments, I relax, let the caffeine move through my body, waking me up at the same time that the sun stretches yellow fingertips of light across the spiky tips of pine trees.

Pinned to a small bulletin board beside my desk is a note. The one that Tate left me before he left Whittier. *I'm sorry. I love you.* It still hurts to read it, because when he left, I felt like I'd lost a part of me. Eventually, I came to understand why he did. His dad's abuse was a suffocating shadow that trailed Tate wherever he went. He had to leave in order to find out who he was. But I was sure he'd come back, and when he didn't, it hurt even more.

After I threw the rock at his dad, Tate and I were hardly ever separated. And when my mom began drinking, we understood each other in a way that welded that connection into an unbreakable bond. Thinking about him now allows other memories to drift to the surface, earlier ones that move through my head in a warm procession, and I smile. When we were kids, skipping rocks at the fishing cove, making bowls out of the spring mud and filling them with leaves and rocks, pretending to have dinner together in our own apartment. As young teens after a bike ride, sitting on a rock side by side, our thighs barely touching, his finger running down my arm until my fist unfurled, and he slipped his hand into mine. Playing basketball in the school gym, our competition always fierce. The feel of his lips against mine, his body long and lean and a perfect match to my own. The way he hugged me like he'd never let me go. Then come the ones that leave me cold. The blackness of the bruised and swelling skin around his eye on that last morning at the Buckner Building. The salty taste of tears and the lemon tang of the tea Ruth fixed me when he was gone.

And then the last memory I have of him. At my master's graduation, seven years after he left Whittier. The pinpricks of electricity that coursed through my skin when I saw him—tall, handsome, *there*. A bubbling of hope that pushed into my heart. He was back! Everything would work out after all. Except this time I was the one who left, hurried, picking up my scattered clothes, wiping the mascara that had bled down my face, because this time I understood the truth. We had nothing in common anymore.

With a sigh, I set the cup down and turn to my work, picking up my notebook for September and laying it open. From a desk drawer I pull out a fresh notebook. On the cover of the new journal, I affix a yellow label, which is the color I've assigned to this year, and below that an orange label, which is the color I've assigned to the month of October. I have piles of notebooks, color coded by year, then month, then numbered by volume if there are multiple notebooks per month. The pages of September are worn from use, a black ring from where I must have set my coffee cup down on the page. I'm careful as I read over the month, making sure I move forward any information, dates, or notes to myself that seem important into the October notebook.

There's a line about teaching guitar lessons that lifts my eyebrows. What in the world made me come up with that kind of idea? Already a memory rises, unbidden. Mom across from me on the floor, a cheap guitar balanced in her lap, the instructional book opened in front of her. *Okay, Claire bear, it says here that every guitar player should start with these eight chords. And today's lesson focuses on two of those chords.* A wrinkle formed between her eyes when she looked at me. *You're missing something.* I sat cross-legged, my elbows resting on my legs, head in my hands, just watching. She was beautiful. Dark hair shiny and thick. Skin glowing and smooth, and the way she looked at me, like I was the most important kid in the whole world. Dad had always told me that when he first saw her, he felt knocked in the gut. It felt that way being her daughter, too, before alcohol took over.

She smiled at me, touched the dimple in my chin with her thumb. *I know what's missing. Go look on your bed.*

I'd scrambled to my feet and raced to my bedroom, squealing when I saw what rested on my pillow. A small guitar. And even better, it was purple. My favorite color.

I returned to the living room, beaming, and took my place on the floor across from her, hugging the guitar to my chest. *I love it!*

She'd touched my face, her eyes bright, and when she spoke her voice was thick. *I love you, Claire.*

I shake my head, wait for the burn in my eyes to fade. I wish these memories didn't still hurt. Haven't I shed enough tears for her?

I breathe in and return to my job, relieved to see I'd crossed the idea out completely. I nod, agreeing with myself. It's a bad idea. But the next note is like a slap across my cheek. *Mom lives in Whittier, and Ruth knows but didn't tell me.* I flip backward through the month. Does Dad know? He must have told me at some point. He would never keep that from me.

I tilt my head when I see the page for September 21. It's been almost entirely marked out with black marker. Nearly an entire day gone. I flip forward from there, stop, my hands hovering over the pages. There are blacked-out sentences on every day since. I suck in my bottom lip. A sadness coils around my heart. Am I this determined to reject her so completely? I feel a twinge of guilt at the idea and an anxiousness that creeps across my skull. I hate that I can't remember.

I sit back in my chair, thinking about Mom and Dad. The way she fell apart was like watching a beautiful flower wilt and die, gradual and painful to witness. She'd been a magnet of genuine warmth that made everyone around her feel important to her in some irreplaceable way. But once she got used to being numbed by vodka, nobody was enough. She was always worse when Dad was driving for long stretches of time, like he was a lifeboat she clung to, falling back into the water as soon as he left.

I didn't realize how bad things had gotten until one morning when I was twelve. I'd had a terrible nightmare that my mother had lost her way in a storm and slipped into the harbor and drowned. I woke up in a cold sweat, scared, frantic. She wasn't in her bed; it looked like she'd never come home. I was crying, hardly able to catch my breath. Tate had met me in the lobby. *She's dead, Tate. She's dead.* The dream was fresh, fueling a panic I couldn't control, because I think deep down I knew that I was losing her. We got to the outside doors and Tate stopped suddenly, flinging one arm back as though to keep me from moving past. *Get R . . . R-uth,* he'd said. Instead, I'd pushed past him and gasped. A woman huddled on the concrete step outside, arms wrapped around the metal post like she was holding on against a hurricane-force wind. I pushed through the doors, and the cold wind stole my breath when I knelt beside her. Her head hung down, hair falling in tangled clumps around her face, and she smelled. Like alcohol and body odor.

I'd pressed my arms into my stomach, thinking I might puke. *Mom?*

She'd lifted up her face and stared at me with bloodshot eyes. *Oh, hi, Claire bear.* She said it like we'd accidentally run into each other at the harbor. Like she wasn't hurting me over and over. Like I was nothing at all. The remnants of my dream vanished, taking with them my fear, and suddenly I was filled with an anger that burned. My hands balled into fists. *What's wrong with you! Why can't you stop? I hate you so much!*

Her body shook like my words were bullets piercing her skin. I'd screamed until my voice was hoarse and I was crying, and Tate led me away and upstairs to my apartment, and then Ruth was there, my head in her lap, a cool washcloth on my forehead.

My phone buzzes in my pocket, and when I reach for it, a note card slides out and falls to the floor. There's a date on one side. Friday, September 21. I pick up the card, flip it over, and find a note to me, short but to the point, and the words dance and blur and whip themselves into a frenzy that rushes to my head in painful stabs. The note card falls from my hand when the desk vibrates with an alarm for Jazzercise. I jump to turn it off, elbowing my coffee cup, which topples over, spreading coffee across the card, my notebook, and phone. I grab the notebook and hurry for a paper towel, biting my lip. I could lose an entire month of memories because of a stupid accident.

A few pages are damp and a three-by-five note card is a sopping brown mess, but for the most part, it doesn't look too bad. Relieved that the damage is minimal, I throw the note card in the trash, wipe off the notebook, and check my phone. I'm going to be late for Jazzercise, and not surprisingly, Ruth hates when people come in late. Says it throws off her whole dance game.

CHAPTER SEVEN

At first, Ruth and Jazzercise don't appear to go hand in hand until you see her leg kicks and spins, which destroy every preconceived notion anyone ever has about sour-faced Ruth from the post office. She holds the class in the school gym, which is located a short distance behind BTI and is accessible by a pedestrian tunnel that connects the two buildings or by a very quick walk outside. We use the tunnel for days when snow pushes up and over our doors, or when the wind slices through the air with gusts capable of taking little ones off their feet. With the nice weather, I decide to walk outside. Fresh air is something I don't take lightly.

I get there just as Ruth's voice booms from the front of the room. "Line up, ladies. Oh, Claire, you've decided to join us. Good. There's a spot by Sefina."

I take my spot, unsure why I'm finding it hard to get a deep breath.

A light touch on my arm. "Are you okay, Claire?" Sefina's face is soft with concern.

I think about her question and give the best answer I can. "I don't know. I feel sad, I think, but I don't know why." I'm confused and feeling exceptionally vulnerable, which is probably why I decide to take a leap and ask, "Do you?"

Her mouth drops open, and she pulls back, eyes darting over my shoulder. I turn, see Ruth, who is talking to my mother. The muscles in my legs go weak. Now I know why I feel this way. "What is she doing here?" I say through clenched teeth.

"She lives here now, Claire." Sefina speaks low, calm. "You know this but I think it's been hard for you to accept. She's different, though, I promise. But I don't think that's why you're—"

Music booms from a large speaker, drowning out whatever else she was going to say. I turn to see my mother has gone, and Ruth is at the front of the room. "Let's stop the chatter, ladies, and work up a sweat instead. I know I need to. Anyone else?"

The few half-hearted *woo-hoos* that float around the room are quickly drowned out by Sefina's exuberant "Hell to the yeah!" shout that earns her a pressed-lips look from Ruth. I laugh and begin to move, and soon the music and my own exertions drown out my breathing, Sefina's grunts, and, most especially, my thoughts. I've done Jazzercise for so long that I don't need to think in here. I can just do, so the time passes and I enjoy the physical effort without the added job of having to think too hard.

"And five, six, seven, eight, now rock lunge, ladies! Side to side. There you go. Pump your elbows. Sefina!" Ruth admonishes. "I said pump your elbows, not dance like a chicken. Heel hop! Squeeze those legs. Heel, together, heel, together. That's better, Ann Marie. Maybe next time wear your hearing aids so you can stay on the beat. I said, next time—oh, forget it!"

I smile. Ruth is still Ruth, even as a Jazzercise instructor.

"Chassé, ladies!"

I fly across the room, my legs moving without me. It's a glorious feeling. I never took dance as a kid; it was too expensive and too far away, but I think I would have been good at it.

Sefina huffs and puffs by my side, her face mottled and shiny from sweat. "You're killing the chassé today, Claire."

I smile and keep moving. For all her long-limbed gracefulness, Sefina can't dance without tripping over her own feet or mine. But my gangly six-foot frame moves with a shocking lightness. I'm not smug about it, but I am, well, proud. I love the feeling I get when I dance. My parents must have loved it, too, because my early memories of their marriage include impromptu dancing in the kitchen, the lobby, the parking lot, anywhere a moment overtook them, and I'd look up to see Dad swinging my mom around like she weighed nothing, her head thrown back and her tinkling laughter mixing into the air around us. The memory hits me with such force I nearly stumble in my chassé, but I recover, and when the music crescendos, I hit every move in time with the beat, nearly crashing into Sefina on my return across the room. She's given up, and she lands in a sweaty heap on the gym floor, one hand raised in surrender. "Cheater. You've been practicing without me, haven't you?"

I shrug. I have no idea. "You know that even if I have, it wouldn't make a difference."

"Likely excuse," she groans.

"Sefina," comes Ruth's stern voice. "Get up! This is dance class, not mat Pilates. We still have our cooldown."

Sefina blows out a forceful breath that lifts a chunk of hair out of her eyes and pushes to her feet, giving me an evil-eye glare before joining the rest of us in our cooldown. I laugh. When it comes to most things, Sefina and I have always been a competitive duo, whether it's racing to the end of a trail run on snowshoes or catching the first fish of the morning or floating across the gym floor in a chassé. It's a consistency I can rely on.

After class, I quickly find my cell phone, and it's buzzing with a reminder. Mom lives in Whittier now, and Ruth knows but didn't tell you. My fingers curl until I'm gripping the phone so hard it hurts. Ruth is obviously protecting Mom, and it stings to read that. I need to talk to Dad. Find out if he knows, because there's no way he wouldn't tell me. Quickly, I add it to my reminders and set an alarm. I can stop by his office now.

Sefina joins me and leans against the wall, glances Ruth's way. "She's crazy, like a Jazzercise dictator." She turns, eyes the bag already on my shoulder, and raises her eyebrows. "Where are you off to so fast? You're still coming over for lunch today, right?"

I check my phone calendar. "Yes, it's right here." Unlike her dancing, Sefina's cooking is excellent, and my mouth already waters from whatever she's planning to fix. "See you then."

Outside, the weather is nicer today, so the kids are on the playground. Their shouts and laughter bounce between the walls of the school and BTI, and the sound lifts my spirits. I feel a tap on my shoulder. Ruth.

"Hi, Ruth," I say.

"What are you doing?"

"Standing outside talking to you."

"Funny. I mean where are you headed now?"

I open my mouth to tell her, but there's a blankness in my brain, an unknowing I can't move past. It turns my breathing shallow, this floating in a sea of un-knowledge. My fingers dig into my palms. I hate it. On my screen are words that sharpen into arrows, stick in my chest. **Mom lives in Whittier now, and Ruth knows but didn't tell you.** There's a heated prickling in my cheeks, and I can't meet Ruth's eyes.

"Oh, Claire."

I look up to find her staring at the screen. Is that pity in her tone? I straighten my shoulders, meet her gaze. The deep lines around her mouth smooth with a softness in her eyes.

I hold up the phone. "Does he know yet?" When she doesn't reply right away, I scan my notebook, but I haven't moved anything forward from September that indicates anyone told me. Frustration at how little I know simmers together with the idea that Ruth would keep something like this from me. I look up, unable to mask my disappointment or a sense of betrayal. Ruth knows how I feel about my mother. "Why, Ruth?"

She breathes out a heavy sigh. "She's sober, Claire, and she has been for years. But don't look at me like that. Vance wanted her back here. He's the one who insisted she come home."

I recoil. Dad *wants* her back? "I don't believe you," I say, my lips tight around the words.

Ruth blinks. "It's true, Claire. Maybe he knew something, I don't know, but he loves you and he loves her, and he wants you all to be together again. And I know that all you remember are her failures." Ruth blinks again, hard, fast. "But she's better, I swear to you." She points to my notebook and her hand shakes, I think from emotion. It surprises me. "And that's something you need to write down until it sticks, because we're all too old to keep lying to ourselves."

My pen shakes over the page and my eyes blur. "So she gets to come home, and suddenly she's the good guy? After everything she did, Ruth? How is that fair?"

Ruth studies me for a long moment. Then she touches my face, and I nearly jerk back, shocked by her gentleness. "It's not, Claire. But most of life isn't. Especially yours. We just need to make the most of whatever we're given." It's classic Ruth. She never sugarcoats and she can always sense when I'm coming undone and says exactly what I need to hear to stop my emotional descent. She's been that person for me since my mom first started drinking. There must have been a well-worn path in the hallway between Ruth's apartment and my own when I was a kid. She was the first door I knocked on when Mom wouldn't get out of bed, the first number I dialed when the vodka bottles collected in the bathroom trash, and the person to ground me when I was fourteen and got caught smoking pot with Tate in the school bathroom. She invited me to dinners, brought over breakfast, and helped Mom shower when she couldn't walk a straight line. All those years, I was never alone when Dad went on the road, because I always had Ruth.

"Claire," she says, evenly and with little emotion. "Look at me."

"Yes?" My voice is an airless squeak.

"Your mom is sober, she lives in Whittier, and she loves you. Nobody is trying to keep anything from you. Okay?"

A cool breeze wraps around me, and a wave of goose bumps raises my skin. There is so much information: on my phone, in my notebook, from Ruth, from the way my heart beats too fast and I can't connect the dots, can't clear my head enough to think. My phone buzzes. Mom lives in Whittier, and Ruth knows but didn't tell you. I back away from Ruth, fueled by a longing to see Dad and a need to get away from her.

"I have to go," I say, and hurry away.

~

I pull open the lobby doors, chanting the plan in my head: *Mom lives in Whittier and Ruth knows but didn't tell you. Talk to Dad.*

Dad's office is just inside one of the lobbies and past a community board littered with flyers for game night and babysitting needs amid new building policies and parking issues. The door is closed. I knock, and when no one answers, I push it open to his small and cluttered office.

"Hello?" I call, but the room can't hide anyone, especially not Dad. I sink into a chair by his desk. My phone buzzes. Mom lives in Whittier, and Ruth knows but didn't tell you. I stare at the screen, grip the phone. Mom's back? My fist hits the desk, sending a few loose papers fluttering to the floor. As usual, his office is a mess. Dad has a penchant for saving every scrap of paper he lays his hands on and then piling those pieces of paper around his office in short stacks that cover nearly every surface, floor included. He says it's his very own system of filing that works just fine for him. And it does. Once, when I came home from college, I asked him to locate data on light bulb purchases for the past year, just to prove his system inept. He found it in minutes. That's not to say there wasn't a certain amount of cursing that accompanied his searching, but he found it nonetheless. I laugh to myself, remembering the way he lifted the spreadsheet in the air, a triumphant smile on his lips.

The memory fades and my laughter ends abruptly when I see a picture lying on top of a pile of papers. It's of Dad when he was much younger—thick head of hair, wearing a dark-blue suit, and dancing with Mom. She's beautiful, her delicate hands clasped in his giant paws, her hair floating down her back in shiny brown waves. In the photo, I see only her face—head against Dad's chest, eyes closed, mouth in a soft smile. They look happy. I let the picture fall to the desk. Of course they were happy. She was sober and they were still in love.

But why was he looking at this? My chest tightens. Does he miss her? Is he lonely? I fall back against the chair. He must be lonely. He cares for me and works his butt off to keep the heat on in this place. My thoughts turn selfishly to my own failed love life. Impossible to resurrect now, but that was probably going to be the case regardless. Tate was my everything and he broke my heart, not once but twice. I'm not sure I would have ever recovered enough to trust anyone else with my heart, and now it's too late.

A buzzing. Mom lives in Whittier, and Ruth knows but didn't tell you. The skin tightens round my mouth. What could have brought her back here? I glance at the picture once more, rub the back of my neck. Dad must know she's back. Why else would he have this picture out? But has he told me? I slide closed the reminder. Have I made it too difficult for him to be honest with me? I pull at the ends of my hair, overcome by a mixture of feelings that twist into a painful knot.

Dad never made excuses for Mom, never pretended that she was anything but a woman with an addiction. But he also never spoke ill of her, never blamed her for leaving us. I wanted him to, though; maybe even a part of me needed him to blame her. Instead, he shouldered what she'd left behind—a broken daughter, a failed marriage, and his own smashed heart—and moved on in his typical good-natured, optimistic Vance Hines way. In the picture, he holds her like she's a delicate flower that might wilt. My heart aches. I don't think he's ever stopped loving her, and I think he's always held out hope that she'd come back. I flick the picture farther away. Did he invite her back? The thought gives me a pang. What if she breaks his heart again? My hands curl into fists. I remember the look on his face when she showed up at graduation: mouth open in a silent shout, hands held out empty in front of him like they were useless.

She will hurt him again; I just know it because I don't think she can help herself. She'll never change. In my notebook I write, *Mom lives in Whittier and Dad knows*—hesitate, then add—*tell Mom to leave before she hurts us all over again.*

I'm walking out when a guy around my height walks into the office, head down, phone resting between his ear and shoulder and flipping through a stack of mail in his hands.

"Again, I'm sorry, but it's n . . . n-ot my job to remove . . . dead flies, Mrs. Johnson."

A warmth radiates from my chest, transforms into a heated jolt that shoots through my body. It can't be. But I would know the familiar cadence of his words anywhere. Tate.

"Yes, yes, I know that Vance always—holy shit!" The phone falls from his hands, and his eyes meet mine, and I can't feel my skin or the floor under my feet, and I don't think I'm breathing.

"Tate?" I whisper, even though I have no doubt from the way he talks, the slant of his eyes in the corners, the shape of his mouth, and his midnight-black hair—

"Oh, Claire, I'm sorry, I didn't know you w . . . w . . . w . . ." He pauses as though what he's trying to say is stuck to the inside of his mouth like peanut butter. "That you're here," he says finally, and it's all so familiar that it warms me instantly.

From the floor comes the squawking of Mrs. Johnson. Without breaking eye contact, Tate picks up the phone, replaces it to his ear. "I'll be up t . . . t-omorrow morning to take care of the flies. Okay?

Yes . . . you're welcome. See you in the morning." He presses end and stands awkwardly between the door and the desk, seeming unsure of what to do next.

I'm staring at him and I can't seem to stop, but I also have no idea what to say, and I'm not even sure where I am or how much time has passed since I told him goodbye with my clothes clutched in a ball against my bare chest. Except he's different, touched by the passing of time in a way I cannot feel, but I can see. I have to place a hand on the desk behind me to steady myself. The Tate I remember was a lankier version of the man in front of me now, but his eyes are very familiar, green like the deep glacier waters that embrace the coast. Suddenly, I am catapulted back to the graduation ceremony my mother ruined, when Tate surprised me by showing up. I hadn't heard a word from him since he'd left Whittier when we were eighteen. But that night I was at a bar with friends after the ceremony, trying to laugh away the spectacle my mother had made, drinking a beer that tasted like sawdust and pasting an armored smile on my face to hide the desolation I felt inside. He'd come up behind me and whispered in my ear.

Hi, Claire.

I'd whipped around, and seeing him chinked my armor, made the tears spill down my cheeks until I was sobbing. Without a word, he'd grasped my hand and led me outside, taking me to a diner around the corner, where we drank cheap coffee, ate late-night eggs and hash browns, and talked about everything and nothing at all. *I had to see you graduate, Claire. I'm so p . . . p-roud of you.* The years since he'd left had melted and I'd stopped thinking about what had happened with my mom and let myself relax, and before I knew it, I was waking up in his hotel bed.

A sinking feeling reminds me of who I am and pulls me back to reality. I can't see Tate right now. And then a horrible thought wiggles its way to the surface. Did Dad call him? I try to move past him, but the office is too small, and he gently grasps my arm to stop me.

"It's okay, Claire. I know about your . . . memory, okay? You don't have to hide it from me." His voice is warm and smooth.

I shake my head. What bothers me isn't my memory but something else entirely, and I should tell him because he deserves to know—he's always deserved to know—but I don't know how, and my throat is closing, making it impossible to speak anyway.

"Are you okay, Claire?" He touches my arm, and it loosens something in me.

It all spills out, pent up inside me for longer than I can remember. "I was pregnant."

Saying it to him is sweet relief mixed with a deep sadness. He might never forgive me for keeping it from him. "It, oh, um . . ." I pull at my fingers. "She, no, Mirabelle." Her name feels foreign in my mouth, but I inhale and keep going. "I was pregnant and the baby was yours. Her name was Mirabelle." Tate isn't reacting and I look down, unable to imagine what he must be feeling inside. Dad's face looms in the air between us. He'd never believed my story about the grad student and read the journal I'd kept when I was younger, hoping to find what he was looking for. The night he confronted me, he'd held the journal in his hands, and I can still feel the anger from his intrusion. *You need to tell Tate. He's a good man, Claire.* I'd snatched it from his hands and slammed the door in his face, refusing to speak to him for nearly an entire week. But I never listened, never called Tate, and Dad had respected my wishes, even if he didn't agree with me.

"I lost her before she got the chance to live." Only a few words, but they fill the room, and my heart aches with yearning, my arms empty. I never got the chance to hold her. "I'm so sorry, Tate." Still not looking at him, I reach for my pen, quickly write down that I've seen him and told him, because I can't forget this. The ridges of the pen dig into the pads of my fingers when I write.

He clears his throat and I look up, notice that his cheeks aren't pale with shock, his eyes aren't darkened with anger; in fact, he looks like I've just given him the weather report. I roll my shoulders. He already knows. Of course he does. My grip on the notebook loosens, and it falls to the floor. Tate picks it up and puts it into my hands, which are shaking.

"Claire, listen, I—"

"Dad told you, didn't he?" I can't think straight, am losing information while I stand here. "When?" I'm an idiot. Of course Dad told him. "Before or after I lost her?"

I move around him, but in the small space, my shoulder brushes against him, and I nearly crumple to the floor, longing to touch him, hug him, anything but this desperate sadness that makes me feel frozen and alone.

"You t . . . t-old me, Claire." His voice is warm, soft, and dripping with what I know is pity. I hate it.

I turn to face him, eyes narrowed, because this I remember. "No, you're wrong. I never told you. You're married, Tate. I wasn't going to ruin that for you. And I didn't need you anymore. I could do it on my own, I . . ." Shame slithers across my skin.

"You t . . . t-old me afterward."

"Oh." My spine rounds forward. I told him. Afterward. And I can't remember that. My vision blurs, but it doesn't stop my hand from flying across the page of my notebook. I need to remember this; I need to remember everything. My hand aches.

"Claire." His voice is sad, plaintive, and he tries to touch my forearm like he wants me to stop writing, but I shake him off, at once hating and clinging to the notebook in my hands because it's the only thing I can depend on, my buffer against the unknown.

"I should have told you before, but now it doesn't matter because she's gone and I'm"—I speak through my teeth—"now I'm me and it's better this way."

I step into the hallway and hurry to the elevator, and when the doors close, I let my knees give way and sink to the floor, still writing, wiping tears off my face to keep the paper dry.

CHAPTER EIGHT

The elevator door opens, and I step into the hallway just as my phone buzzes. Shower then Lunch with Sefina. I look around, unsure—this isn't my floor; I see the number twelve by the elevator. Dad's floor. I'm shaky and breathing too fast and trying to read my notes over and over. I told Tate about the baby, and he's in Whittier. Mom lives in Whittier and everyone knows. A growing confusion winds through my body, wraps around me, and all I want is to be comforted by the booming timbre of Dad's voice, to see his bearded face, to talk to him.

His apartment door is unlocked, so I walk inside. "Hello?" The air tastes of burned toast. I smile. It's a smell that has probably become ingrained in every porous surface in his apartment. Dad and burned toast: his one culinary skill.

I walk into the living room. With the blinds closed and lights off, the apartment is dark and uninviting, with a mustiness that tickles the inside of my nose. I turn on the light by Dad's recliner, thankful for the yellow fingertips of illumination stretching into the room. When I was nine years old, I fell off my bike and landed on rocks that jabbed into the soft parts of my knee and scraped my skin bloody. Dad was there and he picked me up and held me until I stopped crying. He always makes me feel safe, even when everything around us is falling apart.

His heavy flannel, the one with green and blue stripes and a padded inside, lies across the arm of his chair. I pick it up, bring it to my nose, and inhale layers of oak and pine, grease and sweat. Dad's scent. I slide my arms through and pull it closed, sit down in his chair.

A photo album lies on the table beside his chair, one I don't recall ever seeing before. The first picture is of me as a baby, asleep across my mom's chest. She stares down at me, a tender look that pushes her lips out, like she's about to kiss my head. Every page is a photo of me, and most are labeled in her handwriting. *First crawl, first walk, first tooth,* and up through my birthdays. One of my parents hiking with me as an infant strapped to my mother's back, Dad standing beside her with his arm around us both. The next one by a campfire: I'm four or five, and Mom holds me on her lap, kissing my cheek. Then come the older ones. Me standing next to my science-fair project in fifth grade: the volcano that never erupted. Another with Tate in a too-big tuxedo and me in a too-long pink organza formal dress. Mom's handwriting underneath: *Claire and Tate Prom.* My hand hovers over the picture. Is this Mom's photo album? Did Dad send her pictures during that time? I pull at the ends of my hair, thinking about Dad reaching out to her, keeping her involved, when he had every right to cut her loose. I close the album, hold it tight. He loved her.

And Mom. Keeping all these photos. For a moment I soften, think of how her addiction has ruined her life. Then my hands curl into fists. She looked so happy in the photos. Our family looked so happy. Why did she have to ruin everything?

I lay my head back, feeling the exhaustion of a day I can't remember in the stiffness of my bones, the dryness of my eyes, and I snuggle deeper into his shirt, feel my eyelids grow heavy, and with a sweet relief, I let them close.

~

I'm outside BTI, breathing hard, my leg muscles twitching because I sprinted down twelve flights of stairs. I want to run as far and as fast as I can. I want to forget Mom, and mostly I want to forget her words. He's the one who didn't want you, you know. *She's lying; I know this but my teenage heart clamps on to it, holds it close, and already I can feel it spreading like a disease.*

I run until my lungs burn, my legs ache, and my face is dry and sticky. I lean forward, hands on my knees, wait for my breathing to slow down.

I look up. Behind a chain-link fence looms the Buckner Building, staring at me like a giant spider out of dozens of busted-out windows. My sweat dries, leaves my shirt wet and cold in the fall temperature. I shiver and zip up my jacket, slide my hands into the pockets, stand up as tall as I can, and stare back.

Black patches stain the concrete, spreading like a rash. Even from the road I can hear the echoey plink of water that drips inside. The building has sat here alone and wide open to the elements for so long now it seems to have become part of the land.

Grass grows out from doorways, and moss clings to rocks and dirt instead of floors. My skin prickles. Kids say it's haunted, but I think it's just sad and lonely. I think of Mom, the way her eyes close when she takes a drink, like she needs me to disappear. But Dad—I swipe at a tear—Dad always wanted me. I kick the ground and walk over to the fence, thread my fingers through the holes and try to see inside the closest window, but the dim evening turns the insides black.

I can't go home. I can't face him. Can't look him in the eye, because Mom's words put something dark and ugly in me. He didn't want you, you know. *All these years of her drinking, and the only thing that's kept me from wanting to put my fist through a window is Dad. So the thought that once he didn't want me wiggles around my heart like a worm, makes me question everything.*

Down by my knees, I notice that the metal wiring looks warped, but when I look closer, I see that someone's cut the fence, made a little door. I push on the metal, and it gives just enough for me to crawl inside. So I do. The grass is almost to my waist and mixed with weeds. My foot kicks an empty and rusted beer can; it makes a popping sound that bounces off the concrete building, seems to dance around me. It's getting darker, the light more blue than yellow.

I walk up to one of the windows, peer inside. I've never been this close, never wanted to before now, but today I feel like this is exactly where I belong. Inside is a lake that reflects the purple sky behind me. It looks like the forest has moved in, and at first I can't see where the building ends and nature starts. It rains inside, water dripping from everywhere, and my nose fills with the earthy smell of plants and dirt and something else. Mold, I guess. When my eyes finally adjust, I see that what I thought were vines are wires, and tree limbs are pipes dangling from the floor above.

Below the window is a dryish spot, just big enough for me to stand. I grip the windowsill, trying to avoid the piles of dead flies stuck in the crevices, and heft myself up, bringing a leg to rest on the sill. The flies crackle under my knee. I shudder and scramble over the sill, landing on the balls of my feet inside the building, where the water laps against a fake shoreline of rocks and dirt. I breathe out and look around.

I've crossed a border into a hidden world, like Max and the Wild Things. I'm breathing fast, but I don't feel scared—I feel free. Free from my mother's words that glom on to my insides, thick and suffocating. I sink to the floor, press my back into the softness of the moss-covered wall. Night falls and soon I'm sitting in the cold; water drips around me, and darkness makes it impossible to see anything, so I rest my forehead on my knees. The dark makes it hard to tell the passing of time, so I don't know how long I've been sitting there listening to water drop and animal feet skitter across concrete.

"Claire? Claire?" Dad's voice is cracked and worn, like he's been yelling or calling. "Oh, sweetheart. You're freezing cold." His arms surround me, lift me up, so warm they feel hot against me. I clasp my hands behind his neck and try my best to hold on. He lifts me over the window and begins to walk, holding me tight against him. I feel five years old, and I squeeze my eyes shut, never wanting it to end.

"Mom packed a bag," I whisper into his shirt when my lips aren't frozen anymore. "I think she left us."

He doesn't stop walking, but his arms tighten around me. "I know."

His feet crunch on the rocky pavement and wind swishes through the trees, bringing with it the smell of leaves and water and fish. Of home. I nestle my face into his collarbone, let my words fall into his shirt. "She said you didn't want me."

His sigh moves through his chest, rolls against my ear, and he stops walking, sets me down. We're outside BTI now. I keep my eyes trained on the ground, wishing I never said anything, afraid he'll tell me the truth.

He touches my cheek and I look up. Our eyes meet. "You are the best thing that ever happened to me, Claire." He pauses like he's thinking hard about his next words. "Your mom was so young when we married." Something darkens his face. "And her father wasn't a good man. She had nightmares all the time and I knew she needed more help than I could give her, Claire bear, but I couldn't afford it. So I just tried to love her. I thought it would be enough." A breeze rushes cool over my wet cheek. "Then she got pregnant, and, well, I knew that having a baby wasn't what she needed, that she was still too sad, too scared." He inhales a ragged breath, and for a second I think he might cry. I look away because I don't want to see him cry. "She chose you, Claire." Dad wipes a tear from my cheek. "And I've been grateful to her every day since for being strong enough for all three of us."

His words strengthen me, dry my tears, and I straighten my shoulders and say what I know is true. "We're better off without her."

I think my words take something from him, because for a moment he looks like a shell, empty and lost. Then he nods, squeezes my arm. "For now, Claire."

~

I wake up to the phone buzzing against my leg, not knowing where I am and gasping for air, desperately trying to hold on to the tail end of a dream, but it drifts away and I let out a strangled sob.

Breathe in, breathe out, slow and controlled until the facts accumulate. One, I'm in Dad's apartment; I can tell from his chair and the lingering smell of burned toast. Two, I'm wearing pink socks, which means it's Monday, which is also Jazzercise day, and based on the workout leggings I'm wearing, I have gone or was about to go. A buzz from my phone and bingo—Shower then Lunch with Sefina. I need to go home and get ready for lunch. I stand, stretch, notice I'm wearing Dad's flannel, but instead of taking it off, I keep it on, feeling a chill deep in my bones that is warmed by the extra layer. I'll return it later.

~

Sefina's apartment is just like mine except she lives on the fifth floor with a view of the waterfalls behind our building, and her refrigerator is covered with pictures of her girls, not Post-it notes with instructions.

She sets two bowls of beef stew on the table, along with a basket of rustic bread and butter. I dip the bread into the broth, pushing aside carrots and potatoes and hunks of beef, then fill my spoon with the hearty stew. "Really good, Sefina," I say.

"Thanks; glad you like it." She puts her spoon down, leans forward. "I heard you ran into Tate?"

The news is an electric shock that I try to conceal from Sefina by eating a spoonful of stew and training my eyes on the notebook.

Tate Dunn is back and he knows everything. I brush a piece of hair from my face, glance out Sefina's window to collect my thoughts. Outside, the sky is dry but dark with gray clouds that make her apartment light glow in comparison. I stare at my faint reflection in the glass, and it gives me pause. Thin lines weave out from my eyes. I look much the same as I remember but different, too, the impression of the years on my skin in ways I don't feel inside.

Tate Dunn is back and he knows everything. I want to remember this bit, want it seared into my brain. In my mind he stands before me in the lobby of BTI, dark hair long around his face, shoulders broad on a thin frame. I'd sneaked out to meet him when I was fifteen, tiptoed past Ruth asleep on the couch. It was only one of many times we broke the rules together. Mom had been gone for two years by then, and Dad was still driving, waiting for the building manager position to open up. Ruth had fully stepped in, practically moving in when Dad was on the road, making me breakfast every morning before school, dinners at night. I was capable of staying by myself, but Ruth would have none of it. She said a teenage girl needed someone around, and while I loved her for it, my mom's absence had left a hole inside me, and amid hormones and a growing anger, it ached with a loneliness that only Tate seemed able to fill. We went to the Buckner Building with flashlights and blankets and a joint. The scarred and lonely building was our version of a clubhouse, and we went there whenever we needed to get away, never venturing much farther than the loading dock. Outside the building that night, we stood eye to eye, and Tate reached out to tuck a blonde flyaway behind my ear. *You look pretty with your hair like that.* I can still remember the way my skin tingled at his touch and how all I could do was stand there and blink. Then he kissed me—just a brief meeting of our lips, but it flooded me with a sweetness that left me longing for more.

The memory evaporates into a bleakness that is echoed in the gray light outside. I have no right to think of Tate in this way, and I write that in my notebook, underline it three times. I look up; Sefina waits with her arms folded on the table, spoon abandoned in her stew.

I point to my notebook. "Yes, I saw him but we really have nothing in common anymore, Sefina. It was good to see him, though." That's not in my notes, but it's not hard to guess either.

"And Alice? You have it written down that she's back in Whittier, right?"

A cube of beef falls from my spoon, splashes stew onto the table. I put my hands into my lap to stop the shaking. She's moved back? I scan my notebook, see a line about Mom being back and Ruth keeping it from me. I'm suddenly hot, and I slide my arms out of my dad's flannel. "Yes, it's right here, but you know that doesn't change anything, right?" I ask what upsets me the most. "But why didn't Ruth tell me she was back?"

Sefina sighs, takes a long sip of water before answering. "She has, Claire. But it's hard for you to accept, and sometimes you are so distracted trying to write everything down that you miss the really important bits. Like"—her eyebrows raise—"Ruth telling you probably a thousand times by now."

Her words sting, but I write it down anyway, including the fact that Ruth has been trying to tell me the truth. It does soften my uneasiness to know she's tried.

"It would be good for you to try to see Alice more," Sefina says, her voice heavy with something I can't figure out. "She's really changed and she wants to be here for you now that—"

"She's sober?" I finish for her, not entirely sure where it came from but knowing, on some level, that it's true.

Sefina's eyebrows move closer together. "You remember that?"

I shrug. "I guess."

"That's amazing, Claire. Truly." She shakes her head, smiles, and taps her chin like she's thinking. "You know, it's possible to remember some things, like out of habit. I read this article once about a person with amnesia who, in the beginning, had to be told he had lost his short-term memory, so they wrote it on a card that he kept in his shirt pocket." Her face brightens. "You did something similar, I think."

"I did?"

She nods. "Only in the very beginning, before you figured out your notebooks and calendars. But this guy from the article would read the card whenever he needed to be reminded about his memory loss. Eventually, he stopped needing the card to remember. He just knew. He even stopped carrying the card, but whenever he got upset or confused, his hand would automatically touch his shirt pocket. Like it had comforted him in some way, and on some level he remembered that comfort."

I've heard most of what she's said, but only one thing sticks. "You read articles on memory loss?" I pull at the ends of my hair. "Because of me?"

Sefina's face softens. "You're my best friend. I wanted to learn everything I could about what happened to you and figure out how I could support you." She taps my notebook. "Although you left me in the dust years ago with this whole system."

I'm speechless and touched and also horrified to think of how the people I love have had to adapt to me and my needs. Like caregivers. All of them. Dad especially. Suddenly, I'm holding back tears, hating myself for my weakness, desperate to pretend that none of this bothers me. "How does my dad do it?"

Sefina's smile drops. "Do what?"

"Take care of me." I try to picture him as he is now but can't, and the emptiness of my memory taunts me, a gigantic black hole that consumes everything. "Have I ruined his life?"

Sefina reaches across the table and puts her hand on top of mine. "No, Claire. He would have done anything for you. You did not ruin his life. Write that down, okay?"

"Okay." And I do, unable to shake a persistent sadness that envelops me, writing that down, too, so I can figure out why I feel this way.

"I just wish you'd give yourself a break."

I look up, confused by her words. "What do you mean?"

"You work so hard to remember everything with your notebook and calendars and even your phone. And I know it helps you to feel in control, and you are so amazing with how you've dealt with all of this." Sefina tightens her ponytail, smiles, and shrugs. "Sometimes I wish you'd trust me too."

"I don't?" I'm taken aback by her honesty, but I don't know what to do with it, how to absorb it.

"To be your friend, yes, of course. But you stick to such a strict schedule, and we all understand why, and frankly it's what makes you so remarkable, but it seems"—she breathes in—"stressful, and lately, especially, it feels like you're missing out on other kinds of experiences in favor of writing everything down. It seems so overwhelming."

"But how can I experience anything if I don't write it down?" The ground shifts and I struggle to keep hold of this conversation. My blood races around my body, and I jiggle my knee. "How can I remember anything if I don't write it down?" I rub my hands across my thighs, try to make the aggravation I feel go away.

Sefina sits back in her chair, looks unsure of herself. "I mean, sometimes I wonder if you'd get to enjoy life more if you could just experience it and let the people who love you help you to remember it. Not all the time, of course, just some of the time."

I hold up my notebook. "But this is my memory, Sefina. I can trust it."

Sefina doesn't say anything at first, just looks at me. Then she leans forward. "That's my point. Maybe you could trust people too." Her smile touches her eyes. "Like me."

"You?"

She spreads her arms. "All of us." She frowns. "Well, maybe not Karen, because that woman is just plain mean, and certainly not Mr. Needs-to-Keep-His-Hands-to-Himself Joe."

My body tenses at the implication that I need help to remember, but Sefina's joke about Karen and Joe brings a smile to my face. Karen moved in next to Sefina when her girls were little. She shares one wall of Sefina's apartment and goes to great lengths to complain to the homeowners' board about Sefina, her girls, TV levels, cooking smells, anything and everything. One time she even complained because Sefina had cooked something that smelled delicious and didn't offer any to

Karen. And Joe has been interested in Sefina since she first moved here, and she's right: he's just a pervert, plain and simple.

Sefina continues, "But you've got me and Harriet and Ruth and . . ." Her head tilts to the side. "Aren't you going to write this down?"

Suddenly, I am laughing. "You just told me to stop writing everything down!"

Sefina is laughing now too. "Oh, crap; right. Okay, just write this down: 'Sefina wants you to stop writing so much and start experiencing.'"

I do because Sefina is my friend, and I know she means well, even if the idea turns my breathing shallow.

CHAPTER NINE

Today I volunteer in Kiko's classroom. It's on my calendar. Kiko taught third and fourth grade when I was a student here. She is generous, stern when she needs to be, loving to every kid, even the annoying ones like I was, and she gives hugs that make the saddest kid feel important and safe. I help during quiet activity time, when the kids can choose from drawing pictures with the nice art markers, writing stories, doing puzzles, or reading to Ms. Claire. It's in my notes, and it's something I do twice a week. I love it, I'm sure.

I pause and wonder if it's hard for me to be around kids. As a teacher, I enjoyed it, and when I found out I was pregnant, instead of being scared because I was alone, I was elated. Dad was the one who was scared. How was I going to do it on my own? I'd assured him that all I needed was right here in Whittier. I stood tall and poked him in the chest and said, *I'm going to be an amazing mom.* His eyes had gone soft, then, and he'd surrounded me with his arms. *I never doubted that, Claire bear.*

More than anything, I wanted that baby. Wanted to be a mother. I touch my stomach, remembering how I used to imagine what it would be like to hold her. From my notes I discover that I spoke to Tate yesterday, told him about the baby, and he wasn't even surprised. I rub my temples, a headache flirting around the edges of my eyes, shock that Tate is here and already knows, and my mind slips backward to graduation, his hotel room.

I have a job and an apartment, I told him. *Come back with me.* We had been lying naked in bed, his body wound around behind mine, warm and strong, my head cradled in his arms. He felt the same but different too—sturdier, older. Being with him had been like coming home after a long trip, familiar and new, intoxicating in all the right ways. But his words were a slap in the face:

I'm m . . . m-arried, Claire.

You're what? His admission stripped me down, made me feel more naked than my own bare skin. *What's her name?*

Maria.

He wanted someone else, not me. Didn't love me enough. Just like Mom. I'd clutched at my chest, a painful pressure building inside that threatened to overtake me. I had to get out of there, away from him, away from this feeling that I was never good enough. So I fled, ignoring his calls, erasing him from my mind as much as was possible. I didn't need Tate. I didn't need Mom. Everyone and everything I needed was right in Whittier.

Then I discovered I was pregnant.

And instead of making me scared or nervous, the news was sunshine, igniting all that could be good in my life. I could do this. Maybe I was even meant for this. I would love this baby the way a child is supposed to be loved.

I stare at my colored tabs, notebooks, calendars, reminders and slump forward, weighted down by the ugliness of my reality. What kind of life could I have given a baby, anyway? So I wipe my face, sip cold coffee, and return to my notes.

After volunteering at the school, it's *Home for lunch*, followed by my afternoon errands, which include a trip to the market and pharmacy, and after checking the weather, I add *afternoon walk*, and then it's back to my apartment for the evening, which I've blocked off for reading. Sometimes it feels pointless because I can't recall what I've just read, but I still find the act of reading soothing and normal.

I sigh and lean back to survey my preparation. It's a full schedule that fills me with a sense of accomplishment as I set my reminders and make my shopping lists. I should be content with this level of preparation; instead, I feel an expanding emptiness. My arms wrap across my stomach, and I wait for the sensation to pass.

Before it does, there is a knock on my door, and a woman stands opposite me. I grip the doorknob hard, blink fast. She is older, thinner, but with the same dark-blue eyes and thick chestnut hair I remember, even if gray strands run through it. "Mom?"

She hands me a foil-wrapped plate with a note on top and a quote.

The purpose of life is to live it, to taste experience to the utmost, to reach out eagerly and without fear for newer and richer experiences. —Eleanor Roosevelt

I live in Whittier, I'm sober, and I love you, Claire. You amaze me.

The words blur but I don't look up. She doesn't get to see me cry.

"Part of my recovery has been to learn how to live in the moment." Her voice is warm honey, and hearing it, I am six years old again, loved and important to her, and it weakens my resolve to act like I don't care.

I try to keep my face impassive, hard. "What do you mean?"

Lines crease the skin in her forehead. She is older and beautiful in a quiet way that comes with age. "My father was a hard man, Claire. But I had to hit the darkest, rockiest bottom to realize that his demons didn't have to be mine." She wrings her hands, nervous, and I soften. Dad has said as much to me. "In recovery, I learned how to stop letting the past define the person I am now." She tilts her head. "I know that you think you have to compensate for all that you've lost. But I want you to know that the person you are right now, at this exact moment, is beautiful and perfect and exactly right." She taps the note card. "Eleanor was a wise woman."

I don't realize my face is wet, don't understand why my heart squeezes painfully until I taste the years we lost in the aroma of buttery pastry drifting from under the foil. With a gentle smile, she takes the plate from my shaking hands and brings it into my apartment, sets it on my desk, pins the card to my bulletin board, stops when something seems to catch her eye.

"What's this?" She lifts a piece of paper from the wire basket.

I follow, wiping at my face, and shake my head. From the looks of it, it's a flyer. One I must have made, but the knowledge of why or when is barren land inside my head.

INTERESTED IN BEGINNER GUITAR LESSONS?
CONTACT CLAIRE HINES, APARTMENT 1407

My mother is nodding, her eyes shining. "Oh, Claire. This is a wonderful idea! Do you remember how we learned together?"

Of course I do, but it's tainted by my confusion and a flaring anger that this woman standing inside my apartment, who looks and sounds like my mother, is not the woman I know. My hands clench and I shift my weight, suddenly uncomfortable. "Leave, please."

Disappointment flickers in her eyes, but then she nods and hurries to the door, touching my arm when she passes. In the hallway she hesitates, gives me a long look. "I'm different, I promise. And I'm not leaving you ever again."

When the door clicks behind her, I fall into my desk chair, hands open on my lap. The smell from the plate keeps me focused. I lift an edge of the foil. Bear claws. They are Dad's favorite; mine too. Warmth spreads through me at the sentiment and the gift. It's something she was known for before her life imploded, even for a little bit while the seams were coming apart: reaching out to others with her homemade treats, visiting and listening when people needed it. She'd often bring me along on those trips, and I'd sit and listen to the adults talk while she'd scratch my back or run her hand through my hair. I remember one particular winter when much of the town had come down with the flu. It had hit nearly every family, and most of the building was on a self-imposed quarantine. Ruth's husband had just left her. Gone through the tunnel with a woman from the second floor and never came back. The whole town knew about it. They'd lived in Whittier for only a couple of years, coming, like my own father had, to work in the fishing industry but staying for the impossibly low cost of living.

I remember the day so clearly because it was the first time that Tate had spoken to me without stuttering. It wasn't anything special; he'd just leaned over during school and whispered, *Can you pass me the purple crayon?* To me it was magical and made me feel important to him. I'd run home after school to tell Mom and found her in the kitchen, flour dusting her cheeks.

What are you doing? I'd asked.

She'd turned and knelt down, and her breath smelled of yeast and cinnamon, not harshened by the sting of alcohol and mint. *Poor Ruth has the flu, and on top of that, she's alone and her heart hurts because it's been broken in two. She needs a friend. Would you like to come along and help me cheer her up?*

I'd nodded and Mom had touched the dimple on my chin with the pad of her finger, smiled, and handed me a tray of cinnamon-and-raisin scones. *You have the kindest heart, Claire bear.*

My phone buzzes and I shake my head to clear it, record as much as I can about her stopping by with the bear claws before biting into one.

It's an explosion of buttery cinnamon goodness, finished perfectly with a strong cup of coffee. I eat the pastry in a few bites, smile.

It was nice of her to bake these for me.

~

I hurry outside, walking through the dirt parking lot and to the back of BTI, where the school sits. Behind the building, water rushes through worn mountain rock and into the river below. My phone buzzes with a reminder to head to Kiko's classroom, and I get there just as the third and fourth graders are choosing their quiet activity centers. There are only about sixty kids in the entire school, so the grades are often blended, depending on what works best for the students. It's a close-knit school, and the kids know each other and their teachers well.

Kiko smiles when I enter; her eyes nearly disappear into her cheeks when she does, and it is comforting and familiar, reminding me of what it felt like to be her student. She was one of the reasons I wanted to be a teacher here.

"Good morning, Ms. Claire," she says.

The kids repeat, "Good morning, Ms. Claire!" in voices that are high and sweet, with one or two that sound bored and sleepy. I smile and wave and settle into a giant orange beanbag chair. There's a sign taped to the bookshelf above the chair that reads Ms. CLAIRE'S READING CORNER, which makes it a snap to guess that this is the area where I belong.

"Now, who would like to work with Ms. Claire today?"

Half the class raises their hands, one girl in particular trying to raise hers so high I think her arm might come out of its socket. She wears cat-eye glasses that are too big for her face, and her brown hair is tied into a ponytail so high it seems to sprout from the top of her head. Bobby pins poke out from where she's tried to pin down the ends of her ponytail in an effort to create what I can only assume is a bun. I cough to cover a laugh.

"Oooohhh, Ms. Kiko, please!" the girl says. "I wrote a story, and I want to read it to her. Ooooh, ooooh, please pick me, please!"

Anticipation bubbles up. This is what I loved about teaching: kids and their exuberance for even the smallest things, like reading to a memory-addled ex-teacher.

Kiko raises her eyebrows, purses her lips, and waits. The girl lowers her hand and hangs her head between her shoulders. "Oh, yeah, sorry. I'm not supposed to yell out like that. I forgot and stuff, so—oops, sorry, Ms. Kiko."

"Thank you, Maree. And yes, you may read to Ms. Claire today. I know how hard you worked on your story yesterday. After you, Izzie and then Leonora. Okay, class, you have fifteen minutes at your first station."

The girl, Maree, hops to her feet and skips over, a small paper book held together by pink and green staples clasped in her hand. She throws herself into a smaller beanbag chair by my side, sliding her glasses up as she makes a big show of settling herself into the bag until her legs stick out in front of her. She points to her ankles. "Look! I have yellow socks on 'cause it's Tuesday!"

I can only assume that I have told her about my sock system, so I smile and nod, pull up my pant leg to show her my own yellow socks. "That's right!"

"Yeah, I decided to do that, too, 'cause I think it's so smart, and now I always know what day it is unless I forget what the color means, which happens kinda a lot, so I wrote it down in a little notebook. I'm just like you now!"

"That's so great, um . . ." Her name doesn't come to mind, so I say, "Kiddo!"

She frowns when she tilts her head. "My name is Maree, like Mary with a *y* but with two *e*'s 'cause I love *Anne of Green Gables*, and she spells her name with an *e*. I'm writing a book, and it's all about the adventures of my mom, and that's also the title, see?" She holds out the cover, which reads *the advntrs of Uki, my mom who is rely brav.*

I lean forward, hands clasped in my lap. "I'm excited to hear all about your mom."

She gives me a look over her glasses, which have fallen to the tip of her nose. "This is just one story. I have loads more. Do you want to hear all of them?"

"I'd love that, but let's start with this one today, okay?" The girl is cute and precocious, and I wonder how many times we've worked together, because she seems very comfortable with me.

She spreads her book out on her thighs, and I can see that she has colored illustrations in crayon on the page opposite her text. Her glasses fall off her face, and she sighs dramatically and sets them on her lap. "Once upon a time, there was a really brave girl named Uki, and she was an epic hunter who could feed her entire village." She holds up her book and shows me a drawing in brown crayon of a girl—I know because of the triangle skirt she wears on her mostly stick-figure body—holding a pink bow, an arrow cocked and ready. Behind the figure are tall mountains drawn in upside-down *v*'s and colored green. The girl turns the page. "One day, Uki found a boy who was locked in a cave with no food and no water. He was so hungry, and it made her so mad that she screamed into the mountains and brought down an avalanche, and then she made a fire and melted the snow into water. Then she ran out into the forest and brought home some vegetables and hamburger meat and Pop-Tarts and probably some candy and gave them all to the boy, who was never, ever hungry again." She shows me the picture on this page; this one has a drawing of a cow—I'm guessing from the udders, which are drawn with meticulous care—and a box of what I think might be Pop-Tarts, surrounded by multicolored lollipops. She turns the page, and this drawing is simple. A big red heart, colored pink on the inside. "And the boy loved her from that day on." She closes the book, puts her glasses back on, and smiles up at me. "Do you like it?"

I nod, amused by her imagination. "I do, very much. You're a good writer, and your mom sounds like a very brave woman." I hesitate, wondering if I've met her mother before, and decide to ask, "Do I know her?"

She puts one hand on her hip and gives me a look. Annoyance? Pity? It's hard to tell behind her cat-eye glasses, which cover half her face.

Kiko claps her hands. "Okay, kids, time to move to your next station."

The girl puts her small hand on my shoulder and pats me. "I'm sorry about all of your lost memories and stuff. I think that really sucks. My name is Maree, like Mary with a *y* but with two *e*'s instead 'cause of *Anne of Green Gables*. Maybe you'll remember me next time."

The girl skips away, leaving me staring after her, wordless. I'm suddenly overheated and scratching the skin of my arms, hating this moment when the curtain is lifted enough for me to see that I'm nowhere near normal. So I write and write and write as much as I can to try and remember our interaction until another girl settles herself on the beanbag chair beside me.

When the bell rings for the end of school, I make sure my notes are complete, then stand and stretch—the beanbag is not the most comfortable chair for someone my height. I check my phone for my next steps before collecting my things. I give Kiko a wave. "See you later."

She smiles and says in a voice laden with something I don't understand, "See you tonight, Claire."

CHAPTER TEN

Back inside the lobby of BTI, I am met with the murmurs and excited voices from the schoolkids who hang out there after school. The sounds relax me. Kids have that effect on me, despite the fact that they are unpredictable and changing. They quiet as soon as they see me, and I try to suppress a grin. There's a long-standing difference of opinion about allowing the kids to hang out in the lobby. I've always been of the opinion that if they behave respectfully, let them. It's bright and busy with people coming in and out—probably the most action these kids see in our town, especially during the winter months. "Carry on," I say. "It doesn't bother me that you're here. Just pick up any trash before you leave."

I've just turned to walk toward the elevator when a sign on the community board in the lobby stops me. A REMINDER! FOR YOUR OWN SAFETY, PLEASE USE THE TUNNEL TO GET TO SCHOOL. Huh. We had a sign like this for a brief period when I was a kid, but that was right after the bear broke into BTI.

"It's because of some bear that's hanging around." A boy's voice. I turn to see him staring at me from under his brimmed winter hat.

"I don't get why someone doesn't just shoot him." A teenage girl, her blonde hair shaved into a long Mohawk on top. "That's what my dad says, anyway."

The boy gives her a look. "'Cause he hasn't hurt anybody, Tasha. He's just hanging around looking for food."

I nod. "We had a bear like that when I was a student here. He went away eventually, and nobody ever got hurt." I tap the sign. "But it's good to use the school tunnel while he's around; best not to give the bears any ideas before they hibernate."

The girl giggles behind her hand, and the boy nods. I stand there, suddenly unsure of where to turn.

The boy pipes up. "On your way to the market, Ms. H.?"

"Yes, that's right, I am," I answer, and work my jaw, trying to place his face. His eyes are a soft brown, kind, the tips of his fingers stained with color, and a camo backpack is splayed open at his feet, where I spy a folder labeled Algebra in black Sharpie. Something I can work with. "Have you mastered linear equations yet?"

Giggles from the girl again.

"Shut up, Tasha," he hisses, then turns back to me. "Nah, Ms. H., we've moved on to quadratic equations."

"Ms. H.," says the girl, Tasha, "you said the exact same thing yesterday and the day before that—"

"Shut up, Tasha," says the boy. "She's new here; sorry, Ms. H."

I can see that the boy is trying to help me, but with his giggling sidekick, the effect is that of a spotlight. The idea that I do something over and over and that these kids have watched me makes my skin crawl and reminds me that everything I do to live a normal life is an absolute farce. I scratch at the back of my neck, completely lost in the useless matter inside my brain, but I try to ignore the girl, focus on the black staining the tips of the boy's fingers, the side of his hand. An artist. I take another leap. "How's the art coming?"

His eyebrows arch up with his wide smile, and he leans over and pulls a black notebook from behind the Algebra folder. Holding the notebook open in front of him, he steps toward me. One page is covered in tiny geometric shapes in varying shades of pencil gray that combine to form a larger pattern. "Kinda like M. C. Escher," I say, trying to let my eyes cross in case the kid has created a picture within a picture.

"Huh?" he says.

On the opposite page is another pencil drawing of a dragon, but even in gray shades it's a beautifully detailed picture, with dark eyes that stare at me from above a long scaled snout. "You're really good."

"Thanks, Ms. H.!" He closes the notebook and slides it into his backpack.

Another flyer tacked to the board grabs my attention, and when I see it, my back muscles stiffen.

INTERESTED IN BEGINNER GUITAR LESSONS? CONTACT CLAIRE HINES, APARTMENT 1407

I'm squinting, reading it over and over. It's my name and apartment number, but I couldn't have put this here. Could I? I open my notebook, flipping through the pages, finding nothing. My face hardens with the idea that what I can't remember is separated by such a thin veneer. "Who put this here?"

I don't realize I've spoken out loud until a boy beside me says, "The woman who bakes all the time."

Standing beside him is a girl whose mouth hangs open. She closes it enough to say, "Yeah, isn't that your mom?"

My feet root to the floor. My mother? I want to flip through my notebook, figure out why there is a flyer for guitar lessons with me, why this girl is talking about my mother, but I am numbed by too much information to do anything more than stand in place.

"I think it'd be cool to take guitar lessons," says the girl with the blonde Mohawk. She reaches up and tears off a small sliver of paper that has my name and number on it, then looks at me, eyes narrowed. "But you can't remember Anthony, and he talks to you every day." Her head moves to indicate the boy beside her. "Can you actually teach guitar?"

I'm speechless, face hot with embarrassment, confusion, and a strong desire to leave. I tear the flyer from the board, crumple it up, and throw it into the trash can by the front door. "No, I can't teach ever again." A buzz from my phone.

"On your way to the market, Ms. H.?" The boy shoves his hands deep into his pockets, gives me a small smile that I think looks sheepish, maybe embarrassed. For me? I wonder, but not for long, because he's right. My phone buzzes. Market: tomato soup, canned peas, pasta, and spaghetti sauce.

"Bye, kids."

"Um, Ms. H.?" The boy shifts his weight, looks unsure of himself.

"Yes?"

"My mom and I will be there tonight."

With a town as small and contained as Whittier, we have quite a few community events, everything from movie to craft to trivia nights. So despite the fact that I have no idea what he's talking about, I nod and smile because chances are it's an event I usually attend. "Great. See you then." I turn from the kids, grateful to let the interaction melt away.

~

A bell chimes when I enter the tiny minimarket, which is hardly bigger than my kitchen and living room. Hank sits on a stool behind the counter, reading a *National Enquirer*. He worked for the oil industry for years before retiring to Whittier to live out the rest of his days fishing whenever he—and I quote—"goddamn wanted to." He bought the market when I was in high school because he said he needed a distraction during the long winters here, when fishing was at a minimum.

"Bigfoot again?" I say, putting a can of tomato soup in a small shopping bag.

He folds the paper down, looks at me over the tops of his reading glasses. "Apparently he showed up at a baby shower in Juno."

I shake my head. "Big guy must have run out of diapers."

Hank barks a laugh. "Good to see you, Claire."

"You, too, Hank. How's business?"

"Oh, it's all right." He chews the inside of his cheek. "What're you needing today?"

"Just the usual." I grab pasta and a jar of spaghetti sauce, and when I put the items on the counter, I spy a 3 Musketeers bar under the counter. It's in my hands and on top of the pasta before I can tell myself no. I might be the only human in Alaska and the lower forty-eight who appreciates the nougat-only candy bar, so when Hank brings them back from Anchorage, I can't refuse. "And one of these."

Hank smiles, and when he does, it gives him a twinkle in his blue eyes. With his white hair and a bushy beard that brushes the top of his chest, Hank could be Santa. The little kids in town have always thought so. He counts out my change, drops the coins into my open hand, and his big palm lingers. I can feel the heat of his skin. "Listen, Claire. You've overcome so much already, but I think you're capable of whatever you set your mind to." His gaze doesn't break from mine.

"Well, thank you, Hank; that's really nice of you to say."

"Are you doing okay?" He raises his eyebrows. "With everything? Are you remembering?" He shifts his weight and the movement makes him look uncomfortable, which is far from the man I know, who once stood shoulder to shoulder with my dad, sheltering Tate against his own father.

I smile, amused, and hold up my notebook. "Well, I'm trying."

"I mean with the other, oh"—he clears his throat—"it's in your notebook, I'm sure."

My whole body stiffens, clueless as to what he's talking about, so I turn to my notebook and my eyes widen. My mother lives in Whittier now. The idea shortens my breath. Is that why Hank seems uneasy? I keep reading, desperate to figure it out before he knows how in the dark I am, and I see another note to myself. Tate is in Whittier too. Now I can't hide my surprise, because I can feel it in the tips of my ears. "Oh, are you talking about Tate Dunn? Yes, I know about that." I rock back and forth on my heels. Hank certainly remembers how close I was with Tate. Caught us stealing two backpacks full of chips and soda from the market when we were sixteen. Afterward, he made us work for him for free for an entire week to pay him back. I don't like remembering how little care we had for how we affected others, like Hank. I scrunch my nose. "Have I ever apologized to you for how I behaved as a kid?" His market was the victim of more than one of our shoplifting attempts, and we got caught only that one time.

Hank's eyebrows shoot skyward, as though my question surprises him. "Ah, Claire, that was a long time ago. You and Tate were just kids, and you both turned out all right, didn't you? And you can bet that Vance made sure you apologized to me."

I smile. Of course he did. "Well, I'm sorry now, too, if that makes any difference."

Hank holds his hands out. "You have nothing to be sorry for; Vance raised you . . ." He drops his gaze, folds the paper that's on the counter. "He raised you right, Claire."

The bell above the door chimes.

"Hello, Hank," Ruth says and I turn to see her in her post-office uniform of blue pants and a pressed and starched button-down shirt. "Hi, Claire. Hey, I meant to ask you yesterday . . ." She purses her lips. "Can you please do something to help Sefina stay on the beat?"

I make a face. I don't have to recall what she's talking about to know it has to do with Sefina and her dancing. "She's a lost cause, don't you think?"

Ruth laughs. "I wouldn't tell her that. But you might want to head on over to the clinic now. Sefina needs to close a bit early today." She seems to measure me up. "Would you like for me to walk you over?"

I tilt my head, confused by her question because the city offices are in BTI, just down the hall. "No, Ruth, I think I can—"

She hands me a note card. *The city offices have moved. They are in the new building with the blue roof, across from Whiskey Pete's.*

I shrug, try to act like this information doesn't shift the landscape of my memory. Still, I know where Whiskey Pete's is located, and it's only a short walk. "Oh, no, I'll be just fine. Hard to lose my way around here, right?" I check my phone and slide the market reminder left to clear it, leave the pharmacy reminder up on my screen. "See you later, Hank."

"Bye, Claire. See you tonight," Hank says. I leave but the door to the market doesn't close all the way, and I hear Hank speak quietly to Ruth, who murmurs something in return, and part of me wants to go back and demand to know what they're talking about. But then the part of me that doesn't want to acknowledge how little I remember wins and I walk away.

CHAPTER ELEVEN

It takes only a few minutes to get to the clinic. A warm breeze brushes over me, and I unzip my jacket, enjoy the warmer temperature. Up the hill and to my right stands the Buckner Building. I feel a pang when I glance up at the long stretch of concrete blackened by mold, shattered windows empty and dark. I'm even more like that building now. Once useful and moving forward and now forever frozen in time, a relic of my own past.

As soon as I enter the clinic, I'm met with the powdery smell of latex laced with Vicks VapoRub. Sefina is behind the counter, her straight black hair pinned up on the sides, arms crossed. "I hear you think I'm a lost cause when it comes to dancing. I'll have you know that I am going to start practicing every free minute I get, and then I will challenge you to a Jazzercise dance-off."

One of the reasons I've always loved Whittier—it's as small town as small town gets. I went to college in Anchorage, and while I enjoyed the coffee shops and stores and learning how to be anonymous among so many people, I missed Whittier and the sense of belonging I've always felt here. I hold out my hands. "I'm sorry but I have no idea what you're talking about. I have a significant memory-loss issue, you know." I smile.

She laughs. "Fine, you got me. But I'm still practicing."

I scan my notebook. "So I think the headaches have been worse lately."

"Really?"

"Yeah, and"—I pause, scan the medical file I've brought along with me—"do you think it could have anything to do with the new meds I'm taking?"

"I'm not sure, but I'll put in a call to your doctor's office, okay?" Her face softens. "Have you seen Tate again?"

The question turns my knees to jelly. I ran into Tate? Here? I try not to show it as I flip the pages until I find the notes about our conversation, brief and to the point: *Tate Dunn is back and he knows everything.* My shoulders relax at that, but my mind spins trying to envision how I acted. Was I awkward? Embarrassed?

Sefina waits while I read. "It doesn't look like I've seen him again." I feel a jolt of disappointment, a flutter of shame. He probably doesn't want to see me like this. Can I blame him? Then I stiffen. "He's married."

Sefina shakes her head. "Not anymore."

I nearly smile at the news but quickly cover it up with a cough. "What happened?"

"From what Ruth said, it didn't last very long. She said the woman was no good to begin with." She waggles her eyebrows. "That's good for you, though, huh?"

My cheeks warm. It's a ridiculous thing for her to say, and it bothers me that she speaks so flippantly, as if I'm normal. "Sefina," I say quietly. "Who would ever want to be with someone like me?" I hold out my notebook and phone, see my hands tremble in the air because it upsets me that she even suggested it.

"You are strong and smart and amazing, Claire. If I were gay, I would totally hit that."

And just like that my anger fades because I've never been able to stay mad at Sefina.

She staples the top of a small white bag, smiles. "Hey, Leilani said she saw a flyer on the community board about guitar lessons with you. I had no idea you were thinking about something like that, but I think it's fantastic!"

I'm already flipping through the pages, irked that I can't find anything related to guitar lessons. I can feel myself start to sweat, a twisting in my gut at the idea that I can't develop a system big enough to cover everything I forget. I chew on my nail, thinking about a spreadsheet layout or some kind of innovative design to help me keep better track of things when Sefina speaks.

"Claire?"

"I can't teach, Sefina." My voice is quiet, bitter.

When she doesn't respond I look up to find her watching me, head tilted, her eyes soft. "Do you remember how you called Leilani your magical sprite? You're still her favorite teacher, you know. I have no doubt that if you could handle Leilani, you can do anything." The skin around her eyes crinkles. "And she was quite a handful."

Sweet memories surface of my early teaching days. It dulls my anxiety. I easily recall Sefina's daughter, Leilani, a perfectly tiny version of her mother—dark haired and mischievous—and I was an enthusiastic and inexperienced newbie, completely in love with teaching. "She was just spirited, but I managed her okay," I say, smiling now. "Except for that one time."

Sefina puffs her cheeks out with air. "She'll never forget that day. Wasn't it your first week teaching?"

I laugh, enjoying the freedom of remembering. "I had playground duty. One minute Leilani was sitting beside me eating a sandwich. She asked me if I liked Spam and offered me a bite."

Sefina moans. "That girl and Spam. I'll never understand it."

It's as if I'm standing in the indoor playground, my boots digging into the coarse sand—Sefina fades as I let the memory become a movie I've watched a dozen times. Leilani was barefoot and hanging upside down on the monkey bars. Her waist-length hair fell like a waterfall over her head, shimmering in dark waves with her giggles. But even from across the playground, I saw her legs slipping, and we both screamed out. By the time I got to her, she'd fallen and landed with her arm at an unnatural angle. I knelt beside her and held her until help came, telling her jokes and stories to keep her tears at bay. I was pregnant but not really showing then, except I can remember the heartache at not protecting a child in my care. The worry that overwhelmed me at being a single mom. The guilt I felt. Would I be able to protect my own child if I couldn't even protect little Leilani? I rub my stomach up and down, like I did when the baby was rounded out in front of me. My hand drops and I shift my weight. Sefina watches me, her eyes wet.

"Talk about a failure of a first day," I say. "Poor girl."

Sefina laughs. When she first moved here, Sefina was waif thin and unsmiling. Whittier gave her something good back. "Don't give it a second thought, Claire; that broken arm was a badge of honor for Leilani." She holds out a white paper bag. "Make sure you take these with food. Last time you mentioned that you were feeling a bit nauseous. Even a couple of crackers can make the difference." She uncaps a black pen, writes across the bag. "It's on the bag now too."

My phone buzzes. Go for a walk.

I smile. It must be a nice day today if I scheduled a walk. I leave the clinic and head toward the harbor, inhaling the fresh air. *I'm going for a walk. I'm going for a walk.* I also have a reminder that buzzes me on my phone. You are taking a walk. The cool breeze feels good on my skin, and the clear sky is pale blue above the snowcapped mountains. I keep to the same path when I walk in town, through the pedestrian tunnel that runs under the railyard, down the boardwalk along the harbor, to the inn, turn around, go back through the tunnel, take a left down Whittier Street, past Whiskey Pete's, and up Blackstone Road to the Buckner Building. It's not a long walk, but it's enough to stretch my legs and something I can easily do on my own.

I don't know what it is about the Buckner Building, but I feel a pull to it, a kinship. It was a place I started going to after Mom left, where Tate and I went often because it was the only place we could truly be alone. And now it's just a nice way to end my walk. I reach the top of the hill, stand outside, and look up at the Buckner, a long stretch of concrete stained black, the building stark and pale against the deep-green vegetation that surrounds it. It took several years to build the nearly 275,000-square-foot military building, which included everything from barracks, a movie theater, a bowling alley, hospital, jail cell, even a bakery and a radio station, all connected by elevators and wide stairwells. It was completed in 1953, cost millions of dollars to build, and seven years later it was abandoned when the military deemed the Whittier port strategically unnecessary. I did a project on it in high school, and even now I can remember trying to wrap my mind around why adults would build something so big, so substantial, so useful and then walk away like it meant nothing. Then again, I could relate, and instead of buying into the rumors that it was haunted, I felt sad for the building and for every year it stood there empty and alone.

From inside comes the drip of water and a shuffling sound like wildlife. The hair on the back of my neck stands on end, and I turn to see a bear sitting on the road that winds up and past the Buckner. My heart beats against my ribs. Bears are a common sighting here—they find this building a good place to hunker down on occasion—but I'm still awed by their wildness. Indecision freezes me in place. Should I turn and go or be still and let the bear go on its way? He sits back on his haunches, stares directly at me, and even from this distance I can see his black, pointed ears, the caramel fur around his muzzle, and his eyes, and all I can think about is Dad because he's big and strong like a bear but also kindhearted and gentle too.

Suddenly, I'm not scared, even as my pulse thunders in my ears. The bear gets to his feet and shakes his shiny black coat before sauntering up the road, then breaking into a run. He's beautiful when he moves, and I watch him disappear when the road curves to the right. I'm oddly calm; the experience seems fitting here, in front of the building that stares down at me, empty and alone. I'm turning to leave when a small form darts from around the other side of the building.

It's a child—a girl—with her hair pulled into what I think is a poorly executed beehive, which, combined with her cat-eye glasses, gives her the look of someone who might have roamed this building in its heyday. She's running straight toward me as though she's been waiting for me. Do I know her?

"Oh, crap, Ms. Claire, this place is freaking creepy!"

Question answered: I do, in fact, know her.

"What are you doing here?" I ask, keeping the question general enough to get an answer that might help me connect the dots.

The girl stands with her hands on her hips, her cheeks red, her breathing heavy and exaggerated like she just ran a half marathon. I smile. She's cute.

"I want to go inside, but I'm not allowed to 'cause it's too dangerous."

"Why do you want to go inside?"

She gives me a look like I'm made of something dense.

"I want to see what's in there! Then I saw you walking up here, so I ran as fast as I could, 'cause you're a really tall adult and a teacher, and you could take me in, right?"

The dots are getting easier to connect, but that doesn't mean I understand them any better. "You followed me here?"

She flattens her mouth into the sheepish kind of look I remember seeing on kids' faces when they'd been caught doing something they shouldn't. "Yeah, well, this building is creepy, but it's all alone and I think that's kinda sad 'cause nobody wants it, you know?"

"Yeah, actually, I do know. I think the same thing." I smile at the girl's insight.

"See? So we should go inside together. Can we? Please?"

I'm already shaking my head no when my phone buzzes. You are taking a walk. "Trust me; it's too dangerous inside."

Her eyes widen. "Do you know that 'cause you've been inside?"

"Yes—I mean no. It was built a long time ago, so we have no idea what kind of bad materials could be inside."

"Like what?" She's a curious one.

"Like asbestos, which is really bad for our lungs."

"Like you can't breathe in there or you'll die?" Her voice is awed.

I smile. "Not exactly, but it's a good idea to stay out." I hold up my buzzing phone. "I need to get back and so should you. The bears are still out, and they love this building. You shouldn't be outside alone, okay? Walk back with me."

I start to walk and realize the little girl isn't beside me; I stop and turn to find her where we'd been standing.

"It seemed like you remembered, but you didn't," she says. "You're good at pretending, aren't you?"

Her words are spot on, and I wonder how many times we've interacted. I don't have to wait, though, because the girl has started counting off.

"I've seen you lots since I moved here." She holds up a finger. "I helped you in the gardens once." Raises a second finger. "I read you my story during quiet activity time at school." And a third. "Last Wednesday you caught me trying to grab Oreos out of the vending machine, 'cept my arm is too short, and anyways you told me it was stealing." A pinkie finger. "Once I brought up a basket of your laundry 'cause you forgot what you were doing and started to go back upstairs without your basket, so I followed you and gave it to you at your apartment. It was heavy." She stands taller, obviously proud of herself. "You gave me a dollar and said it was a very nice thing for me to do." She raises her thumb. "And now this time." She purses her lips, scrunches her nose. "But you don't remember me, do you? I'm Maree, like Mary with a *y* 'cept with two *e*'s 'cause I love *Anne of Green Gables*, and she put an *e* at the end of her name, and I think that's really cool."

I'm writing everything she's saying as fast as I can, which is a challenge because the child speaks as though it's all one long sentence. But now all the dots are laid out in a way that I can connect a few, and I look up from my notebook to find the girl staring at me, head tilted, upper lip sucked in.

"Do you always have to do that?"

"Do what?"

"Write everything down? Can't you ever just, you know, do things without having to write it down? 'Cause you rub your hand a lot like it hurts." Her eyes roll to the sky. "And also"—she starts to hop up and down on her feet—"it's really cold out here, and we could have been back to BTI by now if you didn't have to write so much down."

I want to respond, I want to say something to negate her words, but the truth of them strips me down, exposes my farcical system that can't even make a little girl think I'm normal.

She blows air through her lips until they flap. "Oh man; I'm sorry, Ms. Claire. I shouldn't have said that. That's probably a hard thing for you." She shakes her head. "I'm too repulsive."

I'm taken aback and then suddenly laughing because the girl is sincere and yet her words don't fit at all. I cover my mouth to stop myself. "I'm sorry, what did you say?"

She shakes her head and her glasses slide down. "No, that's not it. Ms. Kiko says I can be impossible—no, I mean impulssible—no, not that one either."

Another giggle tries to surface, but I push it down. The girl is so earnest in her attempt to apologize. "Impulsive?"

"Yeah!" She pushes her glasses up with one finger. "That one! You're really smart."

"Thanks."

I try to be nonchalant when I check my notes, but I think she sees right through me. "You should help me in the gardens another time. I like company when I work in there."

She hurries to my side, beaming. "You bet! I can't wait!"

We walk back to BTI, Maree a chattering, skipping presence by my side, and I find her company a soothing balm to an unexpected sting of loneliness.

CHAPTER TWELVE

The girl hops off on the tenth floor, and while the elevator rises, I smile when I read through my notes from the school today. The kids were fun, enthusiastic to be with me and for reading. On paper most of them seem to know me, particularly this one girl who was especially interested in my memory loss. I try to envision my time in the classroom, to stitch together even the thinnest threads into something vibrant and real. But my mind is a blank notebook, and I slump against the elevator wall. It's pointless and the more I try, the more alone I feel in the effort.

When the elevator doors slide open, I walk out with my head down, reading and rereading about the kids, and I walk straight into something solid. "Oh!" I look up and nearly stumble backward, heart racing at the man in front of me, the familiar slope of his jaw, the silky blackness of his hair. My eyes open wide. Tate Dunn.

"Hi, Claire," he says.

With my notebook pressed against my chest, I try to think of something to say that hides the jittery rush spreading through my legs.

"Hi," is all I manage because the smell of him, the space he occupies, the breadth of his shoulders that I want to run my fingers across is something I *know*, and it's overpowering.

His smile deepens the lines around his eyes in that pleasing way that happens when men grow older. Tiny bits of gray paint the fine hairs by his temple. I shift my weight, try to act nonchalant and not like some tongue-tied teenage girl while I furiously flip through my notebook. He's acting comfortable and normal, not at all like this is the first time we've run into each other, which is exactly the feeling that warms my cheeks. I stop searching—there it is, and only yesterday too. Tate has moved back to Whittier, and I've told him about the baby. I nearly sigh with relief. He stands beside me, smiling at me the way he did when we were kids. The same smile that touched his eyes and deepened into something more when we were older. The smile that says I'm his most favorite person in the world.

I'm in overdrive, consumed with memory, trying to fully grasp the idea of the years that span between the last time we were together. Feeling the mixture of longing and sadness I had when I realized that we didn't want the same things anymore, even if my skin felt tattooed with the warmth of his touch. He lived in Idaho with Maria, wanted nothing to do with Whittier or me. I almost snort. At least nothing more than a one-night stand.

"Do you n . . . n-eed to write anything down?" He searches his pockets, comes up with a pen. "Ruth says that's w . . . w-hat you do to remember."

I push a strand of hair behind my ear, try to find my feet even as the ground shifts. How many times have we had this conversation? "How long have you been back?"

"N . . . n-ot long; only a couple of weeks, actually, and in case you're w . . . w-orried"—his smile is warm, eyes soft, and I feel my neck muscles relax the tiniest bit—"we ran into each other for the first t . . . t-ime yesterday. You wrote it down." He shifts his weight, seems hesitant. "Do you, um, do you want to . . ." He pauses again, mouth shaped in a half whistle, and I wait because this I remember so well. The stuttering and the way some words catch in his throat, refusing to come out. When he was a boy, the effort would turn his cheeks red, and he would often give up, choosing silence over talking. But not with me. It never bothered me because I loved whatever he had to say, and I would wait for however long it took for him to say it. Finally, the words escape his mouth: "Have coffee or tea or something?" His hair is cut shorter than when he was younger but messy in the way I remember. My fingers tingle with a desire to run my hands through it. "We have a lot to catch up on, Claire."

"You're married," I say, and nearly wince at how blunt it sounds.

His eyes widen. "I was, but that was a long t . . . t-ime ago, Claire. She'd already left when you called, and n . . . n-ow I have . . ." His mouth is open but nothing comes out.

He only stuttered badly around me when he was nervous. Why is he nervous? I breathe through my teeth. Because I'm brain damaged?

He slumps forward, seems to change tactics. "I didn't w . . . w-ant to run into you like this. I'm sorry." He gives me a look. "Do you w . . . should you write this down, Claire?"

My body jolts into action, and I'm relieved to have something else to focus on. I'm writing before I've even had time to think about the words. *Tate Dunn is back in Whittier and he's old.* I scratch out *old* and write *older.*

"Are you living here now?" I can't meet his eyes, afraid he'll hear the excited thumping of my heart or sense how desperate I am for his answer.

He rubs the back of his neck, shakes his head. "Yes . . . I am."

I tilt my head, skeptical. Tate said he'd never move back to Whittier. Not as long as his dad was alive. "Why?"

"W . . . w-ell, I have a new job and also . . ." Tate stops talking, works his jaw. He used to tell me that when he got stuck on a word, he taught himself to think about a pair of otters gliding through still water, and that image helped him to stop and regroup. But Tate's stuttering was always the worst when he was upset or nervous about something. His dad made him nervous with his mood swings and fits of rage, especially when it came to his stuttering. I feel a pang. I never made him nervous.

I hold my notebook against my chest. "I thought you'd never come back to Whittier."

He shifts his weight before saying, "He died."

I know instantly who. "Your father?"

He nods.

It hits me like a bullet. The man who caused Tate so much pain, the man responsible for driving him away from Whittier—from me—is gone. My thoughts drift back to a summer morning just after Tate's eighteenth birthday. We'd gone to the Buckner Building; it had become a habit of ours—something about its neglected ruins spoke to us. Tate had shown up with a black eye, and we'd sat side by side on the loading dock, legs dangling off the concrete stoop, feet inches above a pile of broken bottles, rusted beer cans, cigarettes. Morning light peeked through the busted-out windows, dusting our skin. Dark maroon stained my fingers—paint that had dripped from the bottle when we sprayed our newest image across the cement walls: a huge fist, middle finger raised.

Tate inhaled off a joint, passed it to me. Our exhales mingled in a cloud, thinning, then disappearing into the cool air.

Remember that night the bear got into the lobby?

I nodded. *That bear was huge.*

Tate inhaled again, held it in until he coughed. *It was my fault.*

The weed moved languidly through my body, dampened my surprise. *How?*

Dad w . . . w-as at the bar, and I didn't think he'd be able to g . . . g-et back in. So I propped the door open.

I laughed. It wasn't funny, except it was. Everything was funny and stupid and tragic, but at least I had Tate. He understood Mom's absence ate at me, left ragged bite marks that festered as I watched Dad's back stoop with every year she broke off a chunk of his heart when she didn't sober up. I remember thinking that in some ways, I was the lucky one because at least she was gone. Tate's dad was as mean and as drunk as ever.

I'd inhaled again, closed my eyes, and let the smoke lay over the places that hurt. Tate fell silent, threw his can of spray paint against the wall. It clunked, then fell with hardly a sound onto the mound of litter below.

I was afraid to look at him, could feel him holding back, and I didn't want to know what it was. I threw my spray can, too, but it hit a wire dangling from the ceiling and just missed the wall.

Finally, he softened into me, rested his hand on top of my thigh, palm up, and I slid my hand into his.

I don't want to be like my dad.

I stiffened. *You're not.*

I need to get away from him, Claire. I have to leave this place.

Not even the floating numbness of weed could keep his words from cutting into me. *You can't leave.*

Come with me.

I remember how I wanted to say yes, imagined myself following him anywhere, maybe even traveling the world like Harriet and Pete had. But then I thought about Dad and Ruth, and my mother, and I swallowed hard. I wasn't weak like her. I didn't need to run, because everything I wanted was right here in Whittier. So I tried to laugh him off, grabbed his face in my hands and kissed him, savoring the roughness of his cheek, the softness of his mouth, the way his hands slid around to my back, pulling me against him, and I remember how it felt both passionate and desperate. Like a first and last kiss.

He stares at me now, so different from my memory, grown-up and confident in a way I've never seen. I feel suddenly shamed, stuck in a past that I thought we'd shared. And now he's back and we couldn't be more different.

My mouth opens but I can't sort out my thoughts; I'm caught in the past, unsure of what we've been talking about. "Um . . ." I search my notes, find what I'm looking for. Bill's dead. "Oh, um, when did he die?"

"Last year. They think he lost his w . . . w-ay home from the bar." Tate makes a noise in his throat. "Not surprising he'd go out . . . like that."

"Oh." I know this; I'm sure I do but I also don't, so I write it down, hating that I have to do it in front of Tate.

I'm flooded with thoughts, not all of them good, and words fall out that feel old, tired, because too much time has passed. "You said you'd never leave me like my mom did, and then you did. You don't call for years, and then out of nowhere you show up at my graduation. We sleep together and *then* you tell me you're married." Letting it out is a release I didn't know I needed and it feels good. And, I realize, I'm not angry with him. Quite the opposite. I'm gratified, like I just discovered a missing limb. Elated because the bond between us, the one that grew from his very first words to me behind the vending machine, feels as strong as ever.

Tate acknowledges it all with a dip of his chin. "You had Vance and Ruth and this whole town, Claire. They were your family. I didn't w . . ." Again he stops, his mouth in a circle until he breathes in and changes tactics. "I don't have an excuse. I thought I'd get my shit t . . . t-ogether and then convince you to come with me. I thought I was w . . . w-eak like my dad; I thought you were better off without me. I was a mess."

I don't know how to respond. Being around him is cold water in the desert, drowning me in memories that are crystal clear and bringing with it the iron tang of loneliness. After Mom left, Tate was a solid presence by my side—one arm slung around me, fingers in my hair, my wet cheek against his bony shoulder. "You were my best friend, not a mess," I say quietly.

He shrugs. "You know I . . . was. Remember the t . . . t-ime I tried to burn down the bar?"

I can't help but laugh. We were sixteen and it was the middle of winter, cold and foggy, with snow coming down in wet chunks. "Yeah, but it didn't take and no one found out."

"Well, I w . . . w-as angry most of the time, except when I . . . except around you, and I knew that if I didn't g . . . g-et away from him, I'd become him."

"And did you?" Without thinking my hand goes to my belly, and my chest tightens. He would have been a wonderful father; I have no doubt. Regret curls my fingers. I should have told him about the baby. I nearly did; so many times I picked up the phone to call, but as soon as I thought about his wife, I hung up. Would things have turned out differently if I had told him? My face hardens. Of course not.

He touches my arm. "No, I didn't, but I g . . . g-uess you knew that all along. It t . . . t-ook me longer to see it."

My hand itches with a desire to run my fingers through his hair, to remember what he felt like under my palms, and I want to write it all down, don't want a second to slip past me, but shame needles into my skin. I don't want him to know how much I can't do, how changed I am from the girl he knew.

"G . . . g-o ahead," he says.

"What?"

"Write it down." His eyes are soft and kind and something else. "I'd like for you to remember. Besides"—his smile is mischievous—"for years, you'd w . . . w-ait until I could form a single word. You . . . never made me feel embarrassed or stupid. You made me feel n . . . n-ormal and I haven't forgotten it." He points to my notebook. "Now I g . . . g-et to return the favor."

A burning sensation sweeps across my cheeks, and I dip my head and write, adding more asterisks than I need to indicate that this part of my day is important. I feel a wrinkle form between my eyes. "Why did you move back to Whittier?"

Tate holds my gaze, and for a minute I don't think he's going to answer me, and when he does, it's a machine-gun patter of "V . . . V . . . V . . . V . . ." until a gate opens and the words he wants are released: "I'm the new harbormaster."

A smile stretches across my face. "That's a big deal. Congratulations, Tate." It's also the kind of job that keeps someone in Whittier, at least until they tire of the ever-present wind and heavy clouds that cling nearly year-round to our town.

But what do I think could happen between us? I know the truth. Nothing can happen anymore, not with me as I am. I turn inward, as though to protect myself because the idea has teeth that bite. "But why here?"

"Well, first because there are some exciting p . . . p-lans for the city, like updating the boat ramps and there's this whole new concept for the waterfront. It's exciting to be a part of the g . . . g-rowth around here."

There's a spark in his eyes when he speaks and an excited lilt to his voice that diminishes the verbal pauses, smooths his words. This is Tate when he's confident and in control. This is the boy I remember. But I find myself lost in the cadence of his words, missing the meaning, and when I try to write down what he's said, my pen doesn't move. "Oh . . ." My face is hot and I can't bring myself to lift my eyes to meet his, don't want to acknowledge the emptiness of my thoughts. I decide to take a stab. "So, um, are you visiting or here to stay?"

The silence is only momentary, but it's soaked through with pity. I don't have to remember to know that people feel sorry for me. And the idea that Tate pities me curls my toes from a rush of embarrassed anger.

"I'm here t . . . t . . ." He pauses and I wait. "Stay."

A buzz from my phone vibrates my pocket, and my shoulders slump with relief at an excuse to end this conversation where the brain-damaged me is on full display to the one guy in the world I most want to see me as normal. I wag the phone in the air and make my way toward my apartment door. "I'd better go now."

"Wait, Claire—here." Tate hands me a business card with his name on it. "I'm the harbormaster. We can t . . . t-alk more about it another . . . time, okay?"

I back into the hallway, nodding and writing it down as fast as I can, trying to keep a smile pasted on my face despite a despondent heaviness in my heart. "I'm glad you're back, Tate. I've missed you." My keys shake when I put them in my door, but I get it open and am inside in seconds, breathing hard against thoughts that run laps in my head and on the page. I have no right to this man. No right to these feelings. Not anymore. Not like this.

~

I look out the peephole. The hallway is empty. I'm not sure how much time has passed or how long I've been sitting on the floor with my back pressed against the front door, but my eyes are dry. My body feels sluggish, the room cold and bleak, and without thinking I rise to my feet and hurry to Ruth's door.

She answers almost immediately, like she's been standing at the door waiting for me.

"Can I come in?"

Her eyes soften, and when she nods her hair doesn't move, the iron-gray waves extra stiff today. Ruth's hair hasn't changed for as long as I've known her. Not the color, not the cut, and not the style. Today it makes me think that she is upset from the way it clings to the sides of her head—unmoving, stubborn. She opens the door all the way. "Of course." I follow her inside, comforted by the blend of grays and browns in her apartment cut through with dark orange or avocado green. Like the seventies never left. But her unchanging decor soothes me with its familiar warmth and dependability.

Ruth hands me a mug of warm water she heats in the microwave and opens up a small tin of tea. I choose a lemon and ginger one and dip the bag in and out of the water while I read through my notes.

She stands opposite me on the kitchen side of her counter, a glob of honey dripping from a spoon that she sinks into her tea. "Talk to me."

"There's so much, Ruth, and I keep reading about it, but I want to remember and I can't." I'm not crying, even if my voice is thin, cracked. "I know Mom is here and"—I read a note from the top of every notebook page—"that you've probably told me dozens of times." I read the next bit from a bulleted list I've made of important facts. "And I told Tate about the baby, but he already knows. He said I told him afterward." I meet her level gaze. Ruth doesn't lie to me. "Did I?" The question hangs in the air between us, and I watch as honey spins a golden thread from the spoon that Ruth hovers over her cup. She stares into her tea as though searching for an answer, and her silence sets my heart beating too fast.

"Ruth?"

"You did. You were confused, Claire. It was about a year afterward, and you were still recovering, trying to get your bearings. That first year was so hard for you."

I feel myself almost physically recoil trying to picture what it was like. "It must have been so hard for Dad and for you," I whisper. "Having to take care of me like that, to remind me about my baby."

Ruth looks up. "That's the thing with you, sweetheart. You always think about others. No matter what, it's where your mind goes first."

I'm not used to endearments from Ruth. It's never been her style, and I never needed it from her because her love came through in the midnight hours when she comforted me from a dream, in her home-cooked meals, the dress she sewed for prom. Hearing it now is a soft blanket around my shoulders.

She continues, "And with the help of your rehab team, you figured out pretty early on how to remind yourself about your memory loss."

My forehead wrinkles. "How?"

"First, with a note card you kept in your pocket. Your doctors suggested you keep it on you with everything you needed to know, and then they would instruct you to read it whenever you were distressed or upset because you couldn't remember." Ruth shrugs. "It worked and eventually you didn't need to read about it anymore; you just knew. You're the one who transferred that idea to your notebooks. Then again, you've always been such an organized and self-contained person, even when you were just a little girl." Her voice is warm, like she's proud of me.

I read again from my notes. "But when did I call Tate?"

"It was later, when you were back home and still adjusting. Vance said it was late one night after he'd gone to bed. He woke up and found you in the kitchen with your notebook, writing the same thing over and over. *Tell Tate about the baby.*" She pauses, sips her tea. "You begged Vance to help you call Tate."

"Oh."

Ruth studies me, like she's trying to decide something. "You know, Vance helped Tate get the harbormaster job."

I write that down. "Why?"

"What you don't know"—Ruth puts her hands out, palm up—"actually, it's something Vance never told you . . . is that he's kept in touch with Tate all these years."

The information spins in my head. "Why?"

"He's worried about that boy since you were both little. Alice too. Well, she did before"—Ruth pauses—"before she went downhill and couldn't focus on anyone but herself." Ruth presses her lips together. "But she's sober now and lives here. You have that in your list, right?"

I nod because I've just read it.

"Alice used to bring him clothes from the Goodwill in Anchorage whenever she went because Bill couldn't be bothered to keep the boy in pants that fit or winter coats without holes. Your dad made sure Bill got

Tate to school when you two were real little and then later when you were teenagers." Her lips quirk up. "Used to wake that boy up himself."

My eyes open wide. "Dad did?"

"Oh yes." Ruth sips her tea. "But when Tate left, Vance worried about him out there, all alone, so he found a way to get in touch." She cups her mug with both hands, looks at me over the rim. "That was after he was already married to that horrible woman."

I write it all down, and while none of it surprises me—especially the part about Dad helping someone, that's just the kind of person he is—my heart is full. Dad also helped Tate because he knew how much I loved him. He did it for me too. The cramping in my hand pauses my writing, and I stop to stretch out my fingers, roll my shoulders and neck.

Ruth sighs. "Oh, Claire," she says and touches my hand, her palm surprisingly warm and soft. "You're trying, sweetheart. It's just not easy, is it? For anyone, especially for you. But you're trying."

"What choice do I have, right, Ruth?"

"I don't think you understand," Ruth says.

Something I've written makes my face feel tight. "Dad met Tate's wife?"

Ruth takes my cup and hers, turns to put them in the sink. "Only once," she says, and I notice that she stands as though she carries a heavy weight across her shoulders.

"Is everything okay, Ruth?"

"I'll be okay."

My phone buzzes. "I should probably go. Thanks for the tea."

She gives me a sad smile. "Anytime. See you tonight, sweetheart."

I slide my bag onto my shoulder and head out, checking my phone as I walk to my apartment to see what plans we have going on for tonight. I hope it's a game night.

CHAPTER THIRTEEN

A loose photo on my desk catches my eye when I walk past on my way to—I stop, rub the back of my neck, momentarily at a loss for what I was doing. I turn in a half circle, hands stretched out in front of me, trying to shake the present like I'm panning for gold. Hoping that the answer to what I was doing will rise golden flecked and shiny above the silt. But nothing. My bladder feels empty, so I wasn't going to the bathroom. A fullness in my stomach means I must have eaten recently. Still, nothing comes to mind, and when my eyes spot the photo again, I pick it up, grateful for something to occupy my thoughts.

I smile. The picture is of me and Dad after I received my graduate degree in elementary education. School was always a safe place for me, and as I grew older it became an easy leap for me to see myself as a teacher. Teachers didn't disappear for days inside their bedrooms or have to leave Whittier to drive a truck for weeks on end. Teachers, at least in Whittier, were around and available for students even when the school was locked up and dark. Plus, teaching came naturally to me, and I loved being around kids, especially the ones who were too loud or troublemakers or angry at the world. I could relate. I look at the picture again. Poor Dad. I put him through so much. Once, I pulled the fire alarm, just for fun, and forced the entire building outside in the middle of a night when the snow flew sideways. I skipped school with Tate more times than I can count, and we shook the vending machine so hard hoping snacks would fall out that we broke it. I can come up with a list of stupid things I did when I was a teenager. I think at one point the homeowners' board wanted to kick us out because of me. But Dad and Ruth were always there, and my antics didn't go unpunished, at least the ones I got caught for.

So it was easy picking my major and later deciding to get my master's in education. Because without all the adults sticking with me, believing in me, and punishing me, too, I might have followed a very different path. Once I was focused, school came easily to me, due much in part to my love of lists and notes and calendars of all kinds. I look again at the picture, remember the proud tautness of Dad's shoulders, so convinced that I would take my education and travel the world. He wanted me far away from Whittier, refusing to ever see how much this town had saved me. I did have friends who left to teach in international schools all over the world, and I could have gone that route, I suppose, but there was a big part of me that yearned to give something back to the kids in Whittier.

I shake my head, blink rapidly. That was all a long time ago, I tell myself.

In some ways I can feel the years that have passed since this photo was taken in the texture of the skin across my arms, the looseness around my eyes, because time itself has changed me even if I don't recall its passing. In other ways, it shocks me to face the truth. The present is liquid, flowing from moment to moment, and I am a raft, drifting with the current, not always connected to the minutes or hours, days and weeks attached to the passing of time, until I stare at a photo like this and am forced to acknowledge how much I have missed. I press my arm against my eyes, wait for the burning to fade before looking at the picture again.

In the picture, I'm wearing a black cap and gown, and Dad has his arm tight around me, his bearded face split in two by his grin. I trace the outline of the two of us with one finger. This was taken right before the ceremony, before my mother's untimely arrival, before I broke the news to Dad about my job in Whittier, and before Tate Dunn walked back into my life.

No, Claire, you can't come back to Whittier. Dad had touched my face like I was delicate and made of glass, a sad wrinkle in his forehead. *It isn't the right place for you. It's too small, honey. I think if I'd been able to afford something better for Alice, maybe things would have been different.*

I'd put my hand on his arm, made him look me in the eye, because I was both angry and saddened by his words. *I'm not her. I'm nothing like her.*

The memory fades and I focus on returning the picture back to where it belongs. That must have been what I was doing in the first place, certainly not dredging up old memories that hurt.

Framed pictures line the hallway, and I let my eyes travel over them, looking for an empty frame where this one might belong. There's a picture with me and Dad by the water, a glistening salmon swinging on a fishing rod between us. Another of me as a toddler—a little monkey clinging to his back during a hike, blonde curls flat against a chubby face. A grainy photo of me standing in the mouth of the Whittier tunnel. Dad took that one the first time he drove me to college. He stopped just before we entered and ordered me out, said he needed photographic evidence that my days of traveling the tunnel were numbered.

My phone buzzes and a reminder pops up on the screen. Relax and read your favorite book, make coffee. I click my tongue and smile. I must have been making coffee; then maybe I got this photo out because I was thinking about him. It's enough of a guess to make me feel grounded, and now I know my next move: go to the kitchen and see if I made the coffee or was in the middle of it.

When I enter the kitchen, I freeze.

A young girl, maybe nine or ten, kneels on the yellow laminate squares, small hands collecting hunks of glass. She looks up when I enter, studies me from behind glasses with frames that are too big for her small round face. Glasses that don't look like the prescription kind.

And her hair. It's piled up on top of her head and appears to have been wound around the cardboard of a toilet paper roll. I can tell because half of the roll is sticking through her hair.

A bubble of laughter fights to escape my mouth. I stop myself. Kids don't like to be laughed at by adults.

"Hi!" I say because I can't think of how else to start this conversation. It's embarrassing to have forgotten why she's here, but something about her puts me at ease. Maybe it's just because I've always been comfortable around kids. "Is everything okay?"

She narrows her eyes, pinches her lips together. "Aw, hell, did you forget about me already?"

I shrug. "Did you forget that kids your age shouldn't use language like that?"

She ducks her head, smiles. "You sound just like Ms. Kiko." Still smiling, she lifts one hand. Blood trickles down from her pinkie in a dotted line. "You were getting me a Band-Aid, and I think you forgot. And also, maybe you forgot that I broke one of your glasses on accident. So I'm sorry, even though I already said that, but you probably forgot that too. And I guess you definitely forgot that you walked me home from the Buckner 'cause you said there were bears who would eat me."

The way she says *forgot* like it's something she knows about me, like it's written across my forehead in thick black letters, inches up my back. But I ignore it because she's just a child, and kids can say all kinds of things they don't mean or completely understand. I grab a paper towel and press it into her palm, examine the cut, which is small and mostly superficial. Just in case, I check my pocket, and to my delight I pull out a slim Band-Aid.

Her eyes widen and I see that they are a dark blue ringed in green. "You didn't actually forget, you just forgot that you remembered! That's great!" She reaches to take it from my hand. "I can do it myself."

"No worries," I say and open the slim package, pull it apart, and have the Band-Aid on her small wound in seconds. "I used to be a teacher, you know."

She holds her hand to her chest, stares at me like perhaps I've grown a pair of purple horns. I touch the top of my head—nope. A chunk of her hair falls away from the toilet paper roll on her head and lands squarely in front of one eye. The cardboard roll, finally released, falls to the floor amid the broken glass between us.

"Aw, hell," she says, and maybe it's the juxtaposition of her kid voice saying an adult word or the fact that I was just like her at that age or that the kid was wearing a toilet paper roll on her head, but a lightness builds inside and I laugh. I try to stop, cover my mouth with one hand—I don't want her to think I'm making fun of her—but the entire situation is so bizarre that I can't help it.

It doesn't seem to matter because the girl laughs, too, small, light giggles that fill the kitchen. It's surreal and sweet, and a lump blooms in my throat.

"What's up with the hair?" I say. I could ask her why she's here, but that would be acknowledging how much I don't know, so instead I play along, figuring that the answers will uncover themselves if I just look for clues. I'm very good at figuring these types of situations out.

"I already told . . ." She wrinkles her nose, stops midsentence, and begins to pick up the glass, throws it into the trash can I pulled out from under my sink, and together we finish cleaning up the mess.

We've both risen to our feet and stand opposite one another in my small kitchen. "I like your glasses," I say.

She nods, her lips quirked up at the sides. The kid is cute, I'll give her that.

There's a name for the shape of her glasses, but I can't get the words to form on my tongue. "I like your glasses," I say, then squeeze my eyes shut because even I can feel the familiarity of the words in my mouth, like I've just said them.

The girl laughs, but it's a sweet infectious sound, like we're enjoying an inside joke. I laugh too. No matter; I *do* like her glasses. I offer her a fact to cover up for my slip. "Cat-eye glasses. They were popular in the sixties."

She giggles, crosses her eyes as if she's trying to look at the glasses on her face. "Yeah, I know; aren't they cool? They're not real, you know. I got them at the Goodwill in Anchorage because they're from the sixties, and I love *everything* sixties. I watch old movies with my dad, so I know a lot about old stuff. And I most especially love everything Audrey Hepburn, you know?"

I nod. "When I was your age, I was into everything seventies— bell-bottoms, braids, tie-dye."

Her eyes grow big behind her glasses, and she looks at me as though seeing someone different. "Cool," she says, then touches a shiny brown curl that hangs below her chin, looks at the fallen cardboard roll on the ground. "Audrey Hepburn wore her hair in a beehive sometimes, and I think it looks cool. I found a YouTube video on how to do it." She picks up the roll, frowns. "I think I need more bobby pins."

I hesitate. I should send her to Sefina, who has two girls of her own. She must have loads of practice doing girls' hair. Besides, this girl can't possibly be here to hang out with me. I turn to lead her out, stop. My mother was a hairdresser, and if there was one thing I learned from her—really one of the only things—it was how to do hair.

"Why don't you let me try?"

The girl stares at me. "Um, okay. Do you want to see the video too?"

I smile, shake my head. "No, I think I can manage on my own." Then I hesitate because I still don't know why she's here, and I'm pretty sure it wasn't so I could do her hair. I glance quickly around the kitchen, see a backpack by the table—not mine, so it must belong to the girl. A crumpled piece of paper sticks out of the unzipped top. I move closer to see whether it can give me any clue, but the girl's next words stop me.

"Is this when you forget everything again?"

I turn, give her a look that is perhaps a bit too sharp, but she's surprised me. "Excuse me?"

"Aw, geez." She scrunches her nose. "Sorry. Nina says you don't remember anything, Tasha says you can remember some things but mostly not much, and Ms. Kiko tells them to hush 'cause she says you're an amazing person who's been through lots." The girl pushes her lips out, tilts her head to the side like she's studying me. "I think probably that Ms. Kiko is right, and besides Nina and Tasha are *teenagers*, so they can be mean for no reason. You know?"

My jaw hinges open at the girl's blatant honesty, and I try not to dwell on the fact that teenagers are talking about me at all. But the effort loosens my hold on this conversation, and I search my brain for something to say that relates to this little girl. *Ms. Kiko.* She's a teacher at the school here in Whittier. I know this is a fact because I taught with her briefly from *before*. "Are you in fourth grade?"

"Yep, me and six others. It's weird here, you know. Real different from my other school."

More information I can use. "So you're new here?"

The girl's eyes grow round. "Wow, yeah! I knew Nina was wrong; you do remember some things. We moved here on September 4, and I remember that date 'cause it's National Wildlife Day. Did you know that?"

I shake my head.

"I do 'cause I have a little flippity calendar that says what's special about the days." Her voice turns serious. "Animals are important on September 4, and I love animals so that's how I remembered it." She seems to be waiting for me to say something, and when I don't she gives an adult sigh and picks up a purple backpack from beside the kitchen table. She pulls out a piece of paper. "I think you probably forgot why I came up here to see you." She hands me the paper, which is crumpled like it had once been a paper ball.

It's a flyer with a picture of a guitar, the kind I could find in clip art, and a few typed sentences.

INTERESTED IN BEGINNER GUITAR LESSONS? CONTACT CLAIRE HINES, APARTMENT 1407

"I'm interested," the girl says. "And my name is Maree, like Mary with a *y* but with two *e*'s like in *Anne of Green Gables*."

I stare at the flyer, biting my lip. The paper is familiar, thicker than regular copy paper, and cream instead of white. I look at my printer, and the skin on my forehead eases with relief because the same paper fills the feeder tray. I tap the flyer. So this *is* from me. But what would put this idea into my head? I can't teach anymore.

I open my notebook but can't find anything related to why or where or anything else that would be helpful to me in this moment when I am faced with the gigantic black hole in my head. I hold out the flyer. "I don't think this is mine."

The girl scrunches her nose. "You're Ms. Claire, and this apartment is 1407, so, um, I think it is." Her eyes roll skyward. "And I want to learn how to play 'cause I think it's cool, and my mom will *love* it. I saw you accidentally throw it in the trash, so I figured I should bring it to you so you know what I'm talking about, since you have your, you know"—she shifts her weight, points to her head—"sucky memory and all."

I'm speechless, trying and failing to put it all together. But from what she's telling me, I gather that I decided to teach beginner guitar lessons, then maybe decided against it, but this girl fished the flyer out of the trash and is now standing in my apartment because she wants to learn how to play. It all feels very sudden but I remind myself that this feeling is peculiar to me alone. "Hold on a sec," I say and head to my desk, frantic to find a folder labeled "Guitar Lessons," because that would be something I would do, but, no, I find nothing. I bite my nail, trying to come up with a plan.

"Ms. Claire?" the girl says.

When I look up, I frown. "Yes?" Something about this girl is familiar, I think, at the same time that I don't recognize her face.

"You don't have to teach me guitar right now. You were gonna put my hair up in a beehive 'cause that's how Audrey Hepburn wore her hair, and I want to look just like her."

Hair. Now that's something I can do. I swivel my chair around until we're face-to-face. My mother was a hairdresser. She'd cut hair in the middle of our living room, and I would sit cross-legged on a kitchen chair, chin in my hands, watching. When I was older, I remember helping her with teenage girls' hair for a school dance. We did buns and braids and swirly updos, and I was her hands because her own shook too much by then.

She follows me to the small bathroom, the one that still has the military-issued cotton candy pink–tiled walls. I bring a kitchen stool and set it in front of the mirror for the girl, who quickly clambers up, still talking.

"This is so great." Her forehead wrinkles when she meets my eyes in the mirror. "Umm, I'm Maree, like Mary with a *y* but with two *e*'s 'cause I like it spelled that way, and I came up here so you can teach me guitar lessons, and then you said you could put my hair in a beehive." She stops to catch her breath. "So that's why we're in your bathroom. Does that help with your lost memory?"

"Yes, Maree, it does. Thank you." Her earnestness is a balm to the unsettling way she brings up my memory, and while a part of me squirms with the implication of what she knows about me, the other part is charmed by her honesty and comfortable with her youthful exuberance. Smiling, I begin carefully sectioning the front of her hair, which is thick and soft, and as I work, the pink of her scalp shows through. From above her I can see the slope of her nose, which ends in an upturned nub. "Can you open the top drawer, Maree, and pull out the box of clips and bobby pins?"

She plops the small plastic box on the counter, looks at me in the mirror. "Why do you have all these hair things when you have such short hair?"

I begin to back-comb the hair at the crown of her head. "When I was little, my mom was a hairstylist. I guess I never got rid of her things after she left." Thinking about her pushes at a door in my mind that swings open far too easily. I am eleven and sitting on a stool in our kitchen. Mom stands behind me, the snip of the scissors loud in the quiet of the kitchen. I wrinkle my nose from the musk of alcohol that surrounds her like a cloud. *You look so much like him, Claire.* My hair was long then, past my shoulders, thick and blonde. She swayed behind me; I could feel it in the movement of the air and the way she grabbed my shoulders to keep from stumbling to the side, swinging the scissors close to my head. *Mom?* She was never violent, but her moods were unpredictable: tears one minute, stone faced and silent the next. And then the loud snip by my ear, and a chunk of hair slid over my shoulder in long golden threads that scattered across the floor. Her cry echoes in my head. *Oh shit, Claire; I'm so sorry. Oh no! I'm so sorry.* She'd collapsed in a heap, slumped over, my hair grasped in her hands like wilted pick-up sticks. I'd scrambled off the stool and knelt beside her, rubbed her back, chewing at a fingernail, because I didn't want her to disappear inside her room for days. *It's okay, Mom. I've always wanted short hair. Let's just cut it all off, and I'll look just like Dad.*

"Oh, my mom had to leave too." A girl's voice brings me back to my bathroom, a comb in one hand, her hair half-teased. I study the girl in the mirror. "Oh geez," she says. "My name is Maree, and you are making my hair into a beehive."

I smile, let my mom slip away, stuffing the pain of her leaving back into its hole, where I try to keep it buried. "I haven't forgotten you yet, Maree, but what did you say about your mom?" I start to pin the back of her hair, and her eyes light up when she sees the beginning of the hive.

"I said my mom left too. Where did yours have to go?"

My grip on the comb loosens, and I step away from the stool, study the girl, who stares at me, her face a mask I don't understand. Ruth's voice bounces around in my head. *She's sick, Claire. She can't get better here, and she doesn't want to keep hurting you.* "Well, sweetheart, she was sick."

Her mouth drops open. "No way! So was my mom."

"Is that so?"

"Yep. A wolf bit her and gave her the America flu."

I nearly drop the comb. "The what?"

Her eyes roll up to the ceiling as though she's thinking hard. "Well, I can't remember exactly, but she's really brave and very strong, and she can't be with me anymore 'cause she hunts wolves so I can be safe."

I raise my eyebrows, unsure of how to respond. The story is fantastical but surely laced with some kind of truth. I just don't think it's my business to ask.

"My dad tells me a story about her every night before I go to bed. Her name is Uki."

I shake my head. "I don't think I've ever met someone named Uki."

She slaps her thigh when she laughs. "But you can't remember, so how would you know if you ever met her? You're really funny."

I can't help but smile. "Thanks."

I push a bobby pin into a section of her hair, not sure what to do with this information about her mom, but my heart squeezes for her because I wonder how close this tale is to my own. She's just been given a better backstory.

She strains her head to look at me over her shoulder, and with her hair pulled out of her eyes, I can see the arch of her thick eyebrows, the light-brown dusting of freckles across her nose and the tops of her cheeks, and I am splintered by a feeling that sends the comb clattering to the floor. I kneel to pick it up and try to squash the sudden desire I have to wrap her into my arms, kiss the very tip of her nose, and ask how school is going. Instead, I cross my arms, plagued by the thought that I could have been a mother today if I'd gone to the doctor when the headaches first started. But I didn't and my baby died. I squeeze the comb in my hand and stand up, focus instead on finishing the beehive.

"Are you okay?"

I look up, nod. "I'm fine. Just been a long day."

She stares at me for a moment, then scratches her nose with the palm of her hand, studies her half-finished bun, and makes a face at herself in the mirror. "No offense, but I think I did better with YouTube."

The edges of my mouth curl into a smile, and I tap her lightly on the shoulder with the comb. "That's because I'm not finished yet, smarty-pants."

She runs a hand across her brow. "Whew." Her eyes brighten. "And my name's Maree, like Mary with a *y* but with two *e*'s. Not Smarty-Pants. And you're doing my hair into a beehive 'cause I suck at it."

I smile at her in the mirror. "Thank you, Maree. I think I'm all up to speed now."

Sometime later I watch Maree sling her backpack onto her shoulders, brown hair pulled into a smooth beehive that would have made my mother proud. I can hear her now. *It's perfect, Claire bear. Do you know how long it took me to learn the beehive? You're just a natural at everything.* I sniff, blink a few times.

The girl pulls a crumpled piece of paper out of her backpack. "You want to teach guitar, and I want to learn. Here." She pulls out a pencil, writes something on the back of the paper. "You have something about it in your notebook 'cause I saw you write it down when I showed you before."

I take the paper: it's a flyer—mine, it looks like—about teaching guitar lessons. The little girl has scribbled her name, spelled M-a-r-e-e, and a short note in her childish scrawl: *Dont forget! I want to be your guitar student.*

"Um." I read the flyer again along with her note. My mother taught me to play. Some of my fondest memories with her include the times spent together hunched over our guitars in the middle of our living room. I was never very good. A fluttering of excitement builds in my chest at the idea. Teach this little girl, Maree, how to play the guitar. I hesitate even though I realize that I want to very much, because the real question is am I able to? Will my system hold up to a situation where someone else is depending on me to get things right? I can feel the impossibility of it in the tightness of my throat battling with the tingle in my fingers at the thought of teaching again in whatever capacity. And the guitar? All I remember about the guitar is what my mother taught me in her imperfect way all those years ago. Will it be enough?

A thought makes my feet feel like they hardly touch the floor: I'm a teacher. It's what I love. I'll find a way to make it work.

The girl has started to spin slowly in circles, hands out on either side like she's trying not to tumble backward from the weight of her backpack. "Maree." I read her name in my notebook, but saying it seems to surprise her, because she stops spinning so abruptly she nearly falls sideways.

"You remembered my name?" she says.

"Well, I think you might be a tough one to forget."

She nods seriously. "I am. My dad says so. And he also says that I'm a real handful."

I laugh quietly, filled with a sudden warmth that minimizes the sharpness of my fingernail pressing into my palm, reminding me to *write this down.*

"So will you teach me guitar?"

A buzz just under my skin. "Yes, I would like that very much." *Write it down, write it down*—a mantra I repeat. *Write it down. Write it down.* "Well, I'd better go—"

The girl gasps. "Oh yeah, you need to write it down. I see you write stuff down all the time, like even in the elevator. You're always writing, and I think that's because of your short memory." Her words come out fast. I'm taken aback but also quite charmed. "You should do that now so you don't forget and stuff." When I don't move right away, she sighs. "Oh, forget it." She plops her backpack on the ground, fumbles around inside, pulls out a notebook and a purple colored pencil, checks the digital watch on her small wrist, and writes something down across the page. She tears it out of the notebook, shoves the paper into my hand, and with much effort, picks the backpack up and slides her arms into the straps.

I read, *You wil teech Maree guitar lesons on Monday at 5.*

"I choose Monday 'cause it's at the beginning of the week, and it starts with an *M* and my name starts with an *M*, so that should be very helpful for you. And then I decided on five o'clock since I get really bored then 'cause it's too early for dinner and too late to have more snacks." She looks up at me, waiting. "So is that okay?"

I grip the paper. I have absolutely no idea, but already I know that I'm not going to tell this little sprite no. That seems about as impossible a task as remembering our conversation. In fact, I find that I would very much like to see her again. "I'll put it into my calendar, um . . ." I scan my notebook.

"Maree," she says. "I'm Maree, and you put my hair in this sweet beehive, and you're also going to teach me guitar lessons on Monday."

I smile. I appreciate her specificity.

With a flip of her beehive, she turns and walks toward the door but stops abruptly because she's staring at a picture.

I follow her eyes. It's a picture of me standing outside the tunnel before I went to college the first time. It's under a framed photo of me and Dad, one taken when I was quite young, with a salmon hanging in the air between us. She looks at me and then again at the picture. "You look the same," she says.

"Do I?" I run a hand through my hair, pull at the ends that are still short and blonde. "That wasn't taken a long time ago, maybe five or . . ." I trail off and for a moment I'm swimming, my mind floating in a black void that turns the edges fuzzy. "That was—"

"Ten years ago," she says.

My eyes narrow. "How did you know that?"

She points to the lower right corner of the photo. Her nail is short, bitten down past the nail bed so that the skin is red, inflamed. "The date is right here." She peers closer at another picture, this one of me on a sled attached to the back of Dad's snow machine. I can't be more than eight, and even though I can't see his face, beside me is my best friend, Tate. I can tell from the too-big and frayed orange snowsuit he wears and the cracked goggles that cover half his face. His dad didn't have a lot, but whatever he did have, he spent on alcohol and cigarettes. My skin tingles with memory: the sting of snow whipping across my face, my nose running from the cold, Tate behind me, screaming in my ear as we flew over the road. "Sledding behind the snow machine. It was my favorite thing to do in winter."

"It looks so fun," she says.

She looks at another picture, this one of Dad standing in front of BTI. I took it after he got the building manager position. "Who's that?" she says. "He's a big guy like you."

Her words warm me. It's an accurate description of my dad, who is larger than life both in physical stature and in his presence. "That's my dad, Vance Hines. He's the building manager here." I look down at her. "Do you know him?"

Her glasses have fallen to the tip of her nose. She pushes them up with one finger, and I notice that her face has lost the cheerful exuberance from a moment ago.

"We made flowers for him today at school, but I didn't know he was your dad."

I press a hand to my chest, touched. "Wow, that's so kind of you. I'm sure he'll love them."

"Oh no, Ms. Claire." Her eyes get wide and her bottom lip trembles, and when she speaks it's hardly more than a whisper. "You don't remember?"

My body goes cold. Tears heat my eyes at the way she says it, with her eyes a brighter blue than before, her mouth twisted, and I don't have to guess because on some level I already know.

CHAPTER FOURTEEN

I don't want to know.

Something writhes in my gut, threatens to cut me open. Sadness weighs upon my skin, and I have to lean against the wall or I'll fall. I am overcome with the feeling that I have lost something I can't ever get back.

A small hand slides into mine, squeezes. Tears streak her small heart-shaped face. "You can come with me, Ms. Claire. Okay? I think Ms. Kiko is upstairs. I'll take you to her. Okay, Ms. Claire?" Her voice is soft, the words lilting up at the end, as though she's speaking to a small child. But I can't feel the sweetness of it—not now, not when I'm afraid to speak. Afraid I'll scream if I do. There's a space inside me that's not filled anymore. I can feel it even if my brain doesn't let me see it. But I don't want to see it, don't want to acknowledge a loss this big. I'd rather forget.

She leads me to the elevator and I stare at the lights as we rise up one floor; then I follow her down the hall to the community room. Inside are voices I know. Ruth, Sefina, Kiko. The girl murmurs something, but I can't string her words together, not over the buzzing in my head.

"I don't understand," I croak.

She stops, turns to face me, her hand on the doorknob. "My name is Maree and you are Ms. Claire, and this is a thing for us to remember your dad."

I can't breathe, can't speak; I hold my stomach because I think I might throw up.

She opens the door. "Ms. Kiko," she calls into the room. "I think I did something really, really bad." She hiccups over her tears. "I didn't know."

Kiko, Ruth, and Sefina rush toward both of us. Maree quickly disappears inside Kiko's hug, but I can still see the girl's back shaking, and I feel a twinge for her sorrow too.

The room is empty of people, but it's filled with rows of chairs, and at the front of the room stands an easel with an enlarged photo of Dad and me on the bank of our favorite fishing cove, a silver salmon hanging in the air between us. The picture is newer; I can tell because I look the same and Dad—I have to swallow a lump because Dad is not the age I remember him. He is older, his once blond hair a silvery gray, beard thick and fuller, longer than I ever remember it being, looking even more the mountain man he already is. The picture and easel are covered in paper flowers, big bright ones of all different sizes and colors, the kind that kids might have made in school as a craft activity.

Ruth steps into my line of vision, and her face fills me with fear, because she's doing something I've never, ever seen her do, not even when her husband disappeared through the tunnel and never came back.

Ruth is crying.

I must make a sound, because Ruth reaches out, grabs hold of my arms. "I'm so sorry, Claire."

I know what I'm seeing. Pictures, flowers, people crying. A memorial. The shifting ground scatters my thoughts, and I clutch at the doorframe, desperate to evoke a memory, no matter how faint, of Dad from today or yesterday or—

A woman appears from behind me, and my chest hurts like I've been stabbed.

Mom.

She's older, brown hair threaded with gray, skin forked in lines that span out from her eyes, down her cheeks. Heavy drinking will do that to a person—peel away all the good stuff, show the wear in their skin and eyes. Except her eyes look clear and still beautiful. Sober, perhaps. My heart hardens.

He's dead and she's alive.

I stumble backward, bump into something small, and hear a crunch. A young girl sprawls on the floor beside me, and her bottom lip trembles. Under my foot is a pair of black glasses, the frames broken in half.

"Claire!" Ruth calls.

I turn away and am heading to the elevators, heart thumping in my ears, when a hand touches my elbow. "Claire." Ruth again, and her voice is a calm breeze in the storm inside my head.

This time I stop, let my head hang. "I don't want him to be gone," I whisper.

"I know," she says. "None of us do."

"Why didn't I know?" I say through my teeth.

"You've been trying to remember. It just upsets you every time. I was going to come and get you, but, well, little Maree brought you instead." I can hear a softness in her voice when she says the name, see her attention turn to the girl. "And that's okay, Maree; you did nothing wrong."

"Claire." My mother's voice. I clench my hands. "Join us," she says.

"Why is she here?" I am overcome by an anger I know isn't fair or right, but it spreads through my body like an infection. "She's the one who broke his heart."

Nobody speaks and the silence lengthens. Mom stands with her feet planted, eyes clear, and it occurs to me that she is not drunk. The thought turns me into a little girl. The one who woke up hopeful every morning that this was the day she'd choose me over alcohol. Her head tilts to the side, and I can see that she wants to say something, and it shatters my illusion because I know that Mom never chooses anyone over alcohol. Ever.

"You're right, Claire. I did break his heart and yours and Ruth's and anybody who ever tried to help me. And you're right; it's not fair that I'm here and he's not." She sucks in air, eyes bright. "But this memorial is meant to honor him, and I am staying to do exactly that. And so should you." Her tone is firm, stern, the one I remember when I was scolded for lying as a little girl.

Ruth straightens her shoulders. "Alice is here because she loved Vance and wanted to be a part of celebrating his life. She has every right to be here." Ruth takes a step toward me. "And so do you, Claire. I know this is painful and horrible and unexpected. I know it doesn't fit within your system and that losing him is so big and deep that we all want to disappear inside of it."

A roaring inside my head drowns her out. Images flash in a merry-go-round parade of Dad. Holding me when I was little, safe inside his arms; fishing together; the frustrated twist of his lips when he had to meet with the teachers again because of something I'd done; the smile that never dimmed when I graduated. A sob wells too big in my throat, and I can't let it out, because I don't think I'll ever stop crying.

Ruth grips my elbow. "Some things, Claire." I see her inhale, and her voice is stronger when she says, "Some *people* are worth remembering even when it hurts." She tucks something into my hand. A notecard with a solitary sentence that slices my heart in two. *Vance died of a heart attack.*

The truth slams into my body, and my only response is to allow myself to be led into the meeting room, where Ruth sits me in a chair in the front row.

I am empty. I am numb. I am lost. I read the note card over and over until the room fills with the quiet sniffles and soft voices of my friends and neighbors.

I don't know how long we sit there, but I listen while half the town gets up to say something about Vance Hines, how he touched their lives in one way or another. Someone tells the story about the bear. Sefina laughs, recounting the punch Dad landed on her ex-husband's nose. Hank remembers Dad pulling his drunk self out of a ditch one freezing winter night. *Saved my life,* Hank says through tears that glisten in his white beard. I am there, I am listening, yet I am frozen, a hard shell surrounding my heart. This loss is new to me alone, and it's a fresh grief that tears me apart at the seams. I rub at my neck, see Ruth dabbing at her eyes, Kiko nodding at something Hank says, and I am an island among them. This moment will stay with them long after they leave, but mine will ebb into the waters that surround me, leaving me to grieve all over again. The thought rolls into a ball, settles into my stomach. I try to write it all down, but I can't possibly record everything, especially this immense feeling of loss. This momentary grief.

Someone sits beside me, leans into me. "I'm so sorry about Vance, Claire."

I turn to see Tate, older but with the same green eyes that seem to read my thoughts, and I cry out, surprised he's here but comforted to share it with him. "He's dead, Tate."

He puts an arm around me, and even though it's been years since I've seen him, touched him, spoken to him, I relax into his embrace because Tate feels like coming home.

There's a notebook in his lap, and with his free hand he's writing furiously.

"What are you doing?"

"I'm trying to record everything for you so you don't have to write, so you can just sit here and t . . . t-ake it all in and listen to how much everyone loved him. When you w . . . w-ant to remember, it will all be in here."

His efforts move me so deeply I feel frozen in his arms. "Thank you," I whisper.

He tightens his arm around me. "You're welcome. And don't worry," he whispers. "I w . . . w-on't miss a thing."

My eyes drift to my own notebook, worn and bent, the pages fluffed out from so much use. It is full of desperate scribbles; my fingers throb from so much writing, and I set the pen down, grateful to rest my aching hand.

I tug at my fingers, repeat a new mantra. *Dad is dead. Dad is dead.* But I can feel that something has come loose inside, like a plug has been pulled. I shift in my seat, unable to fight a rising hysteria that slithers across my skin. My hands shake. *Dad is dead. Dad is dead.* With rubbery legs, I push to standing. "What will I do without him?" I ask no one in particular. Kiko, who stands at the front of the room, stops talking, looks at me with such sadness in her eyes I turn away and scan all the faces. Some I know, many I don't, and it nearly undoes me. I grab on to the back of my chair for support, find Ruth's face. "When did I see him last?" When she doesn't answer right away, I reach for my notebook, flip through it, tearing pages in my desperation because I can't find anything. "Please, tell me when I saw him." Pitiful, pathetic, everything I don't want to be, I sound like in this moment.

"You were with him, Claire. We both were." It's my mother's voice. She stands in front of me. "He wanted to talk to you." She inhales a ragged breath. "About me and about—"

"What about you?" My pen presses into the pages, ready to record everything, but Tate stays my hand, holds up a notebook he has already filled with information. My breathing expands and I let the pen fall away to face my mother.

"He wanted us to be a family again," she says, and her voice is steady even as I see the tiny trembles in her chin. "I know how hard it is for you to accept, but I'm not the same person you remember. And Vance thought it was time to make that stick, to help all of us figure out a way to be together." Her eyes travel over my shoulder. "*All* of us."

Ruth puts an arm around Mom and the gesture surprises me. Mom and Ruth were tight once, but she hurt Ruth with her drinking too. "He was proud of Alice, proud of how hard she's fought to overcome her addiction," says Ruth. "He wanted you to see that too." She glances at Mom. "So much has changed, Claire. Vance had a feeling that it was time to put things right—"

"No, Ruth," Mom says. "Not now."

I've stopped listening because I can't focus on anything other than the fact that Dad is gone. I picture him easily as he is—vibrant in my mind, larger than life—and I can't attach the idea of him dead, gone forever, to that person. A painful fluttering builds in my chest. "Did I get to say goodbye? Hug him one last time? Did I do anything to help him?" My body shakes. No matter how hard I try to scrape off the layer of gunk that clings to my brain, I remember nothing. The blankness is a giant mouth that steals everything from me.

"You did all of that, Claire," Mom says. "He said he was so very proud of you and that only you could have survived and thrived the way you have. He loved you so very much, sweet—"

I inhale sharply, the idea that he's gone fresh pain.

"Claire," she says. "You were his world. He loved you and he loved every minute he spent with you."

We stand there among everyone, some staring at me in pity, others shifting uncomfortably in their seats, but mostly the room is silent, save for the scribbling of pen on paper that comes from the man at my side. I rub at my arms; a coldness pricks at my bones and I shiver. I will forget. I will have to relive this all over again. I clutch at my chest. Dad is my rock, always there to pick me up when I fall, to protect me when I need it. And now he is gone. My body sags. "How am I going to remember?"

Ruth takes the notebook from Tate, touches the one gripped in my hands, and gives me a sad smile. "The way you always have. But with all of our help too."

CHAPTER FIFTEEN

Saturday, February 2

I wake up screaming from a dream I can't remember but that has left me in a cold sweat, and I kick the covers off, needing space, air, anything but this claustrophobic feeling that presses against me. Immediately, I see the whiteboard. *Dad died of a heart attack on September 21.* All that comes out is a broken whimper. I read the journal, which describes my seizure and includes the fact that Dad died of a heart attack. It takes a while for everything to sink in but eventually it does, and the pain ebbs. Today is Saturday, February 2, and I've been waking up the exact same way for four months now.

An ache unfolds across my skull, and I rise unsteadily to my feet. It's past nine in the morning—late for me to be starting my day but it doesn't matter. Dad is dead. I didn't have to read it because I feel the loss of him in the darkness that hovers at the edges of my vision, shrouds my heart.

There's a knock at my door, and I hold my breath because for the briefest of moments I think it's Dad. I read the line again. *Dad died of a heart attack on September 21.* Remind myself that he is forever gone and try to ignore the worn-out stickiness under my eyelids.

I pull on sweatpants and a T-shirt and make my way to my desk. I check the dry-erase calendar. Nothing planned for today or for yesterday. My hair clings, limp and greasy, to my face, and hunger pains suggest I haven't eaten in a while. I move with a sluggish reluctance.

I look through the peephole and pull back at the face I see because I'm surprised to see her . . . but also I'm not. It's written on my whiteboard that my mother lives here now.

"Mom," I say when I open the door. She stands tall—older, her face more rounded, a healthy pallor to her skin. Sober. And here in Whittier. Yet a thick layer surrounds my heart, making it impossible to feel anything but suspicion and disappointment, and for the first time—or for all I know, the hundredth time—I wish I could feel something more for her. "I don't want to see you."

"I'm coming in, Claire."

"Why?"

"You've been holed up in there for weeks now and it's not healthy. I'm making you breakfast, and I'm going to cut your hair. You look like a shaggy dog."

I touch my hair; the ends brush long against the sides of my neck. I feel like a shaggy dog, can smell a staleness that tells me I haven't showered, and I don't know if it's that or the weakness that runs through me when I read *Dad died of a heart attack on September 21*, but I open the door all the way. "Okay," I say.

She arches her eyebrows, surprised—I can guess—that I'm letting her in, and walks past me with a cloth bag slung over her shoulder and a pink-and-white polka-dot carrying case held in her arms. I recognize the case. It held her scissors and trimmers and other supplies. When I was eight she let me pull it down from the shelf in the bathroom and open it for the first time. Tate was coming over. I'd told her that his hair had gotten long and had tangles in it that I tried to get out with my fingers at school. *His hair smells too. I don't think his dad makes him shower like you make me,* I'd whispered to her like I was telling a secret I shouldn't, feeling bad because Tate was my friend.

She'd hugged me. *It's not his fault, Claire bear. Some kids have a hard time at home. Things are tough for little Tate.*

Is that why he's so skinny? I'd noticed how he ate all his school lunch, but he never looked full.

Hmmm, she'd said. *Maybe we can do something to help.*

I could bring him extra from my lunch! I'd been excited by the idea.

That's perfect, sweet girl. You can take him as much as you'd like.

After that, I'd pack two lunches, one for me and one for Tate, always making sure to put in an extra cookie just for him. It stuck, and until we graduated high school, I always packed an extra lunch just for Tate. I'm warmed by the memory.

"Do you remember when you had to give Tate a buzz cut?"

Mom's laugh smooths the lines from her skin, and for a moment she looks just like the woman I remembered from before the drinking. "Poor kid had dreads." Her face darkens. "His father was such a mess."

It's a true statement, but it's ridiculous coming from her, yet instead of feeling angry with her hypocrisy, I snort. "Pot, kettle, Mom?"

She looks at me, mouth hanging open. "I know. I can't believe I just said that. *I* was a mess. Oh, honey, I'm so sorry."

"Yeah, but whenever we rated you, his dad always came up worse." I suck in my bottom lip. "At least, that's what Tate thought. He said there was really no comparison. I disagreed."

Mom gives me a look that I think is amused and touched and sad too. She breathes in and blinks a few times too fast. "Okay, then. Go shower and I'll get breakfast ready." She sets the case on the table and brings the cloth bag over to the kitchen, starts to pull out eggs and bread and milk, cinnamon and sugar.

My stomach growls. "Are you making french toast?" It's such a normal question, such a typical *mom* kind of effort, that it throws me.

She used to make it all the time, and her french toast is fluffy and crispy, with a buttery sweetness so light it doesn't even need syrup.

"Oui!" she says, smiling.

I shower quickly, repeating the same words over and over. *Mom is making breakfast. Mom is making breakfast.* When I'm done, I quietly settle myself on a stool at the kitchen counter and find that Mom is indeed making breakfast. While she cooks, I watch her, looking for anything that gives her away: a stumble here, a nip from a hidden bottle. Nothing but normal mom behavior and reluctantly I record, *She seems different. In a good way.* Then add, because I don't want to give myself false hope, *She forgot I don't like syrup and put it on my french toast.*

After breakfast, she pulls a stool into the middle of my living room floor, places a towel around me, and gently pushes on my shoulders to make sure I'm sitting up straight and even. The familiar routine, her touch and the comfortable quiet between us, is an unexpected balm. I close my eyes, listen to the *snip*, her even breathing. But the moment lulls me away and before everything fades, I pull a note card from my pocket. *Dad died of a heart attack.* My chin trembles and I drop my head and slide the card back into my pocket. When I do, Mom pauses, hands on my shoulders, but doesn't say anything.

"How long have you lived here?" I ask.

The snipping stops. "Not long. Just a few weeks before he died."

"Were you back together?"

"In a way we've never been apart, because that man refused to give up on me." Her voice is hoarse.

My shoulders jerk away from her touch. "You hurt him. I think he was lonely."

She doesn't say anything, but the *snip* continues, and I think I hear her crying, but I don't turn around to look. I don't think I can share in her pain.

Her phone rings. "Hello? Okay, stay there, I'm coming. Yes, I'm glad you called." She finishes with my hair, brushes it out, then quickly packs up her things. "I have to go." She touches my face. "I love you." I don't say anything back.

She leaves behind a lingering aroma of bread and powdered sugar, the tang of orange juice. My fingers run through my hair; it feels fresh and new. I sit on the stool, look out the window. The morning-blue sky is threatened by a distant storm brewing in a roiling mix of gray clouds that skirt the mountaintops. Despite the change outside, an unexpected calm washes over me, and I sit back, buoyed by an irrational surge of hope, and write, *She's different. I think it's real.* Then I shut my notebook and bite my lip. Could she really have changed? I read the note card; my eyes burn when I count how many times I've seen the words before me. Hash marks fill the paper. I stand, ready to crawl back under the covers, to sleep, to be anywhere but here in my living room, alone.

Instead, I force myself to sit down at my desk and make a plan for the day.

~

Sometime later, I have changed into jeans and a flannel shirt, and I think this is a major improvement because the structure of clothes against my body feels good, like I've lived in sweatpants and T-shirts. My hand automatically slides into the pocket of my shirt, pulls out a note card, and I am gutted. *Dad died of a heart attack.* I tell myself to breathe past the sob because this information is not new, even if it feels that way.

I have one activity buzzing on my phone. School Gardens. It's a Saturday, so I should be able to do the job in solitude, which I feel like I need right now.

Today, I opt for the stairwell. It's not always easy to get exercise here, especially with weather that plummets temperatures and dumps snow and rain in huge amounts during the long winter months when the sun refuses to share its light. So even when I was younger, I'd always take whatever opportunity I could to move. I jog down the stairs, listening to faint noises ping and pong against the cement walls of the stairwell. In the lobby I turn toward the exterior doors, intending to get some fresh air on my walk to the school, but a storm swells overhead, suppressing the light and covering the lobby doors in a white veil. I look outside. Gusts of wind slice through the snow, send it plummeting to the ground. I shiver; school tunnel it is, then.

The tunnel stretches long and narrow, with a low ceiling and walls painted in mountain scenes that pale in comparison to the real thing above my head. For someone my height, the tunnel should feel claustrophobic. But this is a journey I took often as a kid and then again as a young adult, just beginning my teaching career.

When I enter the school, I pass by the indoor playground and glance inside—empty, except for a vision of Leilani, swinging on the monkey bars. Her giggles follow me to the hydroponic gardens, where the air is warm, tangy with vegetation, and heavy with humidity. It was once a small setup of buckets and lights and has grown now to include a flood table with a floating platform that the kids built themselves. I know this because there are pictures throughout the space of the kids gardening and building the new system. I'm in some of the pictures too. It's nice to know I had a hand in helping and being a part of its growth.

My phone buzzes. School Garden: water temp, prune, mist.

I take off my flannel shirt and hang it on the back of the door. Already I'm sweating from the added heat in the room, but it's a perfect temperature for the plants.

"Can I help again?"

I turn to the voice. A girl stands in the doorway, her backpack slung around so that she's wearing it with the bulky part resting against her chest. Across the front of the backpack is a strip of silver duct tape, and written in thick black letters on the tape is a name, "Maree." Her words tell me that she's helped me in the garden before, so we know each other. How well, I'm not sure, but her smile tugs gently at my heart. I've always had a soft spot for kids.

"You bet," I say. "This garden belongs to you kids, anyway. I just help when I can."

"Okay, but are you sure you want *me* to help?"

The way she says it, like we are familiar with each other, makes me pause. I have no context for what she might mean. "Yes, I'm sure."

"Yay!" she cheers and sets her backpack on the ground before skipping to my side. On her shirt is another strip of silver duct tape that reads "Maree." She licks her lips, claps her hands, and stares at the rows of plants. "What are we doing?"

"Didn't you say you helped me before?"

She makes a funny face. "Yep, but you were almost done, and it was a while ago, and maybe I wasn't listening so great." She holds her hands out, palms up, and shrugs. "Sorry."

A buzz from my phone. School Garden: water temp, prune, mist.

"Well, let's get started, and this time maybe try to listen a bit harder." I smile, run a hand through my hair, and turn to the garden, check the water temp. The girl is staring at me, frowning, so I point to the thermometer reading. "The temperature needs to stay between sixty-five and eighty degrees." Her mouth hangs open slightly. "Do you know how a hydroponic garden works?" I ask.

She shakes her head.

"Have you ever grown a plant yourself?"

"My dad gave me a little pot that had dirt and seeds to grow a sunflower. I just had to put a little packet of soil in, drop in some seeds, and give it water."

"Sounds fun. How did it turn out?"

Her nose wrinkles. "Nothing happened, but I did accidentally knock it off the windowsill when I got mad about something, and all the dirt spilled out. Probably the seeds, too, I guess."

I lift one corner of my mouth. Cute kid. "That happens. But look here." I point to the rows of plants. "Can you see the difference between your flower and this garden?"

She walks up and down the rows, pinches her lips together as she studies the plants. Suddenly, her eyes grow wide behind her cat-eye glasses, which are taped in the middle like they've been broken at some point. "There's no dirt!"

"Very observant, Maree."

She goes so still I think I've scared her. "You remembered my name," she says quietly.

I chuckle and point to her shirt. "You're wearing a name tag."

"Oh, right," she says, and I feel a twinge because I think I've disappointed her. "I guess the name tag was a good idea. So how does this hypnotize garden work?"

I smile. "A *hydroponic* garden grows plants in a water-based nutrient solution. I come down here to check the water temperature, prune, and mist the plants."

She nods. "Cool. So how come you can work down here and remember what to do and stuff?" I stiffen, and when I don't say anything right away, she takes a step toward me and says in a loud voice, like she thinks I haven't heard her, "You know, because of your short-memory thing and how you can't ever remember my name."

Heat prickles my cheeks. It's not that I'm embarrassed by my condition—well, I mean, of course I *can* be, especially at this moment when a sweet kid is calling into question my ability to do such a simple task.

"Oof, sorry," she says. "Was that a"—she curls her fingers into air quotes—"*rude* question? Ms. Kiko says that sometimes I don't think before I talk, you know?" Maree kicks at the floor. "Sorry if I hurt your feelings and stuff."

I don't like having my memory deficits on full display for anyone, but something about this girl's humbleness puts me at ease, and I find myself comfortably moving into teacher mode. "It's good to ask questions, Maree. That's how we learn, but thanks for asking anyway." I wink. "I'm not offended, just surprised."

"'Cause you can't remember?" she says.

I shake my head; the girl is persistent, a bit like a dog with a bone. "Because it's an intuitive question. I helped get these gardens started when I was a teacher here."

Her eyes widen. "You did?"

I don't add that the reason we were able to get the original equipment in the first place was after a raid on a resident who was growing marijuana in his apartment and who was given a onetime pass if—and only if—he donated the gardening equipment to the kids. "Partly. But it all happened before my accident, and most of those memories I still have." I make a face. "I think."

At that, Maree laughs so hard it comes out as a howl. "You *think* but you don't really know 'cause you can't remember if you remember. That's so funny!" She grabs her sides, gulping for air. "And really confusing!"

A smile curls the edges of my lips. The girl's reaction takes me by surprise, but it's also refreshingly innocent, and sharing this moment with her is an unexpected pause in the predictability and order I usually seek. Her comfort level with me also makes me suspect I've interacted with her on more than a couple of occasions. "So how do we know each other, Maree?"

"I read to you at quiet activity time, but you haven't been coming because of your dad and stuff, and Ms. Kiko says you need time to be sad."

My hand goes to my pocket, and I pull out a note card. *Dad died from a heart attack on September 21.* It hurts to read, physically aches to have to stand in front of this girl and not give in to a weakness in my legs. But I make a hash mark on the card, can see that I've read it dozens and dozens of times, can see that it's not new to me even if it feels that way. I breathe in, notice that the girl's eyebrows are wriggled together in concern.

"It's okay if you're still sad, Ms. Claire. You don't have to be happy just 'cause everyone says you should. I'm still sad about my mom being gone all the time, and that's been my whole life, so." She shrugs.

Her kindness touches me. "Thank you, Maree. That's a very sweet thing to say." I don't ask about her mom, because I don't think it's wise of me to ask personal questions—not at the moment, anyway.

She kicks at the floor, eyes trained on her shoes. "I've missed you," she says softly, and the sincerity behind her words surprises me, but before I can reply with anything, she looks up, puts her hands on her hips, and says, "So do you want to teach me how to take care of these plants?"

I smile. "I'd love to. You can follow along beside me and do what I do. Sound good?"

We set to work side by side. She's quiet but seems to pick up on finding the dead leaves quickly. I think her favorite part is misting the plants, which she does with abandon, getting about as much water on herself as on the plants. She giggles easily and I am soothed by the sound.

When we finish, I pat her shoulder. "Great work today."

"Thanks," she says, and the tops of her cheeks turn a slight pink.

We wash our hands and head down the tunnel together, but when we get to the elevator, there are a few kids in the lobby, and with a wave to me, she heads in their direction.

CHAPTER SIXTEEN

I'm walking into my apartment, bags from the market swinging off my arms, when I hear a voice that I would know anywhere.

"Hi, Claire."

I turn sharply and the bags swing with me, one hitting the wall with a soft thump. Tate.

He's holding out a note card, but I'm focused on the angle of his jaw, the green of his eyes, and then I'm thinking about the last time I saw him, and my eyes fly open because—

"I know all about the baby. You t . . . t-old me."

I move back into my apartment, set the bags on the counter, and take the card he holds out. *I live in Whittier and I work as the harbormaster and I'm not married anymore. I know about the baby and I understand. I love you, Claire.*

A blush spreads across my cheeks, and I focus on my hands. We said it to each other as kids, but now, as adults, it feels different to me, important in a way I don't think he feels.

"I thought you could add it to the one you k . . . k-eep in your pocket about Vance." His voice is calm, but I think he's nervous too.

There is a card in my pocket. I pull it out; one hand goes to my chest, and I have to blink hard, stare at the card until the words blur together. Then I grab a pen and make a hash mark. Yes, I know this; I'm sure I know this.

I look again at the card from Tate, feel a twinge at the kindness in his gesture. "Do you want to come in?" I ask, suddenly shy, touching my hair and wondering if I bothered to make it look nice today or, God forbid, did I even shower? I hope for the best, not daring to sniff my armpits to find out.

I put the few groceries I have away, acutely aware of Tate sitting on a stool at the counter, watching me. Do I look old to him? The same? Different? Does he pity me? My mind is full of questions, most of which I can answer with a disheartened yes. I don't want to turn around, until a sardonic voice inside reminds me that he's not here to make mad, passionate love to me. He's here because he'll always be my friend, and he more than likely feels sorry for me. I stand tall and turn to face him, but his full lips part into a wide smile that only highlights his cheekbones and eyes and, oh, that hair that I want to run my fingers through—

"Claire?"

Scattered thoughts in my mind that make me cross and uncross my arms, embarrassed and unsure what to do with myself.

"I have an idea," he says. On the counter in front of him is a small rectangular device.

"What's that?" I ask, coming closer, my interest piqued.

"It's an iPad, basically like your phone but a little bigger, and it can do a bit more. It came out around the t . . . t-ime when, um"—he clears his throat—"when you were p . . . p-regnant."

I'm nodding because, yes, I remember this part. "With your baby," I say.

He nods. "Right."

"And I've already told you," I read from the note card.

He looks proud of himself, and it makes me smile. "Yes."

He opens a program on the device that looks like a piece of notebook paper. "There's a program on here, really similar to your n . . . n-otebooks, except you can organize it into categories that you can sort and search. You can even color code it the same w . . . w-ay. Here, see?"

He taps a line that reads *Vance's Memorial Service*, and up pops an entire screen full of notes—typed, not handwritten.

My forehead wrinkles. "How do I know if I wrote this?"

"You didn't. I t . . . t-ook these notes for you. I w . . . w-anted you to be able to take everything in. These are for you to read now and whenever you . . . like."

I bite my lip, touched and confused and fighting a reflex to pick up my notebook and transfer everything from the screen onto paper. But I don't, because I couldn't bear to ruin the hopeful look on his face. Instead, I say, "Thank you." I didn't use much technology when it was available to me in college, much preferring the old-school methods of paper planner, pens, and pencils. But I take a sticky note, write *Tate gave this to you, it's like a notebook and a phone*, and stick it to the screen.

Tate stands, holds out his hand. "Come on."

I hesitate. "Where?"

"Ruth made dinner and invited us over."

I check my phone and the dry-erase board on my desk. "But it's not on the calendar."

Tate laughs and it's a hearty, welcome sound that vibrates through my body. "I know, but it's already done, and she's w . . . w-aiting for us."

I touch my hair. "Us?" Feeling every bit the blushing teenager.

He grabs my hand and pulls me toward the door. "Yes, and we're not in trouble or anything."

I smile, enjoy the warmth of his hand clasped over mine. "That must be a first," I say.

We're both laughing when Ruth opens her door, and she gives us each a look that takes me back to the time she discovered us smoking cigarettes in the laundry room. She's wearing an apron with a pink ruffled hem, like a tutu. The splash of color is an odd choice for Ruth, who has favored the more somber hues of brown and gray ever since her husband went through the tunnel and never came back.

I point to the floaty layers of pink tulle. "What's with the apron, Ruth?"

She gives me a look that lightens my mood even more. "You gave it to me a couple of Christmases ago."

"Did I?" I study the layers of tulle. "Well, it looks nice on you. I obviously have great taste."

Inside, she hands me a plate of pasta with fried bacon bits, tomatoes, basil, and cubes of mozzarella along with a scoop of green salad. We all sit at her small table, but before she eats she reaches over and touches my arm. "I'm glad you're here."

I pull back, surprised by her sudden tenderness. "Me too."

She gives me a tight smile, then stabs the pasta with her fork. "Your hair looks nice. Alice said she cut it for you this morning."

A prickle of heat runs across my scalp, and I'm opening my notebook but Ruth is still talking.

"She lives in Whittier now and she's sober."

I'm nodding; even if I don't know this, I don't think it shocks me. My hand retreats from the pages, and I turn to the plate of food in front of me.

Tate smiles, points to my notebook. "You've always been so organized. Do you remember how you used to keep a rating system for my w . . . w-eed?"

Ruth groans. "I'm glad those days are over."

I play with a strand of my hair, smile, letting the memory wash over me. "One was for chill, two for sleepy chill, three dopehead chill, and four . . ." I tap my chin, thinking.

"Four w . . . w-as for mostly dead chill."

We both laugh; Ruth shakes her head, eats a tomato.

"I wasn't that creative, was I?" I look down and try to ignore my racing pulse.

He leans across the table, and the air around me fills with the light scent of sandalwood and leather. His eyes are a deep green that glows next to his black hair. I look away, pull on a loose blue thread poking out of the cuff of my shirt, and try to remember that I am a thirty-six-year-old woman with no real future, not a teenage girl with everything ahead of her.

Tate's smile creases the skin around his eyes in pleasant lines. "Do you remember that t . . . t-ime we snuck into the reindeer pen and tried to . . . take the biggest one for a walk?"

It comes easily to me—most memories with Tate do—and my back muscles relax. "Using a pair of Ruth's pantyhose."

Tate eases back against his chair, laughs. "Why didn't we think to find a rope?"

"Why did we think to do it at all?"

It was on a late Alaskan summer night when the sky was perpetually light, and Tate and I were into nothing but trouble. We'd tiptoed through the reindeer pen, nearly overpowered by the heady musk of mud and excrement. The reindeer stared at us through dark eyes and didn't move a muscle while Tate tied the legs of the hose around his neck. "Do you remember how docile he was?" I say, and Tate nods, eyes bright, smile wide.

"Until we stepped out of the p . . . p-en and he t . . . t . . . ran off!" Tate laughs so hard he stops talking. "But you held on."

"And Ruth's pantyhose stretched nearly the entire length of Kenai Street before they snapped out of my hands." A helium weightlessness fills my insides. I laugh so hard it brings tears to my eyes.

"Do they still call it P . . . p-antyhose Avenue?"

Ruth sets a carrot cake, small plates, and forks onto the table. "That's quite enough from you two. It's like no time has passed when you get together."

I dip my head, don't add that to me it doesn't feel like any time has passed.

We eat the cake and I enjoy the easy quiet that comes with people I know well, awash in memories that flow naturally. I finish the last bite, savoring the sweetness of the carrots and the tang of ginger combined with the creamy, sour kick of the cream cheese frosting. "Did Mom make this?"

Ruth's fork freezes halfway to her mouth. Tate swallows so loud I can hear it.

"What?" I ask.

"You remember?"

The question is a worm, wiggling through holes inside my brain. "Um, well, Mom loves to bake, so . . ." It's such a direct question, and I can't figure out what Ruth is asking of me.

Her face softens. "I'm sorry, Claire. That wasn't fair of me. It's just that your mom lives here now, and it just seemed like maybe you knew."

"Mom lives here?" I say, and my hands clench, but I'm thinking of her gentleness and the way she could brush through my thick, tangled hair without pulling too hard or making my sensitive scalp ache. I rub my neck, confused at my thoughts because they don't have the shadow of anger that's trailed me since my thirteenth birthday. "Am I still angry with her?"

Before Ruth can answer, a device on the table in front of me lights up. A sticky note on the screen reads *Tate gave this to you, it's like a notebook and a phone.* I pick it up, slide open the button, and the screen is filled with a notebook-paper graphic and the date, Saturday, February 2. Writing appears on the screen. Alice is sober. She lives in Whittier and she's the mom you remember.

My head shoots up. Tate is typing into a device similar to mine. He smiles into the screen, and more words appear on mine. Your hair smells like apples and your skin is smooth and soft and is that same shade of peach that glows. You are more beautiful now than ever. That's what Tate thinks.

My heart rate slows. Tate used to run his hands up and down my arms, leaving a trail of goose bumps across my flesh. He said he loved the feel of my skin. I pick up the device. "What is this?"

His chest broadens. "I'd like t . . . t-o help you remember, also, if that's okay, Claire."

A coldness pierces my skin, steals the warmth from before, but Tate's eyes meet mine squarely, and instead of pity I sense respect—admiration, even—in his stare.

"I do that already."

"Yes, and you're amazing at it, but it seems like you might be missing out . . . sometimes."

I cross my arms, made vulnerable by his words. "How?"

"On experiencing the moment more instead of trying to write it all down." He holds up his device. "But w . . . w . . . all of us can help." He types again, and I look at the screen.

> This is a shared document. So I can add to your online notebook, giving you a different perspective from the pieces of your day that include me.

There is a bubble by the entry with his name. Another bubble pops up.

I can too. This one has Ruth's name, and when I look up, I see that she's left the table and is sitting over by her desk, in front of a desktop, peering down through reading glasses perched at the end of her nose.

Tate touches my hand. "I can g . . . g-ive access to whoever you trust." He shrugs, seems to wait for me to speak, but I'm frozen, unsure of how to respond to a gesture at once grand and sweet but also invasive and exposing.

When I don't speak, Tate seems to shrink. "I'm s . . . s . . . I apologize. Is it t . . . t-oo much?"

Maybe it's the stutter, a reminder of the boy inside the man, or maybe it's the overload of information that threatens to wash me out or the idea that anyone would go to such lengths for me, but I feel myself shaking my head no, then standing and moving toward him, mouth clamped shut, and tears brimming. When he stands I hug him, and it must surprise him because at first he doesn't move. Then his arms wrap around me and he holds me tight, and I breathe out and lean into the feeling of him, the heat of his body against mine, muscular and strong, and I relish the sensation that swaddles me.

I feel normal.

CHAPTER SEVENTEEN

Friday, February 8

Therapist Kate sips her tea and studies her notes, giving me a chance to read over mine one more time.

"It's been hard," I say. My notes are filled with dark thoughts, and it's difficult to read through them, to experience the emotion all over again. I blink hard but it doesn't stop my eyes from burning. It's been over four months since Dad died, and while I can accept it as part of my reality, the loss is fresh, grief a close friend. I suspect this feeling is not much different for people without brain injuries.

"What did you bring with you today?" She points to the file sticking out of my bag.

I have to check my notes. "Oh, um, I'm not really sure. I guess I was going to give beginner guitar lessons. A little girl was interested." I show her the writing on the flyer. *Dont forget! I want to be your guitar student. Maree.*

"Are you planning to start the lessons, then?" I notice a hopeful lift in Kate's voice, which I ignore.

"I don't know."

"Do you think you might enjoy doing something different from your normal routine?"

I give her a look. "I have no idea."

Kate seems to regroup. "What do you want, Claire?"

I glance down at my notebook. There are three indisputable facts that I keep at the top of every page. They are listed in order:

1. *Dad died of a heart attack on September 21.*
2. *Mom lives in Whittier and she's different.*
3. *Tate Dunn lives in Whittier and is the new harbormaster. You told him about the baby. You are friends.*

Each one of them is a blow to my body. "I want things to go back to the way they were."

"Before your seizure?"

The unfairness of everything simmers into a boil, heats up my skin. "Before Dad died, before Mom started drinking, before Tate left me. Before, when I had a future." Kate doesn't say anything; she's quiet, letting me process. I doodle in the margins of my notebook. "Do you think this does anything for me?"

Her eyebrows raise. "Therapy?"

I nod.

She sits back, seems to consider. "Honestly? This is as far from therapy as it gets." She smiles and so do I. "But your father was a persuasive person, and he felt that this was exactly what you needed." Her face softens. "Vance was a good man and a good friend to my husband when he needed one the most."

Kate's husband served three tours in Iraq and suffers from PTSD that deeply alters the man he was. They lived in Whittier when I was in high school, and Dad reached out, hoping to help the man, whose depression had become a monster he couldn't control anymore. I always thought Dad was trying to make up for not helping Mom in the way he was always trying to help others.

156

"Are things better now for him?" I ask because while I think they are, I also can't recall.

Kate's smile is warm and generous. "Yes, much better. And we both credit Vance for helping him find a way." Her face turns serious. "As far as therapy for you goes, I think that deep down, Vance hoped that it would eventually lead to you forgiving Alice."

I scratch my head and let my eyes slide back to the notebook, but I don't have to read anything there to know how I feel.

"I'm afraid to trust her. Old habits are hard to break, and drinking is the oldest of habits for her." I fiddle with the pen in my hand. "Do you know where she was the night that bear got into our lobby?"

Kate looks at me, and it's not hard to guess I've already told her this, but I do anyway. "At the bar, so wasted that Dad had to go pick her up later and carry her home. It's why he was looking out the window in the first place and saw the bear. He was looking for Mom." I read the fact at the top of the page. *Dad is dead. He died of a heart attack on September 21.* My heart shrivels. "He protected everyone and now he's gone, and Mom wants back into my life. Why does she think she deserves that?"

I can't summon up enough vitriol to match my words. Instead, I think of the time a harbor seal washed up near one of our fishing coves, injured, hardly breathing. Mom knelt beside the animal, running her fingers gently over its head, murmuring, *It's okay, buddy. It's okay.* I blink back tears, busy myself with the notebook. "My mom is coming over in the mornings to talk and have coffee." I point to a line, can already taste her baked goods. "This morning she brought doughnuts."

Kate's face brightens. "How did it go?"

"I don't know but I don't feel angry when I think about her. I always remember how angry I'd get whenever I saw her or just thought about her."

"It's good, don't you think?" Kate says. "Not to feel angry?"

When I don't answer, she continues, "You know, there was a patient many years ago with anterograde amnesia like yours. She could never remember her doctor and would greet him every time she saw him as though it were for the first time."

I wince, thinking how close to reality this must be for me, not liking to picture myself in that way.

"Until this one day, her doctor hid a stickpin in his fingers, and when he shook her hand to say hello, it pricked her skin and caused her brief pain. Afterward, the woman refused to shake his hand."

I straighten in my chair, interested. "She remembered?"

Kate shakes her head. "She couldn't remember it happening, but when they asked her why she refused, she asked if perhaps he held a pin in his hand." She leans forward, her elbows on her knees. "I think that's similar to how you're feeling about your mom, but in reverse."

I take the pen cap on and off, unable to see her connection and frustrated by her comparison. "I don't understand."

Kate's voice softens. "What I mean is that your mom has been sober for nearly ten years now, lives in Whittier, and has taken an active role in your life. I think that on some level, like the stickpin, you've registered this change."

My chest tightens and I can't respond or do more than sit here trying to process.

She picks up a device from the table beside her. "May I?" It's similar to the one in my lap. The one with the sticky note that says it's from Tate and that I brought along with my paper notebook but haven't used. Now it lights up and writing appears on the notebook graphic next to a bubble that says "Therapist Kate."

You had positive thoughts about Alice today. You
don't feel angry with her, you know that she's sober.
You're still working on trusting her but you've come

a long way, Claire. And you mentioned having coffee and doughnuts with her this morning. Next
time, please bring one of her doughnuts to me. ☺

I am warmed by her note. It feels inclusive, like we're part of the
same team. Like I'm not alone. "Thank you," I say.

She looks up from the device, tilts her head. "When we started
therapy after your seizure, you would say the same thing to me at every
visit, and you say it even today."

"What's that?"

"That you want to be normal again."

I nod, swallow hard, because I do want that.

"You've worked so hard to remember like a normal person, to
appear normal to even your close friends and family." She pauses,
inhales. "Maybe being normal isn't the point."

"What do you mean?"

She leans forward and clasps her hands. "Maybe you're meant to be
extraordinary. And if that's the case, then you're already there."

I open and then close my mouth, my mind a blank. What can I say
to that? So I write it down because of all the things I record, this seems
like the most important to remember.

CHAPTER EIGHTEEN

I've returned home from seeing Kate, and instead of pushing fourteen on the elevator, I push twelve. I know he's gone. I've written it on a note card I carry with me, plus it's a line of text that I made as the background on my screen. But I'm standing in front of Dad's door anyway, hoping for what? That it was all a nightmare?

The door is open a crack, and inside it's dark, and cool air slips through the opening, touches the tip of my nose. I push against the door and freeze. A woman stands by Dad's small dining table, one hand stretching out like she means to stop me from entering, a cardboard box lying open on the floor at her feet.

"Mom?" I can't breathe.

I cross my arms against the heavy beating of my heart. She looks the same and also different. Worn, older, but clear-eyed, not the same woman who left when I was thirteen, nothing like the drunken woman who tackled me at my graduation when I was twenty-five. Images and thoughts tangle into ideas that make no sense except that I don't feel heated pricks across my scalp, just a deep sadness, like I've lost something. I touch my pocket.

"You live here now?"

She nods and I stand there, not surprised but unable to find context. Boxes are strewn about Dad's floor, but Dad died, so—my mouth goes dry. "Are you packing up his things?"

"I've tried." Her arm gestures to the mostly empty boxes. "I just can't seem to do it." She wipes her eyes. "Would you like to help?"

I step inside, a heaviness pulling at my legs. "Sure."

She hands me a box and directs me to his bookshelf. I notice that other things dot the apartment, feminine touches that don't belong to my father. The dots connect easily. "Are you living here?"

"I was, we were—" She wets her lips. "He always believed in me, Claire; told me he'd wait his entire life for me if that's what it took for me to get sober."

"It did," I say, but I wince at the harshness in those two little words. She takes a step back, like I've punched her.

My hands tremble from a mixture of emotions. "Do you know how hard it was for him after you left?"

"Claire," she says and the voice is hers, but it's smoother than I remember, unhindered by the slur of alcohol. "I know, honey."

I think my face is wet, but I wipe it with the back of my sleeve and pretend it's not. "He never cried; he tried to pretend that he was fine for me, but at night he would sit in his chair and stare at his hands. I used to watch him. He'd do that for hours." I straighten to my full height, which towers over her, but she doesn't cower or look away; instead, she keeps her eyes glued to mine. It softens me and I have to look away. "Why are you back?" I am thirteen, watching her pack a suitcase and walk out the door.

"For you." When her eyes meet mine, they are unwavering, steel-like. My heart thumps painfully at the sudden glimpse of her as the mom I remember. The one who sat with Ruth after her husband left, the one who comforted a dying seal, the one who made sure Tate had clothes to wear and a good haircut. The one who loved me.

"And for Vance. But it was just too damn late." Her face crumples and she grabs for the back of the closest chair, falls into it as though the strength has drained from her legs.

A current of pain runs through me at her grief.

"But it's not too late for you, Claire, and I'll be damned if I'm going to waste this precious second chance." She sits up straight. "Do you remember my nightmares?"

I give a tight nod. They were always worse when Dad was on the road. I'd climb into bed with her and stroke her hair, try to comfort her. She would never wake up, but eventually she'd stop whimpering.

"I'd wake up to your skinny little arms around my neck, your chubby face pressed into mine." She's smiling, even if her eyes glisten. "You were always there for me, sweetheart, and I was too weak to be your mother. It's the greatest regret of my life." She stands, breathes in. "But I don't live in the past anymore. I live for this moment, right now." She approaches me, takes my hands in her own, and standing in front of her, I feel big and clumsy—a child. "I'm not going anywhere, Claire. And I don't need for you to be normal or perfect, because I love you exactly as you are right now in this minute, and I'll keep telling you that until my last breath."

My emotions are rocks that collect in a pile on the ground at my feet, and I don't know what to do with them. My mother is not the woman I remember most vividly; this remorseful, sober, *loving* woman is the one whose ghost used to haunt my dreams with memories of songs and kisses and nightly tuck-ins. It's an overwhelming blend that pelts me with the rocks, starts my thoughts spinning a vortex around me until I am left confused and standing in a cold apartment, with the snow tapping against the window like something wants to get in, and staring at a woman who looks like my mother.

I rub my head, pull at the ends of my hair. The last time I saw her, she was stumbling toward me at graduation. But now we're in Dad's apartment; I know for sure because of the lingering smell of burned toast in the air and his favorite chair under the window. "Mom? What are you doing here?"

She squeezes my hand before pulling something from my pocket. A note card with three facts printed across the front:

1. *Dad died of a heart attack on September 21.*
2. *Mom lives in Whittier and she's different.*
3. *Tate Dunn lives in Whittier and is the new harbormaster.*
    You told him about the baby. You are friends.

I press a hand to my chest, but this information is not new. I can feel it, even it if fills me with a noxious blend of grief and hope. There are boxes scattered in the apartment. "Are you packing up his things?"

She holds out her hand. "I thought you'd like to help me."

Despite an aching in my chest, I nod, and together we kneel in front of his bookshelves and start there.

CHAPTER NINETEEN

Monday, February 11

The lobby is louder than normal with kids hanging out after school, sitting in twos and threes, talking, doing homework together. It brings a smile to my face.

Just as I turn toward the market, I glimpse a small form in the corner, away from the kids who laugh easily together. She's got her knees drawn up and a booklet tucked on her thighs, eyes focused on whatever she's writing or drawing. She can't be more than ten, but she's dressed in black pants and a black sweatshirt, and her dark hair is pulled into a high ponytail that curls around her head on one side. Maybe it's the picture of her alone against the backdrop of comfortable banter and easy friendships, but something draws me toward the girl.

My phone vibrates with instructions. Market, Gardens. A twist in my belly reminds me to do what I have planned because going off schedule is murky territory where I easily lose focus.

I take a deep breath, slide my phone into my pocket, and head in her direction. The kids' chatter fades as I approach, and I feel their eyes glom on to me. In some ways, I can imagine how I might appear to others. I'm different, a freak to some. I don't blame teens—or adults, for that matter—for not knowing how to interact with me. It must be difficult, I'm sure.

A few giggles come my way, but I lift my head and keep my teacher smile in place. I don't know the faces that observe me, can feel the tiny bites of panic that come with being in a roomful of strangers.

When I get close to the girl, I slow, hesitate; she hasn't looked up from her booklet, and I'm doubting my intentions. Thoughts dance in my head and make it hard to pin down what I was thinking a few minutes ago. Why did I come over here, anyway? Because the girl looked lonely—that's right. But how can someone like me do anything more than embarrass her?

"What are you working on?" I say.

The girl looks up and I see that she wears cat-eye glasses, only the lenses are missing and the frames are taped in the middle like they've been broken in half. The whole effect is charming, if not a little bit sad.

"Oh, hi, Ms. Claire," she says, and I try not to show my surprise that she knows my name. "I'm just working on my book about *The Adventures of Uki*, my mom." She scrunches her nose, I think to move her glasses up the bridge. "Are you feeling better now?"

Giggles from behind me, and I turn to see a teenage girl with short sandy hair that's shaved on both sides. She looks to be about thirteen or so.

"Hey, Ms. H.," she says.

Another girl giggles beside her.

"You put your flyer back up," the first teenage girl says. "And I still want lessons."

My smile feels as blank as my brain. "Okay," I say, hoping she'll lay out more clues for me.

"So can I?"

The girl beside her giggles behind her hand, points to the community board on the wall.

INTERESTED IN BEGINNER GUITAR LESSONS?
CONTACT CLAIRE HINES, APARTMENT 1407

Huh, when did I do that? I roll my shoulders, not upset by the idea. It sounds fun. "My mother taught me," I say. "But I'm not very good."

The giggling girl squints her eyes. "If you suck, why are you giving lessons?"

It's a fair question and one I have no answer to, but before I can respond, a girl's voice pipes up from behind me.

"You're a mean girl, Nina!" I turn to find the little girl in cat-eye glasses has risen to her feet, her eyes blazing.

"No, please don't, kiddo, not for me." The last thing I want is to start a fight among the kids.

The little girl in black looks at me, her eyes soft. "I think you're going to the market and then to the school gardens. But it's probably on your phone."

"Yes, of course, thank you, uh, um—"

"Maree!" say Nina and the other girl in tandem, followed by Nina's giggles. "Her *name* is Maree!"

I give the kids a thumbs-up for their assist. "Thanks, Maree." Then to the teenager: "Stop by if you're interested in lessons. I might not be very good at it, but I'm probably the only choice you have around here, right?"

I wave goodbye and head to the market, where Hank sits behind the counter, reading a *National Enquirer*.

"Another Bigfoot sighting?" I say.

Hank nods. "Last spotted wrestling a grizzly bear."

"Who won?"

He peruses the paper, lifts his eyes, and winks. "Doesn't say." We both laugh and Hank's bearded face softens. "Kids giving you a hard time, Claire? I'll speak to their parents."

I shake my head. "Nah. They're just curious about me. Actually, I'm kinda like a teenager myself."

Hank's big eyebrows meet. "How's that?"

I smile. "I could be angry one minute, sad the next, happy right after and have no idea why the people around me look exhausted."

Hank laughs, a deep rumble that shakes his beard. "You always know how to look on the bright side, Claire."

~

A little girl is waiting outside the market with her hands on her hips. "Sorry about those stupid girls," she says.

I shrug. "What girls?"

Her lips quirk up. "Stupid one and stupid two," she says.

I laugh. "It's okay; I've already forgotten all about the stupids."

The girl's eyes widen. "You can forget mean people? That's like having a superpower!"

"It is, isn't it?" I smile. "I like the way you think. What's your name?"

Disappointment flashes across her face, but she covers it up quickly with a smile and an enthusiastic, "Maree! Like Mary with a *y* but with two *e*'s 'cause of *Anne of Green Gables* and stuff."

"Well, hi, Maree." My phone buzzes—Gardens—and something about her comfort level with me, or her blue eyes that are so dark they almost look black, makes me want to invite her. "Would you like to come to the gardens with me?"

"Yeah!"

As soon as we enter the room, the sticky moisture clings to my skin, beads into condensation that slips down my back. She picks up an apron and slides it on, then starts rooting around the plants, picking off dead leaves. I raise my eyebrows. Okay, seems like we've done this before.

I join her, and for a few minutes, we work in silence.

"Ms. Claire?"

"Yes?"

"Do you think we can do the guitar lessons like we were going to before I ruined everything?"

I freeze.

"Oh, sorry; here." From her backpack she pulls a flyer that does look like something I've put together. "You were going to teach me, and then Ms. Kiko told me that you needed space, but you seem better and maybe now you don't need so much space?"

I write everything I can into my notebook, but the thought of teaching sounds just like something I'd like to do, so I take a leap. "You know, yes, I think I'd really like to do this." I check my phone. "Can you do tomorrow, Tuesday? At five?"

Her eyes get big. "Tomorrow! Oh, hell yeah—oops. Sorry, I mean, heck yes!" She looks at me expectantly, her eyes going from me to the notebook, back and forth like a cartoon character. "Did you write it down? Can you do that now so you won't forget?"

I do, amused, feeling a tingle of excitement run through my arms. I'm going to teach.

~

Before I leave the gardens, I record the interaction with the girl, Maree, and when I get home, I'm pleased to discover a GUITAR LESSONS file folder in the wire slot holder on my desk. I nearly pat myself on the back for my organization. When I open it, I see that I already have one student, who started over the weekend. His name is Jarrod, and he works as boat watch during the winter, which means he keeps an eye on the boats in the harbor, sweeping off snow as necessary so they don't sink. But his true calling, he says, is to be the next Bob Dylan and also, my eyebrows rise, he writes poetry. I can't help but smile. The window presses inward from a gust of wind, creaking softly. I wrap a blanket around my shoulders and stare outside. The yellow glow of Whiskey Pete's is one of the few lights that penetrates the deep afternoon dark.

A soft knock at my door.

Mom, holding a plate of cookies. My eyes widen, but before I say anything, she hands me a card.

Happiness, not in another place but this place . . . not for another hour, but this hour. —*Walt Whitman*

I live in Whittier now and I'm sober. I love you and I'm not going anywhere. Love, Mom

She holds the cookies out. "These were your favorite when you were three." She smiles. "Until you turned four and decided you hated raisins."

I take the plate, balance the note on top, and I find my smile is easy and comfortable. "Thanks." I hold up the card. "Walt Whitman?"

"I recovered one day at a time, and it's become kind of my thing."

My forehead wrinkles. "Your thing?"

She smiles. "Yes, I bake and dispense sage advice about living in the moment, you know, like a recovered Martha Stewart Buddha."

She's making a joke about recovery. My mother the alcoholic—who stands here clear-eyed, hair dark and full around her heart-shaped face—is being funny. It starts in my toes, this lightness that dances up my legs, through my arms, and into my whole body, swimming around in delightful bubbles, and I'm laughing with her. For some reason I have an impulse to share something with her. "Do you remember how you taught us both how to play the guitar?"

There's something in her eyes, an expression—surprise? "I do. You were quite good."

I peek at my notes to get it right. "Well, I'm teaching someone named Jarrod, and tomorrow I'm going to start teaching a little girl named Maree."

Mom leans against the doorway. "I think that's great, Claire. Really great. Especially with Maree; she's got quite a bit of energy, but you'll do just fine with her." She sucks in her bottom lip, looks unsure of herself. "Speaking of, I still play—well, I picked it back up as part of my rehab, gave me something to focus on, and I'm playing at open-mic night at Pete's."

It's a part of my mother I know nothing about, and it stings just a bit. "When?"

"Next Wednesday, February 20, around seven or whenever Pete decides to start it. There's never more than me and maybe Hank if he's got his harmonica on him." I think she's blushing, embarrassed? "I'd love it if you could be there."

"At a bar, Mom? Is that a good idea?" I know it's a rude question, possibly hurtful, but I can't help but ask.

Instead of looking offended, she nods. "Fair question, Claire. I always go with friends, never alone. Ruth and Harriet will be there. Ruth said she could pick you up at 6:45."

I add it to my calendar. "I'll be there."

CHAPTER TWENTY

Tuesday, February 12

I open the door, and before I can say a word, the girl smiles, points to her glasses, and says, "It's me, Maree, like Mary with a *y* but with two *e*'s instead 'cause I love *Anne of Green Gables*, and she put an *e* at the end of her name, so I decided to also 'cept Dad said it had to be two *e*'s so people knew to make it sound like a *y*. I have no idea what that means." The girl pauses her monologue. "You knew I was coming, right?" She breathes through her mouth, little huffs between her words. I nod, hide a smile. She really wants to learn how to play the guitar.

I check my phone, show her the screen, and nod approvingly. "You're right on time. Very punctual."

She hops up and down on her toes, glances down the hallway, then toward the other end of the hallway, where Ruth lives. She sucks on her bottom lip so hard it makes her bucktoothed.

"Are you waiting for someone else?" I ask and can't help but look down the hallway too. It's empty. "I didn't have anyone else on the calendar."

The girl stops fidgeting, stares up at me. "No, it's just me. But I don't want Ruth to see me. She doesn't think I should be here." Her eyes go round, and she lowers her voice but not by much, because I think the girl has no understanding of volume control. "Ecausebay eshay oesnday wantay me to—" She blows air out her nose. "Pig Latin is too hard. Ruth is worried that I'm too much for you 'cause I'm a real handful." The girl looks at me through the empty lenses of her too-big glasses.

I smile. "Ruth thinks all kids are a real handful, but that's only because I was. Come in, Maree. Let's see how big a handful you really are."

The girl turns her body to show a small guitar slung beside her backpack.

"I like your guitar," I say.

"Thanks! The cookie lady gave it to me." The girl shrugs.

"The cookie lady?"

Maree narrows her eyes, tilts her head. "Yeah. Isn't she your mom?"

A tingling runs across my back, and my hand is already pulling out a note card from my pocket and it tells me . . . no—I dig my nails into my palm—*reminds* me about Dad and Mom and Tate. Hash marks cover the note card; I've read it dozens and dozens of times. "My mom does love to bake."

"Oh boy, does she. On Saturdays, she bakes cookies with any kids in the building who want to eat cookies." Her eyes roll to the ceiling. "Who doesn't want to eat free cookies? Can we start now?"

I move out of the way, and when she skips past me, I smell flowers tinged with something sweet, like licorice. A perfect kid kind of smell. I take a moment before following her, lean back against the door, breathe deep, and with my eyes closed visualize my notebook and the file folder with Maree's name written across the tab, because I'm sure I've prepared that. I'm going to start by teaching her the way I learned with Mom.

On our first lesson together, I'd scooted so close to my mother that my toe could wiggle across her shin. She was relaxed, beautiful, and untroubled, but even then it felt temporary, like trying to hold water in my palms. Sometimes she'd be sad, and nothing seemed to make her smile. On this day, though, we were a team, learning together, and she was happy. I could tell by the easy smile on her face. In a rush of emotion that made my throat too tight to speak, I'd dropped my guitar and flung my arms around her. Her hair smelled like cinnamon candy. I'd felt her breathe in, her arms squeezing me in a hug. *Thank you, Claire bear.* And then she released me, wiping a hand across her eyes before turning back to the music booklet. *Let's see here; first, we have to make sure our guitars are tuned.* Her eyes opened wide. *How the hell do we do that?* There was a pause, a moment when I was sure she'd close the book and say it was a bad idea. I'd gripped my guitar tightly. Instead, she'd started laughing, hunched over her cheap guitar, her shoulders shaking, and the sound was so infectious that I started laughing, too. *I have no idea how to tune a damn guitar, Claire bear!*

The moment fades and I am left standing in the doorway to my apartment, arms wrapped across my body, heart pushing painfully against my ribs.

"Hey, Ms. Claire." There's a little girl seated at my table, backpack splayed on the floor at her feet, looking for all the world like she belongs there. She blows air from her cheeks, making them big and round. It's comical. "Did you lose your memory again?" She places a hand on her chest. "*I* am Maree and *you* are Ms. Claire, and today you are teaching me guitar lessons."

"Yes, thank you, Maree." I move directly to my desk, and there is a file folder with the girl's name spelled out on the tab and my notebook. Satisfied, I turn to the girl, who has a notebook of her own opened in front of her beside a camera, the instant kind that shoots pictures out of a thin slot.

"What's the camera for?" I ask.

"I thought I could take pictures of me and the guitar and stuff, and then"—she pulls a ringed album out of her backpack, grunting with the effort—"Ms. Kiko had an extra one of these and said I could use it to make a scrapbook thing or something, and that's how you can really remember me for next time, you know, like how I look and stuff." She stops abruptly, looking pleased with herself, then picks up the camera and snaps a picture of me. The flash stains my vision with black spots.

"Whoa, okay, little warning next time. Not a bad idea, though. I like it!" I clap my hands. "Ready to get started?"

The girl waves the picture back and forth in the air, checks it, seems satisfied, and tapes it onto a fresh sheet of paper on the first page of her scrapbook. With a pink colored pencil, she scribbles under the picture, *Guitar Leson #1 with Maree.*

Then she opens her own notebook and hovers the sharpened tip above the page, looks up at me expectantly.

"What are you doing?" I ask.

She wrinkles her nose, and her glasses slide away from her face. With one finger, she pushes them back into place. "I'm ready to learn."

I motion with one hand toward the living room. "Great; follow me."

She gets up from the table so fast she knocks her chair backward, the notebook gripped in one hand, colored pencil in the other.

"It's not the SAT, kiddo." I settle onto the floor and point to the space beside me.

She sits down, eyes blinking behind her glasses, which are far too big for her small face. "SAT?"

I laugh. She's too young to know anything about that. "I mean, relax. You're not going to take notes, and I'm not going to test you. You're going to learn as you play. But first we need to tune it." After our first lesson together, Mom found an old tuner and taught herself and me how to use it. I pick up the girl's guitar, run my fingers along the wood underneath, and get to work.

It doesn't take too long, but when I look up from the guitar, the girl is staring at me. "My name is Maree," she says, loudly and with emphasis on each syllable, like I'm hard of hearing. "Like Mary with a *y*, but with *e*'s instead. Ms. Kiko said to remind you, but not too much. Is this too much?"

Her utter lack of guile brings an easy smile to my lips. "No, not too much. Thank you for reminding me, Maree."

"I'm getting pretty good at it, I think." She tilts her head. "Do you remember how come you started playing guitar in the first place?"

"My mother taught me."

Maree's eyes widen. "She did?"

I nod and my ears fill with the harmonic sounds of Mom plucking away at the old guitar she'd traded with somebody in exchange for a month's supply of her chocolate chip cookies. "She taught herself and taught me at the same time," I say.

The girl hunches over, pulling at a loose thread of carpet. "My mom left me."

The sad tone in her voice scratches at my heart, revealing my own feelings of abandonment. I can relate more than this girl could know.

I reach out and touch her shoulder, knowing instinctively that she needs someone to listen. I did at her age.

The girl plucks at the strings of the guitar while she talks. "Dad says she was too sick to be my mom, so she had to leave. But you said once that your mom was sick and had to leave, and she came back as the cookie lady, right? So maybe my mom will come back too."

Something Ruth used to say to me when I was a young girl crying in the middle of the night pops into my head. "Your mother must have loved you with her whole heart."

The girl raises her head to pin me with a stare. "That's what my dad says."

I nod. "And he would know that best, wouldn't he?"

She shrugs. "Yeah, I guess. He says that she didn't have a choice."

I want to reassure her, say anything that can erase the sad look in her eyes, but I can't because the truth is probably closer to my own, and I know more than most that not all mothers are meant for the job.

My phone buzzes. **Guitar lesson with Maree. Lesson #1 G to Em.** The directive is a bowling ball, scattering my thoughts like pins. She stares at me, slumped over a guitar balanced in her lap. The buzz again, and while I've lost the fine threads of our conversation, I turn my thoughts to the task at hand. "Ready to get started?" I say.

Maree and I spend forty minutes together, which I know because I set a timer on my phone. I fill a page of my notebook with notes on what Maree did well and where she struggled, and I even include a line at the end that I think is very important information, so I draw a small star beside it: *Maree loves her cat-eye glasses and Audrey Hepburn.* It occurs to me when I'm writing that it feels close to the preparations I might have taken as a schoolteacher, and the idea that I'm teaching again in whatever capacity feels good.

"What are you doing?" Maree asks. We're sitting in the kitchen now, and she leans over the table, elbows spread out like a newborn calf trying to stand. "That's a lot of writing. What's it about?"

"You," I say with a smile. "If I keep good notes, then I'll be more prepared for next time; plus there's a few things you told me that I want to remember. Like the fact that you really love everything Audrey Hepburn."

"Oh, wow! That's great!" She pushes over a three-ringed scrapbook. "I'll put that stuff in here, too, with my pictures." She leans over the book to write, and her glasses slide off her face and hit the table with a plastic clunk. In one quick movement, she swoops them up and slides them back on her face. "How about we write some other things about me?"

I raise my eyebrows. "Like what?"

She shrugs, sticks out her bottom lip, and holds up her pointer finger. "One, I was born on February 23"—lifts the middle finger beside the first—"Two, I'm a pescatarian"—up goes her ring finger—"And three, my mom used a slingshot to take down a giant. But that's not really about me, 'cept it is, kinda."

The last one makes me pause, and my pen hovers above the page, my mouth opening to say something. She looks at me—blinking once, twice, behind the broken lenses of her too-big glasses—and I'm not at all sure how to respond. It's a lot of information at once, so I dutifully write each one down before it slips from my head. I hear Maree pull in a sip of air like she's going to say more.

"Only three?"

Her chin juts out when she leans over to read what I've written. She chews off a nail while she thinks, shrugs. "I guess," she says.

I point to number two. "Pescatarian?"

"Yup, it means vegetarian 'cept I eat fish. My dad fishes all the time." She rolls her eyes when she says *all*. "And I also think that killing animals is wrong, 'cept fish 'cause they're so yum, you know? And there's a lot of them, too, but killing animals isn't okay. Especially baby animals."

It's a lot of information, but I jot a few notes under pescatarian because I think her social stand is sweet, if slightly misguided, and obviously important to her. My eyes slide over number three: *my mom used a slingshot to take down a giant*. It's loaded with nuance, and I don't have enough information to know exactly what to ask, but I take a stab at it anyway. "So what's this about your mom and the giant?"

A smile spreads across her face, and she rushes to her feet. "Oh yeah, that's the best one. I'm writing a book about it at school. I can read it to you when you come in to volunteer tomorrow." She pushes a scrapbook across the table. "I'll leave this here so you can stare at my face some more, and maybe it'll burn into your brain like the camera does, okay?"

My fingers itch to turn back the pages of my notebook, to read everything we've done, to make my notes on this girl, to *remember* as much as I possibly can about her. Instead, I fold my arms over the notebook and take her scrapbook into my hands. "Thanks, Maree, I look forward to staring at your face."

She giggles. "You're funny."

CHAPTER TWENTY-ONE

Wednesday, February 13

I have a date. Well, no, not a date, I remind myself—an early dinner with Tate Dunn, who is the new harbormaster and lives here now. My palms turn sweaty at the thought of seeing him again, after all this . . . no—I pull out the note card in my pocket, its edges worn and thin— he's lived here for a few months, and I'm sure I've seen him multiple times given the number of hash marks that fill the note card.

When I open the door to the restaurant, my face is warmed by the heated air that floats out. I'm early, so I choose a table by the window that overlooks the boats in the harbor. Wet snow pockmarks the water, and a light mist crawls down the mountainside, dances across the undulating surface of the bay.

My phone buzzes. **Dinner with Tate Dunn at Pete's, 5 p.m.** He left a message on my phone asking if I'd like to meet him, and I'm looking forward to seeing him, wondering how different he looks from how I remember him. I touch the butterfly clip in my hair, straighten out my blouse that's come untucked from my jeans, and try not to allow the stubborn tentacles of hope to root into my heart. The best outcome I can imagine is that we can be friends again. I've missed his friendship.

I start to pull out my notebook, stop, and instead reach for the device with a sticky note attached that says it's a gift from Tate. A graphic of notebook paper with colored tabs across the side appears on the screen. One says Movie Date with Tate. My arm muscles tingle when I click it, but it's empty, save for one line. Pick one: Go to Anchorage to see a movie or stay in and watch at your place. I'll make dinner.

A smile spreads across my face. I type, My place, you cook. I have no idea if Tate's a good cook or not, but I'm not one to say no to a free dinner. Then I add, it's not a date, we're just friends. It dampens the excitement I feel, but it's the truth, and I'm a fool to think otherwise.

My hand hovers above the screen. There's another tab: Things Tate wants to know about you. I click on it, curious. It's a list of questions—some short, others longer.

What is your favorite memory and why? What's a perfect day for you? If you could change one thing about yourself, what would it be? (You can't say memory!)

That one stops me, makes me laugh, because of course that's the first thing I was going to say. But a perfect day. What would that look like? I wiggle my fingers at the idea of getting to choose anything I want to do, and suddenly my mind expands to include the things I loved doing *before*. Snow machining, I type, or skiing or anything outside, fresh air, glacier kayaking, seal watching, hiking . . . the list keeps going because I can't seem to stop once I've allowed myself to think beyond systems and calendars and memory. I'm still typing when a woman's voice interrupts me.

"Can I get you water or iced tea while you wait?"

I freeze. Mom. I look up and she stands at the table, wearing the server's uniform of black shirt and black pants, short white apron around her waist. Her hair is pulled into a bun at the nape of her neck, and the light makeup she wears accentuates her dark-blue eyes, which are as beautiful as I remember.

"Mom," I say, reaching into my pocket as she slides a note card onto the place mat in front of me.

The meeting of two eternities, the past and the future . . . is precisely the present moment. —Henry David Thoreau

Dear Claire, I'm sober and I live in Whittier now. You are strong, kind, resilient, and everything I wished I could have been. You amaze me and I'm so proud of the woman you are, right at this moment. I love you and I'm here for you. Love, Mom

I read it again and again until it hurts to breathe, and when I start to give it back to her, she covers my hand with hers. "No, you keep it. I have a whole stack of them." She smiles and suddenly I am in footed jammies, and she is humming while she tucks the covers around the outline of my small body, kisses me on my forehead. *Snug as a bug, Claire bear.*

"Don't worry; this is just one of many." Then she winks, and I can't speak because in that moment she is exactly as I remember her.

Another figure appears, takes the chair opposite me, and fills it far more substantially than I ever remembered. He wears a thick blue sweater that hugs his broad shoulders. Tate as a man. He resembles the younger version I knew intimately even if his squared jaw and straight nose seem somehow more manly, older, but in all the right ways. I uncross and recross my legs, try not to mess with my hair.

"I'll bring you both some iced tea," Mom says.

Tate sets a note card on top of the one Mom gave to me.

I live in Whittier now and I'm the new harbormaster and I'm not married anymore. I know all about the baby and I'm not upset or angry with you. I understand. We were different then, just kids with screwed-up childhoods. But you were my best friend then and we are friends now. You're amazing, Claire. Love, Tate

Wordless, I move to return his note card.

"Keep it. It was Alice's idea to keep g . . . g-iving them to you. Since we're new to your schedule, she thinks we should g . . . hand you one every time we see you. So you have a record of when you see us and maybe with . . . time"—he shrugs—"it sticks somehow." He leans forward. "But it doesn't have to. I w . . . w-ant to know you just as you are."

My lips quirk up and I sit back, relaxed. "Did you just kind of quote *Bridget Jones* to me?"

"Well, yes, and it w . . . w-orked." Tate smiles. "Just like Sefina said."

"Worked?"

"It made you smile."

My cheeks warm and I read his note card again. "You're not married anymore."

"Correct." He looks down at his hands, nods. "At your graduation, I'm not . . . proud of it, Claire. I should have t . . . t-old you. But . . ." He looks up to meet my gaze, green eyes bright against his black hair. "And in some . . . ways this makes me a terrible person, but I've never regretted being with you that n . . . n-ight. Ever. I just wish I'd been honest about Maria."

Hearing her name makes it real, and I shift back in my chair, wanting distance from him. I pull out my notebook, write this bit down because I want to remember that all we can ever be is friends. "How did you meet her?"

He sighs. "You know, I thought . . . when I left here that things would get magically better. Like the distance from my dad would be all I n . . . n-needed." He gives a bitter laugh. "But I was just a stupid kid with no p . . . p-lan and no idea how truly hard things could be. I couldn't get a job at first . . ." He stops, swallows, continues, "I couldn't g . . . g-et through a single interview without stuttering so hard I nearly choked. My money ran out fast and things were . . . hard, and then I met Maria." He waits while I write. "We . . . were both running from something. We were both alone. I was all she had."

"Did you love her?" I whisper.

He looks out the window, seems to search for his answer in the snow and the waves. "I did. But n . . . n-ever in the way I loved you."

My breath catches, and I return to my notes. Something in there that Ruth told me makes me pause. "My dad helped you?"

His smile touches his eyes. "Yeah, he called out of the blue. I have no idea how he g . . . g-ot my number. I had a job at a lumber mill by then, was sharing a crappy apartment with Maria. Vance sent me money after that—not much, but enough to keep me g . . . g-oing. Kept encouraging me to . . . go to a community college, helped me figure out student loans, vouched for me."

As I write I feel a warmth envelop me. None of it surprises me, but all of it touches me deeply.

"Here's your iced teas." I look up, startled to see my mother dressed all in black, like a waiter. She sets an iced tea in front of me—along with a note card—smiles, and walks away. I read the note card, notice there's a number written in the upper right-hand corner.

"The . . . numbers are so you can easily keep track of how often you've run into Alice or me." He points to another note card on my place mat, this one from him, with the number one written in the corner. "Technically, we've seen each other multiple t . . . t-imes before this, but since this is my first note card, I'm starting with one."

I take several sips of tea, check my notes. "What happened with Maria?"

"We grew apart, w . . . w-anted different things." There's an intensity to his gaze that I don't understand. "She had her own demons, and things with her became . . . too familiar, and I wasn't about to put anyone through that. I tried to help, but she—once everything hap-pened, she left, I think because she understood."

"Understood what?"

"That I still love you."

I'm grateful for the distraction of my notebook right then because the speed of my pulse is affecting my breathing and makes my face warm and cold at the same time.

Tate continues, "And now I'm here. Eighteen years . . . too late, of course."

I look up. His smile sends goose bumps down my arms.

"I'm sorry it took me so long, Claire. The time just never seemed right, not w . . . w-ith my father still living here or Maria . . ." He shakes his head, touches my hand. "Until now."

I want to twine my fingers through his, pull him to me, feel his lips on mine, because being with him again, sitting so close our knees keep brushing under the table, I understand that I've never stopped loving him. Not even a little. And he's sitting here telling me he loves me, tell-ing me he's back and looking at me like we can pick up exactly where we left off. A space inside my chest fills with hope. Could Tate still love me in the way he used to? I squeeze the plastic pen in my hand, touch the smoothness of the notebook paper. Like this?

His fingers touch my face, run along my jaw, bring my face up so I'm staring into his cold-water green eyes. "Let's start over, get to know each other again. Will you go on a date with me, Claire?"

A thought tempers the longing that unwinds inside me. "But how will I remember you?"

He smiles. "Over and over again."

CHAPTER TWENTY-TWO

Thursday, February 14

Journal, shower, dressed, coffee, schedule. Check, check, check, and I still have a few hours to go before I volunteer in Kiko's classroom.

There is a knock at my door, and I open it to find a plate of cheese Danish on my doormat with a note.

What day is it? asked Pooh.

It's today, squeaked Piglet.

My favorite day, said Pooh. (A. A. Milne)

Dear Claire, I live in Whittier and I've been sober for ten years. You are strong and amazing and you redefine courage. I'm here for you and I'm not going anywhere. And I hope, like Pooh, that today is your favorite day too. Love, Mom.

Her words are touching and take me back to a time when I was very little and would sit on a kitchen stool eating cereal while she sipped coffee beside me and *Winnie the Pooh* played on a small TV on the counter. I take the Danish inside, holding the card to my chest, warmed through and wondering what Mom looks like now.

Outside, a winter storm rocks our small town, surrounding BTI in a wall of black cotton. With the wind pushing against the building, I brew a pot of coffee and slide a cheese Danish onto a plate, happy to be inside, and sink my teeth into the treat. The pastry is creamy and crispy and doughy in the right places, and the tang of the cream cheese blends smoothly with the bitterness of the coffee. It's a perfect pairing, and when I close my eyes to savor it, I am five years old, sitting on my knees in a kitchen chair, making trails with my finger in a bowl through paths of icing until I have a big enough glob to eat. A hand touches my cheek, followed by the cool wetness of a washcloth. *Silly girl, you've got more sugar on your cheeks than in your mouth.* I giggle and my mother laughs—a warm untroubled sound.

The window is a kaleidoscope of white and black, and I sit back and watch the wet snow slide down the glass. I used to wonder what would have happened if Dad had been able to get the building manager job sooner. If he'd been home, I wonder whether Mom would have leaned on him instead of alcohol. I vividly recall the look on his face when he told her that he was going to apply for the manager job as soon as it opened up. I was twelve, long legged and clumsy and wanting nothing more than for my dad to live at home all the time. I was convinced that if he was around more, she'd be sober, happier. He'd stood in front of her, hands touching her shoulders and his smile so wide it nearly cleaved his beard in two.

If I get it, I'll be around more, Alice. His eyes were bright with hope. *I can help you get better, honey, so we can be a real family again.* He'd pulled her toward him until she had to crane her neck to look up at him. He was much taller than her, and for a second I saw what they'd been like once, before me, before Mom got sad and drunk. And then it was gone, and they were just two people with nothing in common anymore.

It's too late, Vance, she'd said and listed to the side out of his embrace, drunk already. Dad had winced, letting his hands fall away from her and hang long by his sides.

His voice had lowered then. I was supposed to be asleep; instead, I was spying on them through a crack in my bedroom door. *You're not your father, Alice.* There was a note of desperation in his voice, something I'd never heard before in him, like it was something he didn't believe himself anymore. *This is your choice, your future, your daughter, our marriage.* I'd heard liquid pouring into a glass, could only assume it was my mother and her vodka. A hardness had entered Dad's words. *There's an AA meeting in Girdwood. I want you to go as much as you need. Every day, if that's what it takes. Ruth said she'll take you. When I get back, Alice.* Here his voice had stretched so thin it made my eyes wet. *I love you, honey, but it's hurting Claire, and I can't let anything happen to her.*

In the silence that followed, I imagined my mother throwing the bottle out the window, flinging herself into his arms, and begging for his forgiveness. I dug my fingers into my thighs, imagining the wrinkle between my father's eyes—the one that had become a permanent worry line—easing back into his skin with his relief. Instead, she walked into their bedroom, bottle in hand, tumbler in the other, closing and locking the door behind her. I climbed into bed, pulled the covers over my head, and lay awake for the entire night.

The memory dissolves when my phone buzzes with a reminder. **Volunteer in Kiko's classroom.** My jaw unclenches and I sit up, wondering how bad things must have been for Mom by then; how sad, how hopeless, how alone she was to have made the choices she did. I feel a twinge and wish—maybe for the first time—that I could have been old enough to help her through it.

~

The beanbag chair feels lumpy, so I adjust my frame until I can get just the right amount of lean without feeling like I'm going to tip backward. I wonder whether I've spoken to Kiko about getting a different kind of chair for me. I might be a tad too tall for a beanbag chair, even if it is giant size. When I'm more comfortable I quickly review my notes, see that I've worked with two kids this morning—one a sweet boy with a terrible cold, who kept trying to sneeze into his elbow but missed every single time. And now the last kid of the day is walking my way: cat-eye glasses, hair in a beautiful updo, surprisingly elegant for elementary school, and a name tag that spells out *Maree*. Immediately, I am smiling, and when she settles herself on the smaller beanbag, I say, "So do you like *Anne of Green Gables*? I could read that to you today, if you'd like."

Her mouth hangs open slightly and she stares at me, one hand touching her name tag. "Um, wow, that's just—wow, Ms. Claire. Is that you remembering me? 'Cause—um, wow—that's just the best ever, 'cept I have more of my story that I wrote, and I really, really want to read it to you today. Can I?"

I'm thrown by what she says, except I do know this kid, see it recorded in my preparation notes for today. *Might see Maree at school volunteering today. You teach her guitar lessons and also see her at the school gardens and around town quite often.* Huh. Nothing about *Anne of Green Gables*, though. "Yes, I'd like that very much."

She opens up a little paper booklet with pink and green staples. Flips forward a few pages to one with Chapter Two written in uneven letters across the top.

"Once upon a time, a big ugly, smelly giant found his way inside Uki's village." She pauses to show me the picture of a thick-legged, one-eyed giant who appears to be wearing a diaper. "And the giant had a heart that was a big black piece of coal, and he stomped around the entire town like a giant baby." She smiles. "I like that part."

She turns the page. "So everybody in the village was hiding from him, 'cept for one little boy who didn't know any better. The giant saw the boy, and he grabbed for him 'cause giants eat kids 'cause we're delicious and taste like candy."

I hide my smile and notice how her writing is uneven and messy, the sentences curving down the page.

The next page has an illustration of a pink stick-figure girl with long hair and what I think is a pink cape. "So Uki picked up the biggest rock she could find and put it into her slingshot. 'Let go of that boy,' she yelled. But the giant didn't listen, so she pulled her slingshot way, way back and let the rock fly. And it hit him in the forehead and knocked him out."

I can see that she ran out of space, turning her writing into tiny, minuscule print to keep it on the page. "When the giant fell the whole village shook like there was an earthquake."

She turns the page to a big heart and one large-printed sentence. "And the boy loved her from that day on."

"You're a great storyteller," I say.

"Thanks!" She touches her head. "Do you like my hair?"

"I do; it's very beautiful. Did you do it yourself?"

She shakes her head. "Nope."

"Time to move on, class. Everyone say thank you to Ms. Claire, please."

The little girl hops up and hugs me. I smell hairspray and vanilla, and I am touched by her sudden affection. "Thank you," she whispers against my shoulder. I touch her hair—it is stiff and full of bobby pins—before she pulls away and skips back to her seat.

∼

I'm in the school tunnel heading in the direction of BTI. Glimpses of my purple socks remind me that it's a Thursday. My phone tells me the time and buzzes with a reminder of what I'm doing. Home for lunch and shower. A woman walks toward me from the other end of the tunnel.

I squint—it's my mother, and I immediately pull out a note card from my pocket, glance over the three lines to me, feel a pang even if I already know that she's here and Dad is dead. When we meet in the middle, she smiles and hands me a note card. *I live in Whittier and I'm sober. I watch you manage your days with skill and grace and confidence. You amaze me. Love, Mom.*

The note card has the number twelve in the corner, and the message sprinkles a warm feeling over my skin. "Hi, Mom," I say and it feels natural. I like it. "Where are you going?"

She's holding a pan that's covered with a plastic lid. "There's a boy in Kiko's class, and the poor kid is allergic to peanuts, dairy, and gluten, and it's his birthday today. She asked if I could make something for him that he could share with the class." She lifts the tray, smiling. "Nut-free, dairy-free, and gluten-free, and they are so good, too, if I do say so myself."

"That's great." The interaction is normal and yet surreal, and I can't help but feel the loss of the years that her alcoholism laid to waste. It makes a lump grow in my throat.

She touches my shoulder when she moves past me. "You've got guitar lessons with Maree later, is that right? She loves her lessons with you."

"Oh," I say, and feel my shoulders lift. "That's nice." A buzz from my phone. "I'd better go. Bye, Mom."

I walk on, but when I reach the doors to BTI, I look back and see her standing in the middle of the tunnel, staring after me.

CHAPTER
TWENTY-THREE

Saturday, February 16

I'm walking next to Sefina out the doors of BTI and into a bitterly cold but clear day, the winter sun a chronic underachiever. I'm wearing snow pants, a winter coat, and waterproof mittens. Even with all the warm gear, my nose drips and the skin on my cheeks tingles. Snow piles high up the concrete stairs, giving the abandoned boats that litter the property across from our building a winter-wonderland effect. It's beautiful and I'm enjoying the walk. But where Sefina and I are going is the question I can't currently answer.

"Are we going to lunch?" I say.

"We're going snow machining with Tate Dunn," she says, her voice muffled by a fleece gaiter she wears around her neck and the lower half of her face. "And then he wanted to take us out to eat." She looks up at me, her movements stiff from the layers around her head and neck. "He lives here now, and he's the harbormaster."

"Oh." My stomach flip-flops as I try to picture Tate as being old enough or responsible enough for that kind of a job. But the first image that comes to mind is him at seventeen: tall and lanky, his eye black and swollen, saying goodbye to me in the early hours before school.

"Snow machining?" I say.

"Up Shotgun Cove Road," she says from behind her gaiter. "He thinks you need to get out of BTI more. He says that the fresh air and experiences are good for you, even if you can't remember having them."

I feel a pang and have to stop walking, rub my arms. "It sounds fun, but I can't take notes while I'm on a snow machine." I shift my weight; the idea puts me into free fall. Remembering my time with Tate is something I want to keep with me.

Beside me, Sefina inhales, touches my arm. "Claire," she says evenly. "This is about giving you experiences—and you deserve to have experiences—to enjoy it in the moment, as Alice is so fond of saying."

That diverts my attention. "Alice?" My hand slides to my pocket, but in my mittens and snowsuit, I can't find it.

"Alice lives here now; she's sober and kind, and she loves you. I didn't know the woman who drank for years, but I can promise you that the woman she is today is exactly the kind of mother I imagined would have raised someone like you."

The news of Mom living here doesn't hit me as hard as I'd expect. "Someone like me?"

She elbows me. "Yeah, kick-ass and strong, but she's a much better baker." I can hear her smile in her voice. "No offense. But, hey, look at you! You just trusted me to tell you about Alice without having to look at your note card or notebook." She squeezes my arm. "Progress."

We keep walking, my mind repeating the activity. We're going snow machining with Tate. Snow machining with Tate. "Whose idea was this?" I wonder out loud.

"Yours, actually. Tate asked what kinds of things you'd like to do on a date, and this was one of them. He said that Vance used to take the two of you sledding behind the snow machine. Said it was some of his best memories from his childhood. He's a great guy, Claire. And he's got all kinds of adventures planned for you."

My face burns now despite the cold, and a sinking feeling pulls at my legs. It's not hard to put it all together. Tate and Sefina. Of course. She's beautiful and kind and lovely and normal. My head falls toward my chest. My two best friends, and now they watch out for me, make sure their brain-damaged, pathetic friend goes for a walk. I should be happy for them, not feeling sorry for myself. I breathe in and smile behind my gaiter. "That's great, Sefina; I'm really happy for you."

"Happy for me? What?"

"You and Tate. It's great, really." I start to walk again, but Sefina pulls at my arm to stop me.

"Wait, hold up. You've got it all wrong, Claire."

I shake my head, look at my feet instead of her. "No, it's okay. You two are both amazing people. I mean, I don't know him anymore, but I know you, and I always knew that he would grow up to become a good man."

Sefina groans. "Oh, for Pete's sake, Claire. Stop using your memory as an excuse for why nobody is allowed to care about you."

For a moment I can't speak because she's more right than she knows. After Tate left, I held everyone—maybe even Dad at times—far away from my tender spots, afraid that what was left of my heart would wreck completely if someone else I loved left me. Do I do that even now?

"That man has been in love with you his whole life. But you refuse to believe that you deserve his love, so you tell yourself you're not good enough. Self-sabotaging at its absolute finest." She punches me lightly in the arm. "When are you going to stop lying to yourself and just accept the fact that Tate loves you just as you are?"

I raise my eyebrows, the heaviness from before lightened by her words. "Did you just quote *Bridget Jones* to me?"

She laughs. "You bet your ass I did. If Mark Darcy can't get through to you, who can?"

I listen to the snow crunch under our feet, the cold sting of flakes bouncing off my nose, feel the warmth of my friend walking beside me, and enjoy the moment for as long as I can.

~

I sit behind Tate, arms around his waist, feeling the snow machine glide over the frozen landscape. My fingers tingle to write about the trees flying past us, branches laden with clumps of snow. The depthless blue green of the water in Passage Canal. Or the way Billings Glacier juts off the mountain in the distance, the tip of it floating in the air like the prow of a ship.

But I can't write it down, not with the jerking of the snow machine, so I hold tight to Tate and let myself experience every second, hoping that on some level it sticks.

After lunch, Tate walks me to the entrance of BTI. The wind has kicked up, brushing over the water in broad strokes that carry droplets in the air, stings our faces. I observe Tate from behind my face mask. He's older, comfortable in his own skin, and handsome in that weathered way that Alaskan men get as they age. And while I can't remember the details of the time we spent together, the air between us is laden with something warm and sweet, familiar in the relaxed slouch of his shoulders, the smoothness of his words. He's comfortable with me.

"I'd like to come over sometime, if . . . that's okay?" His question makes me fidget, blush like a teenage girl, so that I'm grateful for the mask. "Hang out, watch a movie? Maybe g . . . g-o to Alyeska and ski?"

I nod, try to ignore the jittery tap of my toes on the concrete. "I don't think I smoke weed anymore, though, Tate."

He laughs. "Me either." And then his lips brush my cheek through my face mask, his arms circle me in a hug, and it's normal and natural even if it feels like the first time. "And I've sent you some pictures on the tablet I gave to you. It's on your kitchen counter with a sticky note on the screen. You can't miss it."

"What pictures?"

"It's from snow machining today p . . . p-lus a video from my phone. I did it during lunch, so it's . . . nothing professional, but I think it's a start."

I touch my legs, feel the plush waterproof material of snow pants, the tight band of goggles strapped to my head. It's what I would wear for snow machining. "That must have been fun," I say, and hope that he can't hear the sadness I feel at not being able to remember.

"It was. You laughed nearly the entire time. It's a start."

My eyebrows meet. "A start?"

He pulls me closer, and it's not the cold that sends shivers across my back. "To get to know each other. I want to know you again, Claire."

I'm thankful for the gaiter that hides my frown. "But how can I get to know you, Tate, if I can't remember?"

Cracks run out from his eyes when he smiles. "If you can trust me, I'm hoping the p . . . p-ictures and videos will take some of the burden of remembering off you. Plus, I'm . . . pretty hard to forget."

This fits with the Tate I remember—sweet, thoughtful, funny, and maybe just a tad cocky, but in the cute kind of way—and I can't help but smile.

CHAPTER TWENTY-FOUR

Monday, February 18

I've been waiting for Maree to knock on my door, and when she does, I'm struck by how badly I want to see her and know her—and I do, but only from my notes and the pictures I've been staring at for the past half hour. Without those, I'd walk right past her in the hallway, not a beat of recognition other than from the photos I hold in my hand.

But the girl outside my door doesn't resemble the one from the photos, who makes goofy faces and smiles like she's trying to split her face in two. It's like someone blew out a light inside her.

"Hi, Maree," I say.

"Hi," she says and walks past me, shoulders slumped, not a smile or spark of enthusiasm about her.

"Is everything okay?"

When she looks up, her eyes are extra bright behind her glasses, the lids swollen and red. She presses her lips together and shakes her head.

I bend down until I'm nearly eye level with her. "You look like you need a hug. Can I give you one of those?"

She looks at the floor, nods.

I put my arms around her and pull her toward me until her cheek rests against my shoulder and her brown locks tickle my chin. I inhale Froot Loops and soap and feel the light weight of her body press into mine; her arms circle around me as far as they will go. We stay like that for a few breaths, and I have to swallow hard because I am overcome with a tenderness that feels so natural it makes my chest ache.

I pat her back. "Feel any better?"

She pulls away, gives me a one-eyed look that darts to the kitchen counter behind me. "Can I have a cookie? That would probably make me feel a lot better."

"Sure."

She sits at the table, and I bring her the plate of cookies along with a cold glass of milk. A cookie is in her hand in seconds, dipping in and out of the milk before getting popped into her mouth.

"Mmmm, yummy." She drinks the rest of the milk in a loud gulp, leaving a white mustache across her upper lip. "Do you want one?" she says, and wipes the milk away with the back of her sleeve.

I suppress a smile. "Maybe later. Are you okay?" I say. It's a risk to ask this. I'm not really the best person to confide in. I reconsider. Or maybe I am if a person just needs someone to listen, because that I can do very well.

She frowns. "Oh yeah, I was really sad. But you made me feel better with the cookies, and besides, she just doesn't understand."

"Who?"

"My best friend, Leonora."

Conversations are waves that move up and down, and if I don't stay on top of them, the details wash over my head. This feels like a detail I've missed, but it's not hard to guess that Leonora is another little girl who must have said something to upset Maree. Tate used to get made fun of by a boy in our class, mostly for his stuttering but also because his pants were always to his ankles and he was so skinny his bones poked out. We were in the seventh grade when Tate's stuttering became so bad he refused to speak to anybody but me, and all that combined to make him an easy target. I can't recall the boy's name anymore or the color of his hair, but I do remember the size of his bottom because I'd wanted to make sure I had enough glue. I felt so justified. Nobody picked on Tate.

That day, I sat beside the boy, and when he went to the bathroom, I emptied almost a whole bottle of superglue onto his seat. It was the kind of desk that was attached to the chair, so when he stood up later, the entire desk came with him. He never bothered Tate again, and I never felt bad about the incident like I do now when I think about it. I shift in my seat, sigh; kids can be mean, even when they don't intend to be or, like me, when they think they have a reason to be. Which is another reason I would have made a good teacher: my empathy for kids in general. I look at the little girl, chomping a second cookie that she thinks I didn't see her take, and I puff up. Maybe I can still be a good teacher, even now. "Do you want to talk about it?"

She shrugs. "I don't know, I guess. Leonora said my stories are all fake 'cause my mom's a drug addict."

I tilt my head, concerned because it's a little more serious than I could have imagined, and I can't ignore a side of me that would like to take Leonora by the ear and give her a piece of my mind. Not very teacherly of me. "Did Leonora know your mom?"

"No."

"Then it sounds like Leonora is making up stories of her own."

Maree presses her finger into a cookie crumb on the table until pieces of it stick to her skin. "Yeah, maybe." She uses the very tip of her front teeth to bite a minuscule crumb off her finger, then another.

I hand her a cookie, smile. "Why don't you eat the crumbs all at once?"

She giggles when she takes the cookie. "Thanks." She finishes it and wipes her mouth. "Do you think we could go see the reindeer?"

The reindeer belong to a longtime resident of Whittier. Tourists love to take pictures with the animals, and when they get paraded around town, it's quite the photo op. By winter, they spend much of their time in their pen, which sits across from BTI. I'm not sure how to respond to Maree's request because my likely answer is no, given my limitations, except I don't want to tell her no. I look outside. Dusk bruises the sky into deep purples and grays. Winter nights in Alaska are a solid presence—inky, dark, and unyielding. "Now?"

"Sure, yeah, that would be awesome. My dad said I can't go alone or with other kids 'cause of that bear who won't go to sleep, but it's okay if I go with a teacher; plus, you're so tall that no bear would mess with you anyways." She springs to her feet. "Let's go!"

She's already at the door, Polaroid camera slung around her neck, and my pulse speeds up. It's too sudden, too quick a change in direction, and I feel myself lose the grip on my thoughts. I'm turning to my notebook when I feel a hand on my arm, and I look down to see the girl, her face calm, staring at me behind cat-eye glasses that are taped in the middle.

"I can take pictures with my camera so you won't forget, okay? If you have to write everything down, it will be too late. I talk a lot—that's what Ms. Kiko says—so I can keep you remembering all the way there. Okay, Ms. Claire?"

Her sweetness eases the tension in my forehead.

"We're going to see the reindeer," she says with such earnestness I want to touch the dimple on her chin.

Reindeer, reindeer, reindeer. A mantra I repeat. So we're going outside. I frown when I look at her thin long-sleeved shirt. "Do you have a coat?" From a hook by the door, I grab a sweatshirt. "You can wear this; it looks cold out."

Reindeer, reindeer, reindeer. I start to walk down the hallway, hesitate. Tate and I always took carrots to them. I hurry to the fridge, pleased to find that I have a couple in the crisper, and hurry back to join the girl in the hallway, who's wearing one of my sweatshirts, and it's so big on her small frame that the cuffs brush the floor, giving her the look of a little monkey.

"We're going to see the reindeer, Ms. Claire."

"Okay, um—"

She looks down, frowns, unzips the sweatshirt, and pulls a silver piece of duct tape off her shirt, reaffixes it to the outside of the sweatshirt. "There; I'm Maree, in case you already forgot." She says this with so much earnestness in her upturned face it gives me a pang.

"Thank you, Maree. Now I won't forget!"

Her lips quirk up at the edges. "So my idea with the pictures was good and stuff, huh?"

"What pictures?"

She laughs so hard her glasses come off. "Holy crap, you're so funny, Ms. Claire." She pulls on my sleeve and rushes us to the elevator, pushes the down button repeatedly. "Hurry; let's go before your memory wears off!"

I chuckle, enjoying the girl's antics, opting not to correct her language. Her frankness is startling and charming and mostly unexpected. I love it.

Outside, the sun has nearly set, turning the light into moody shades of gray with clouds that hang over the mountains, skirting over bald peaks and rocky crevasses. Wind whips off the water, frigid and stinging. The reindeer pen sits across from BTI, so we don't have far to go.

The little girl talks all the way, a running commentary on our progress. "We're in the elevator, Ms. Claire; now we're in the lobby; now we're outside and walking down the stairs." She holds my hand as we go; it's small but fits perfectly inside my palm. "And I'm Maree, like Mary with a *y* but with two *e*'s, 'cause of *Anne of Green Gables* and . . ." She stops, leans over, hands on her knees, back heaving up and down. "All that talking is taking my breathing away!"

We stand in front of the pen; the reindeer have sequestered themselves around a small shelter to get out of the wind. One turns his head, antlers rising up like a small tree, then eyes the little girl and turns back.

"Aw, damn, I should have grabbed carrots," she says.

"You should think about the words you use," I say.

She looks up, gives me a side smile. "You sound just like Ms. Kiko!" Her fingers weave into the fence, bend over the wire, her eyes on the reindeer. "Too bad we don't have carrots."

My hand goes to my pocket, and to my delight I pull out a couple of carrots. "Here you go . . ." A total blank. I stare at her, my tongue wanting to say her name, my brain refusing to release it, and my pulse speeds up at the uselessness of my thoughts.

She points to her name tag. "Maree; I'm Maree, and you're teaching me how to play the guitar and stuff, except today we're on a field trip to see the reindeer 'cause I asked and you said yes." She smiles, looking quite pleased with herself.

"Thank you, Maree," I say, amused by her efforts.

The smallest of the reindeer begins to make his way over to us, his hooves squishing into the muddy earth, antlers rising above his head. Maree hops up and down on her toes, holding the carrot through the fence, teeth chattering in the cold air.

"Here he comes! Oh, he's so small!" she squeals. "He's the smallest!" She clicks her tongue, but instead of a sharp sound, it comes out mushy. The reindeer plods over regardless, and Maree jumps up and down, the carrot wiggling in the air. "Here, little baby buddy, here!" He eats it in two bites, leafy green hair and all, and stays still long enough for Maree to pet the velvet tip of his nose. A larger reindeer moves toward us now, ears pricked forward. "Feed the big guy, Ms. Claire!" She struggles to take her camera from her neck while still petting her little buddy. "I'll take a picture of us." She tries to hold the camera up and away, another selfie, and I have to keep from laughing at her efforts. *Click!*

"How about I take one of you?" I say.

She hands me the camera, then stands in between the two reindeer who are lingering at the fence, no doubt hoping for another carrot. Maree holds her arms out on either side and smiles wide. I snap the picture.

"You have long arms; you could do a selfie with both of us in it."

I kneel beside her and hold the camera out as far as I can. She rests one small hand on my shoulder and leans into me until our faces are side by side. "Cheese!" we both say and I push the button, watch the film slide out. Maree grabs it quick and flaps it back and forth in the air.

"Hey, you did it; you got both of us!" She holds the partially developed picture out, and I can just make out the top half of us, our faces side by side, her head tilted toward me, glasses hanging on to the tip of her nose.

I study the image as it comes into focus, and I'm punctured by how happy I look in the photo, cheek to cheek with this girl who wears a name tag for me, a reindeer nose popping over my shoulder.

She pockets the photos, pulls the camera strap over her neck, then points to the duct tape. "My name is Maree. You took me outside to see the reindeer 'cause I asked. But, um, I think we need to go back inside for our guitar lesson."

I wink and make a clicking sound. "Still with you, Maree."

She throws her arms around me, squeezes. "Wow, that's so great! Maybe your memory is getting better."

Tears prick my eyes at her efforts to do something I know is impossible. "We'd better go inside—"

"Holy shit!" she says, her eyes wide, finger pointing at something behind me.

I turn and immediately put my body in front of hers because loping toward us is a huge bear, his fur rippling with each stride he takes. The hairs on the back of my neck stand on end. "That bear should be hibernating," I whisper.

"That's why we're supposed to always take the tunnel." Maree whispers, too, even though it's about as loud as her speaking voice. From the corner of my eye, I see the tip of an orange carrot slide past my arm. "Aw, he's so cute! Poor buddy. Maybe he's just hungry like the reindeer and 'cause of hibernation and stuff." She makes the mushy clicking sound again.

I groan and grab the carrot from her hand, shove it into my pocket. The bear halts a few yards from us, and when he sniffs the air, he makes a loud huffing sound that echoes in the stillness. Adrenaline courses through me, electrifying my skin. Beside us, the reindeer have retreated to their pen. "Maree," I say between clenched teeth, "we are going to walk slowly back to the building. Stay behind me, okay?"

"Okay," she says in a small, breathless voice.

I reach back and touch her shoulder but continue to keep myself between her and the bear, who is swaying from side to side like he's deciding on whether to charge or turn and run. Dad pops into my head. From the night he scared the bear, how he stood tall and looked the bear straight in the eyes. He was my hero that day. "Let's walk nice and slow, and stay behind me."

The wind picks up, rushes around us, lifts the hair away from my face, and turns my breath shallow from its coldness. When we near BTI, the outside lights surround us, making it harder to see the bear, who lingers in the twilight shadows but stays back, still swaying side to side. The door is within reach, and I yank it open, shoving the girl inside before me, my pulse racing. When it closes behind us, I slump forward, relieved, and turn to see whether the bear has left. Instead, he sits at the bottom of the concrete stairs, so close I can see mud caked around sharp claws and the pointed tips of his ears.

Through the window, I meet his gaze, see my dad in his red boxers on that night in the lobby, standing tall against a bear, remember his solid protectiveness and how sure I was that with Dad, nothing bad would ever happen to me. I press my fingers against the glass, not scared anymore.

"Wow, that was a close call," the girl whispers beside me. "You're so brave, Ms. Claire. Just like your dad from that story you tell all the time."

I look at her sharply, wonder whether I've been thinking out loud. "What did you say?"

She squints up at me, wrinkles her nose. "You tell that story a lot 'cause I think it's one of your favoritist memories. One time Ms. Kiko asked you to tell it to our class. Everyone loved it."

Outside, the bear turns and sprints away, disappearing into the woods beyond our building and leaving me with my thoughts and a fading sensation that I'm uncomfortable in my own skin. I sit down in one of the chairs in the lobby, hoping the sensation that I've lost something will go away because it writhes in my gut, so I close my eyes, rub at my face, and remind myself to breathe.

Someone tugs at my sleeve, and I open my eyes to find a young girl in a brown sweatshirt I'm sure is mine with a silver tag that reads "Maree." Her eyebrows raise high, and her arms are extended in front of her, palms up, waiting, I assume, for me to speak. When I don't she sighs and says, "My name is Maree and you're Ms. Claire, and you're teaching me how to play the guitar, but first we fed the reindeer 'cept we almost got eaten by a bear until you saved my life by being so tall and brave and smart." She wipes a hand across her forehead. "Whew, it's hard work to keep you remembering!"

I stand, surprised when she takes my hand, and we head for the elevator while Maree recounts the story about the bear who nearly ate us.

CHAPTER
TWENTY-FIVE

Tuesday, February 19

I wake up with my head against the glass window of—I sit up and take in my surroundings—a pickup truck window. I look beside me and nearly jump out of my skin because Tate Dunn is driving. My hands go to my face, feel my clothes. We could be seventeen or twenty or—no, I'm not seventeen. I'm older and I'm different and—I look closer at Tate—so is he.

Tate looks sideways at me, a comfortable smile playing around his lips, and it eases the twisting in my gut. His hair sticks up on the top like he's been wearing a hat, but the ebony tresses are just as I remember them, still fill me with the desire to run my fingers through them.

"Have a good n . . . n-ap, Rip Van Winkle?" he says and hands me a note card.

I take it, suck in my top lip. "Rip Van Winkle?"

"Read the note card, Claire." He concentrates on the road, and his profile magnifies the line of his jaw, makes pleasing lines around his mouth. Oh, he's so handsome. "Claire," he laughs. "Read the . . . note card."

I do. *I live in Whittier now and I know about the baby. We went skiing and sometimes I think you use your notebook to keep people out, so I
convinced you to leave it at home.*

My eyes widen when I look at him. "Why?"

"I w . . . w-want you to trust me with your . . ." His mouth is frozen, lips together, and I wait, so familiar with his stuttering it's second
nature for me. Part of me wants to crumple the note card, throw it at
him for suggesting I want to keep people out. But I can sense his nerves
in the stuttering, can see that he's doing this for me. "I want you to
experience life instead of having to write every minute down," he says.
"Not all the t . . . t-ime, just some of it."

I look down to find that I'm in an underlayer of leggings and a long-
sleeved T-shirt, ski socks pulled up to my knees, winter coat smushed
behind me in the seat. The tunnel is up ahead, but we are on the side
that leads into Whittier. I sag against the door. "Did we already go?"

"Yes."

"But I can't remembe—" As the words leave my mouth, I stop
because it hits me that I do in a way. In the tautness of my quads, the
ache running up my calves, a lingering coldness in the tips of my toes,
the chapped feel of the skin across my cheeks.

"Here." He hands me a tablet, quickly swipes it open, then instructs
me to push play on a video. There I am, top of the mountain, helmet
and goggles covering most of my face except my mouth, which is spread
into a wide grin. On the video, Tate's voice booms out, "Having fun?"

I lift my face to the sky, ski poles in the air. "It's perfect, Tate. Thank
you!" Then I push off and fly down the hill.

The camera wobbles violently, and I hear Tate mumble, "Oh . . .
shit, she's f . . . f-ast."

"I have others from today, that's just all I had . . . time to upload
before we left."

I play it again, see the look on my face, feel a prickling of warmth
run down my back. There's more. This one from a day of snow

machining. I'm on the back, clinging to Tate, and Sefina's voice calls out, "Grab his ass, Claire!" I throw my head back when I laugh and then give her what I'm assuming is the middle finger in a pair of mittens. The camera shakes with her giggles.

"Thank you," I whisper.

"You're welcome."

I read the note card again. "You think I use my notebooks to keep people away?"

He shifts in his seat, sighs. "You can't write every minute down . . . you know? I know that means you'll make mistakes or . . . r-epeat yourself, but Claire, you're amazing to be around. You're funny and interesting, and I know you hate for others to see you forgetting things, but you are lovely and that hasn't changed. Besides, your hand hurts all the t . . . t-ime; we all see it."

I stiffen at the implication that I am on display. "We?"

He gives me a sideways glance. "Me, Ruth, Sefina, Harriet, Alice."

My face turns to stone. "Mom lives in Whittier?"

"Yes, and she's sober and g . . . g-ood. She's better now, Claire. You should be proud of her."

In my mind I see the way the light spun golden threads in her dark hair right before she left. Still feel the way my heart sliced open. "Why does she deserve that?" I say it quietly, and picture Tate with fingerprints of bruises across his arms that turned yellow, then green, before they disappeared. Anger rushes hot through my veins at what his father did to him. "Could you ever be proud of your father if he was better?"

"My . . . dad was different than Alice, Claire, and you know that." He speaks softly but firmly, and my spine curves forward with shame. He's right. His father was violent and spiteful and spared not a single drop of love for his son.

"I'm sorry."

"But I did try to understand him." He eyes my empty hand, looks sheepish. "Okay, you should write this p . . . p-art down so you remember it. I did bring your notebook along, well, kind of. Here."

He pulls the truck to the side of the road, picks up the tablet in my lap, opens it to a program that has a notebook-paper graphic. He switches dictation on, looks up at me, eyebrows raised. "This way I can t . . . t-alk, but it's getting recorded in your notebook—well, this version of your . . . notebook, if you like it, or you can always recopy it to your p . . . p-aper one, after you ride home in your horse and buggy, of course."

A playfulness lights up his eyes, and instead of being upset, I am warmed by his humor. I've always recognized my antiquated ways.

He pulls back onto the road, taps the steering wheel while he talks. "It was a few years ago. I came back because I thought that . . . seeing him would heal something in me. And maybe I thought he'd be man enough to say he was sorry." Tate rubs the stubble on his cheek. "He had n . . . n-othing to say to me except more of the same, and do you know what I did? I started laughing."

I want to touch his face, put my arms around him, hold him. "Why?" I ask.

"In my head he'd always been a g . . . g-iant, a monster who held all the power. He was a man and I was n . . . n-othing. But I finally saw him for . . . what he truly was."

"And what was that?"

"N . . . n-othing, Claire. Only a shriveled bit of human flesh. Pathetic and alone. N . . . n-ot a monster at all. Just a man who'd made all the wrong decisions and hurt anyone who loved him."

"Oh."

"Yeah, oh. But your mom, Claire, she's different."

"How?"

"She loves you, for one."

My heart beats steadily, shoulders are relaxed away from my ears, hands lightly holding the tablet. It occurs to me that I'm not angry. I think about Mom and I see my hands reaching out, empty, as the door closes behind her, and I'm holding my breath because I do understand what I feel now that I'm told she's back in my life. "I'm scared she'll leave again, Tate."

We're in the tunnel; lights clip past the truck like the rolling of an old-time film. I watch the snow melt into pathways on the window that break apart, form glassy balls that spiral down in twisted droplets.

"She w . . . w-won't," he says with such conviction it lifts the heaviness around my heart.

"How do you know that?"

"Because she left when she couldn't . . . get better *and* be your mom." He smiles at me before turning back to navigate the narrow tunnel in front of us. "She fought her w . . . w-ay to sobriety, Claire, and I think she deserves a second chance to be your mom. Don't you?"

On the tablet screen, his last words finish typing themselves out on the notebook-paper graphic.

deserves a second chance to be your mom

A calm rushes over me, slides down to where it settles inside my chest, and I lean into the seat, enjoying the moment. I press the screen and it brings up a keyboard. My name appears in a bubble on the screen, and I type, give Mom a chance. Then I look up from the tablet and outside the window to the water, flat and still, protected by a sheer gray mist that moves languidly above it.

We're coming into Whittier now, parking in the gravel lot on the side of BTI, when Tate shuts off the car and turns to me, forehead creased.

"There's something I n . . . n-eed to tell you, Claire. I've been meaning to tell you for some . . . time now but—"

"Is that Mom?" She's across the parking lot, arm in arm with another woman, both swaying, listing to one side, then the other. I know the walk. My nostrils flare and I'm out of the truck, hurrying across the lot toward the pair.

"Claire! Wait!"

I ignore him. "Mom!"

They both turn to face me, the woman beside her hardly able to keep her eyes focused, but Mom is clear-eyed and looks tired. "Claire?"

The school playground is behind the parking lot, and I can hear the delighted screams of kids playing outside, but they get drowned out by a buzzing that builds in my head. The smell of alcohol kicks up with the wind, surrounds me in memories and feelings that curdle in my stomach. "You're drinking?"

The woman, hardly dressed for a winter day, no matter how nice the weather today, leans heavily against Mom.

"It's not what you think, Claire. I'm helping Jory, and I need to get her home, okay? I'll stop by this afternoon." They walk away, passing a little girl, who hops up in the air with a wave at the pair before heading in my direction.

"Ms. Claire! Hi!" She's dressed in a thick pink winter coat, mittens, and a hat that sits high on her forehead to accommodate her large cat-eye glasses. "It's me, Maree, from guitar lessons and quiet activity time, and—oh, hi, Daddy! What are you guys doing here?"

I turn around but all I see is Tate smiling at the girl, who runs to hug him around his legs.

My body turns cold, too heavy to move even though I want to run.

Tate leans down to pick her up, but his eyes flick toward me, the corners pulled down in a worried slant. "You're supposed to be at the playground, Maree. I can see Ms. Kiko doesn't look very happy."

"Oh, yikes! Okay, see you after school! Bye!"

Suddenly, I'm thrust back in time, standing in a hotel room, shirt clutched to my bare chest, face wet. *I'm . . . married, Claire. Her n . . .*

n-ame is Maria. I'm sorry. I should have t . . . t-old you. I love you. I'll always love you. You know that, right? I'd run, not wanting to hear his excuse, afraid that nobody would ever love me enough to stay.

I look from the girl to Tate, see the resemblance in her dark hair, the shape of her nose.

Tate is looking at me, and he seems . . . afraid? As though he's worried that, what? I can't figure it out, so I reach for my notebook, but I don't have my bag or my phone, and I'm wearing leggings and a long-sleeved shirt, ski socks tight on my calves, and despite the clothing I am naked and vulnerable, an interloper in lives I have no right to be a part of. I back away, hope that he will just let me go.

The little girl hops down from her father's arms and waves at me. "Bye, Ms. Claire!" She spins around and jogs backward to add, "I'm Maree from guitar lessons and when you volunteer and stuff!" With another wave, she turns and runs to the playground.

"Claire," Tate says, gentle but firm.

I stare at the ground, shiver, realize I'm standing in the parking lot of BTI without a coat. A cold wind bites through my cotton top, and I wrap my arms across my body. Tate is married.

As if he reads my mind, he says, "I'm not married anymore, Claire. It was over a long time ago."

"Her name is Maria," I say.

He nods.

"And Maree is your daughter."

Another nod, slower this time, like he thinks I'm a wild animal, about to run away or attack. I don't know. I can't focus and I can't identify enough clues to connect the dots. I breathe in, remind myself of who I am now. A broken woman with no memory and no life. Frozen in the present. I have no right to be angry with Tate. Not anymore. I try to smile but it slips away. "I'm happy for you, Tate, really happy for you. She seems like a lovely girl."

His eyes are soft and pained, and I don't want to stand here a minute longer. "Thanks for . . . um . . ." I don't know what we're doing standing in the parking lot. "Oh."

"We went skiing." His voice is strained.

"Skiing. Okay, I'm uh . . ." I can't finish because I need to be away from him. I need to be alone. I walk away, a sob trapped inside. *You're better off alone. You're better off alone.* A mantra I repeat all the way home.

CHAPTER TWENTY-SIX

I'm lying on my bed, reading fragmented thoughts captured inside the pages of my notebook. *Tate had a daughter with his wife. His daughter is Maree, the girl you give guitar lessons to.* A sinking feeling makes me question what I should already know. Was he keeping it from me? The shock I feel battles with a genuine happiness that Tate is a father. I always knew he'd make an incredible one.

There's a knocking on my door that I ignore, and I stay on my bed with an arm slung across my eyes. I just want to go to sleep. But the door opens to Ruth's voice.

"Claire?"

"Back here," I call, keeping my eyes covered, too damn tired to pretend I'm not upset.

"It's open-mic night tonight. Did you forget?"

I slide my arm away, give her a look. "Hah," I say, and turn on my side with my back to Ruth.

"You're still in your ski clothes?"

"Tate is a father."

I feel the bed move when Ruth sits, her hand on my shoulder. "He wanted to tell you. I think he wanted to find the right time."

I flip over, meet her gaze. "Did you ever tell me?"

She shakes her head. "No, I didn't think it was my place."

I add it to my notebook, not disagreeing with Ruth's decision. It really wouldn't have been her place to tell me. I breathe in and sit up, trying to ignore the pounding in my temples. "Where are we going?"

From the living room booms Harriet's voice. "Open mic at the bar tonight."

Ruth stands. "I think one of your guitar students is playing."

I bite my lip, wonder how many guitar students I have, decide to let the question go and get ready instead.

~

We leave BTI and head into the frigid wind of another cold and dark winter evening. The weather is harsh here, near-constant wind, snow, rain, clouds, and fog. It's not for delicate flowers. But even those of us seasoned by the climate can still feel the cold deep in our bones, especially on an evening like this when we're outside instead of staying in.

Ruth and Harriet flank me on either side. Ruth has on her winter coat, which falls to her ankles, inhibiting her from taking full strides so that she ends up walking in small, stuttering steps. It's comical, but I try not to laugh. She wears a yellow winter hat pulled low and under a fur-lined hood, and her scarf is wrapped twice around her face so that all I can see are the wedges of her eyes peeking through the layers. She grumbles as we walk. "Why didn't we drive? It's too dang cold out here."

Harriet gives the kind of sigh that means she's heard this more than once from Ruth. "It would take us longer to scrape the ice from our windshields and warm the car than it takes to walk." She also wears a long coat with a heavy scarf wrapped around her neck and over her hair, earmuffs, and winter mittens that might be bigger than her head. "You know, when Pete and I were living in tents in Iceland, we taught our bodies how to acclimate to the coldest of temperatures. This feels like a day at the beach to me." The scarf muffles her voice, and the wind dissolves the volume, but I still hear her.

Ruth groans. "Harriet, was Iceland before or after the time you camped inside an active volcano?"

I laugh. Harriet and Pete had many adventures before settling in Whittier, but Ruth is of the opinion that they are also purveyors of tall tales.

"Oh, Ruth," Harriet says. "After, of course, but before the archeological dig in Belize."

Ruth barks a laugh, and despite the temperatures, their company adds a lightness to my step. We are walking in the direction of Whiskey Pete's, but I can't recall why, so I take a guess. "Is Dad joining us for dinner?" The question feels wrong, the words like blocks in my mouth.

Harriet and Ruth don't answer at first, and with the wind, I'm not sure they've heard me. Their coats make a loud shuffling sound.

Ruth touches my arm. "Vance died five months ago from a heart attack, Claire. It's something you know. I'm so sorry, sweetheart."

My legs feel heavy and I want to sit down, but I tell myself that I know this, because Ruth would never lie to me about something like that. *Dad died from a heart attack.* I inhale, repeat it silently while we walk the rest of the way against the wind, fighting to keep our layers in place.

Harriet pulls open the door to Whiskey Pete's, and I'm met with warm air layered in fryer grease and popcorn oil. Our boots squeak across the sticky wood floor when we make our way to the bar. Pete stands with his back to us, pouring beer from a wall tap into a smudged pint glass. He turns, raises one eyebrow.

"You three look like the zombie apocalypse if zombies couldn't hack the cold."

Harriet laughs, unwinding her scarf and setting her earmuffs on the counter. "Nice to see you, too, handsome."

Ruth unbuttons her coat first, leaving her scarf in place so that her eyes are the only visible part of her, making her look more like a mummy. "You're lucky to have us, Pete." She swings her head around the mostly empty bar. "We've just tripled your sales."

Once we've finally shed our layers, we choose a table by the bar, loading our coats and mittens and scarves in the empty fourth chair. I lay out my phone, open my notebook and pen. Harriet places a paper boat full of popcorn in the center of the table, and Ruth sets down three glasses of sweet iced tea.

"Your mom is playing the guitar for the open mic tonight," Ruth says. "She's not half-bad, actually; she even sings too."

My mouth falls open and I touch my pocket, pull out a note card with three facts, feeling a pang when I read each one, freeze when I see the one about Tate. He's a father now.

Harriet leans over to me, her eyes bright. "You remember the time you snuck out to come here with Tate?"

"Of course," I say. "I had to sneak out because Dad had grounded me for something or other."

Ruth shakes her head. "Both. He grounded you for something *and* the other. You and Tate were such troublemakers."

I shake my head. "I don't know how you put up with us."

"The two of you waltzed right in here like you owned the place. Somehow you'd forgotten how small this town is and that Pete knew you were grounded. He called Vance when you were trying to pick a song from the jukebox." Harriet shakes her head with a laugh. "Was that after the time Vance found you smoking pot with Tate?"

"Sure was," says Ruth. "And the other was when he saw her kiss the boy." She sips her tea. "Vance came over and paced a hole in my floor. He said he had no idea raising a teenage girl would be so hard." Ruth is laughing—a rare occasion, but it utterly transforms her face, makes her eyes squint shut, her cheeks round.

"I told Dad he was the one," I say, shifting in my seat when I think about how deeply I believed that, having to fight the feeling even now.

"Even back then?" says Harriet. "Skinny little Tate?"

I nod. "He said all he wanted was to live in Whittier."

"That's all you talked about," says Ruth.

Harriet nods. "You never wanted to leave."

I take a long drink of tea, let the sweetness roll around on my tongue. "What does Dad think about Tate being back . . ." I hesitate because something isn't right; I sense it from the deep wrinkle in Harriet's forehead.

Ruth covers my hand. "Vance died from a heart attack five months ago, but you're working really hard to remember that."

I inhale; yes, I know this, damn it. I dig my fingernails into my thigh. I have to know it.

"It's okay, Claire," Ruth says. "And Vance was thrilled when Tate moved back." She pauses, raises her eyebrows, but the note card is sitting out on the table, and I've just read the bit about Tate and his daughter.

She continues, "Right before Vance died"—she coughs and blinks hard—"he said you'd all wasted too much time being apart. That everyone needed to be together again."

"I have all of you," I say.

Harriet touches my arm. "But you deserve to have everything, Claire."

I read the line about Tate and his daughter, try to feel happy for him and ignore a terrible loneliness that expands into self-pity. But I keep reading the note card, and a piece of me falls away. Tears collect in my eyelashes, and I swipe at them, angry for this surge of emotion that makes me feel weak. I slide my glass to the side, turn to get Pete's attention.

"Another one, Claire?" he calls.

"Whiskey this time, Pete."

"Claire." Ruth says my name low, a warning tone I remember from my childhood like it was yesterday. "Easy. You came to hear Alice and one of your students play."

"Here you go, Claire." Pete sets it on the table.

It's gone before he turns to go. "Another one, please." He gives Ruth a wary eye, so I tap the glass on the table once, hard. I'm not sure what's gotten into me, but I can't seem to stop myself.

From the direction of the stage comes a scuffling sound. I look up to see a tall skinny guy with a guitar strapped to his back drag a stool to the middle of the stage and set it under the microphone.

"Here you go, Claire." Pete sets a small tumbler in front of me; ice cubes clink against the glass, and my attention diverts. I inhale smoky fumes. Mmm, whiskey.

Pete's hand is still on the tumbler, eyes dancing from Ruth to Harriet, and the idea that I'm being censured in some way raises the hair on my arms. "Maybe you should stop at one, you know, with Alice here and all and . . ." He trails off, an eye toward Harriet, and the look makes it clear that I'm doing something that bothers them. It fuels a guilty churning in my stomach.

But it doesn't stop me. I pull the glass from his hand and force a smile. "Thank you, Pete."

He bows his head and steps back. Thick salt-and-pepper hair piles around his ears and the back of his head in unruly waves. Deep creases pan out from his blue eyes. Pete's the kind of Alaskan old that weathers like the rocks along the shoreline, the years wearing upon him slowly, taking only a little bit at a time.

The first sip burns. The next is smooth, with hints of apple and woodsmoke.

Harriet and Ruth stare at me. I wonder how long it's been since I've had whiskey. I take another sip and can already feel the alcohol spreading its fingers through my limbs, touching my lips, making the note card on the table that tells me Tate moved on and has everything I wanted with him blur.

"One more please, Pete."

Ruth makes a noise, but I ignore her and smile, look around, take in the guy playing a scratchy tune—some Bob Dylan song, I think, but the young guy's voice is no Bob Dylan. Too high, more boy-band material, and his guitar playing is mediocre, beginner at best—no match for the song he's attempting. I sit back in the chair. "He's not very good," I say in a low voice.

"He should have listened to you, Claire," Ruth says.

"Listened to me what?"

"He's your guitar student. You suggested he wait before he signed up to play open mic. Told him he needed much more practice."

My head is already spinning from the alcohol, and the idea that I'm teaching this guy how to play the guitar only adds to it.

Harriet clears her throat and tries to find something positive. "But his guitar playing is better on this song, isn't it? I mean, he's not having to stop and find the right notes, so good for him!"

Ruth grunts and I eat a whiskey-soaked ice cube.

The door opens, bringing in a blast of cold and a woman wearing nothing more than a light jacket, no hat or gloves, her cheeks ruddy and heavily lined. She walks with her head low, makes a beeline for a barstool. There's a tightness in my chest. "Who's that?" I ask.

Ruth makes a clucking sound. "Jory Woods. Her husband just up and left her when the fishing season ended, and her mother died last year. She's got two young ones at the school, but this winter has been hard on her. I thought she was trying to quit. Hmmm, where's Alice?"

I'm staring at the bottom of a glass; ice cubes slide down and hit my teeth, bringing with them the watery taste of whiskey. I set the glass down, chomp on an ice cube, and look around. Whiskey Pete's. My head swims the tiniest bit but enough to tell me that I shouldn't have another whiskey.

Harriet hands me a water; her eyes are narrowed with what I'm thinking is concern for me, which makes sense because drinking too much probably isn't the best idea. "Thanks," I say and take the water, draining half of it before setting it on the table.

She frowns. "Two drinks should probably be your limit."

"Or none at all," mumbles Ruth.

The guy onstage stands, slings his guitar to his back, and leans into the microphone. "That's my set. I'm Jarrod, and I want to dedicate tonight to Claire."

I'm startled to find the young guy holding up his beer bottle toward me.

An old man in the corner booth gives a half-hearted clap. Harriet leans into me. "You're teaching young Jarrod there how to play the guitar, Claire. His playing is no reflection on your teaching, by the way."

Ruth snorts and I start to smile, amused and trying to piece it all together, when a woman at the bar starts to cry, bent over, shoulders shaking. The sound is pathetic and so lost it hits me right in the gut, and all I can think about is my mom and how alone in her own tortured thoughts she must have been to have gotten so lost like that.

Pete heads her way, pats her lightly on the shoulder. "Okay, now, Jory." His voice is low and comforting.

Ruth shakes her head. "Poor woman." Harriet makes a sympathetic sound in agreement.

"Here you go, Jory, drink this." Pete sets a soda on the bar before heading back to help another customer.

I still can't take my eyes off the woman, can't stop imagining my mother like that.

"Is Alice up next, Pete?" Ruth says.

"Rick's up doing Elvis covers, then Alice."

Harriet hoots. "Rick? The guy who plays death-metal tunes on the jukebox every damn chance he gets?" She slaps her knee. "Come on, ladies, this we've got to hear."

"But where is Alice?" Ruth says, and I can hear a note of concern in her voice that sets the hairs on the back of my neck on end.

"Alice lives here now, Claire," Harriet says, patting my hand.

I'm nodding because yes, I know this. Don't I?

A phone rings and the woman at the bar answers loud. "Yeah, okay, outside." She lurches to her feet and stumbles out the door.

I've already thrown on my coat, hat and scarf, gloves. "I'm not feeling so well."

"Whiskey," Harriet says.

"Stay, Claire. You're here to see your mom play," Ruth says. "Alice was really excited that you were coming."

"Yeah." I sound a bit gruff and short, but I want to get out of there. I want to go home. It's been a long day—I can feel it in the softness of my bones, the weariness that hangs from my arms. I try to soften my voice. "Sorry, Ruth. I'm just tired, okay?"

There's no wind when I step outside the bar, and I'm grateful for the reprieve. My mouth is dry, sticky with the taste of whiskey, and my temples pound. Why did I drink whiskey? I feel a sudden light-headedness I didn't notice inside. *I'm going home. I'm going home,* I sing to myself. A woman is crying and the sound draws me around the corner to the back entrance of the restaurant.

"I'm sosorry to keep draggin' you into this, Alice. I'mamess." The woman's words slur together.

"It's okay, Jory. We're not perfect; nobody is, and setbacks don't mean anything other than a new challenge, right?" My mother's voice.

I press a hand to my mouth to keep from crying out. She's bundled up but her face is exposed, and she looks so much like the woman who once laughed and danced with Dad, who rocked me to sleep and baked the best chocolate chip cookies in Whittier. Seeing her now, combined with the cloying taste of whiskey in my mouth, makes tears slide down my cheeks. "Mom?"

She turns, and when she sees me, her head tilts. "Hi, Claire bear. Are you okay?"

I stumble to the side, the whiskey running a winning loop inside my body, and I shake my head. "I don't think so, Mom."

The door to Whiskey Pete's slams open, and out come Harriet and Ruth, bundled and walking with a purpose.

"You go on ahead with our Claire, Alice," Harriet says. "I'll help Jory home."

Mom slides her arm around my waist, and with Ruth flanking my other side, we hurry to BTI. In the elevator, I look down at Mom and feel the years we've lost in a sour queasiness that waters my mouth. "What are you doing here?"

"I live here now, and I'm taking you home, sweetheart."

"I've missed you, Mom."

Her arm squeezes my waist. "I know, honey. But I'm not going anywhere ever again. Okay?"

"Okay." And then I'm in my apartment and running to the bathroom, head in the toilet while Mom rubs a cool washcloth across the back of my neck.

"What happened?" I ask.

"Whiskey," comes Ruth's voice from outside the bathroom.

Mom wets the washcloth again, wrings it out. "What got into you?"

"Maybe it was Bob Dylan," Ruth says. "His music could make anybody drink."

I push to standing, wincing at an ache that spreads across my forehead. "Bob Dylan?" I say and sink into the couch.

Ruth takes a seat on one of the barstools.

Mom hands me a glass of water and two pills. "Drink this and take these."

I do as I'm told, and while my head is fuzzy, an odd thought springs to mind. "I feel like a teenager again."

Ruth frowns. "You acted like a teenager again."

I look at Mom and I'm surprised at the warm feeling spreading through my limbs. Her hair is down, washed and dried in shiny waves, and she wears a soft lavender sweatshirt that brings out a healthy pink tone in her skin. I have to swallow past a lump. "But you weren't here when I was a teenager," I say.

Mom's dark-blue eyes crinkle when she smiles. "Well, I'm here now."

CHAPTER TWENTY-SEVEN

Wednesday, February 20

When I get to Kiko's classroom, I easily locate my spot, Ms. CLAIRE's READING CORNER, and settle into the beanbag chair, moving my tall form around until I squish it into a comfortable-enough seat. While Kiko instructs the class, I scan my notes, blink against a pressure in my eyes when I read that Tate is a father. He's a good one, I have no doubt, and his daughter, Maree, sits across the classroom now, squirming in her seat, with a name tag made of silver duct tape affixed to her shirt.

There's a tenderness I feel toward the girl that is mirrored in my notes from previous times we've spent together. I wonder if on some level I sensed the connection. Tate and I were as close as two people can be. It wouldn't surprise me if that connection extends to his daughter.

Kiko announces quiet activity time, and the little girl with cat-eye glasses picks up her backpack and zooms over to my corner, jumping into the smaller beanbag chair beside me. Maree. I smile.

She points to her name tag. "I'm Maree, like Mary with a *y* 'cept with two *e*'s 'cause I love—"

"*Anne of Green Gables*," I say, and I don't know where it comes from but it feels right and it apparently delights the girl, who has covered her mouth with one hand.

"Oh my God. That is so amazing. Maybe I should be a doctor when I grow up!"

I laugh, having no idea what she's talking about but thoroughly enjoying her enthusiasm.

"Oh, guess what," she says. "My birthday's on Saturday."

She talks as though we are old friends, and something about her comfort with me is at once familiar and devastatingly out of my reach. "And how old are you going to be, Maree?"

"Two digits, Ms. Claire! Finally!" From her backpack, she slides out a ziplock bag, places it carefully on her lap with a furtive glance toward Kiko. "I made lemon bars for the class. It's just stuff that's in a box, but I think they're pretty yummy. Want to try one?"

I nod and she hands me a napkin with a doughy lump that's more round than square and drenched in powdered sugar. I take a bite and she stares at me, eyebrows arched high in anticipation.

"Delicious!" I say.

She blows air through her nose and leans all the way back in her beanbag, looking relieved. "I knew it! Leonora said they were gross, but I knew she was lying." She makes a face at a girl who sits in front of a desktop computer wearing headphones.

I try to change the subject. "So what are you going to do for your birthday?"

She shrugs. "Maybe something with my best friend, Leonora." She leans close, lowers her voice. "'Cept sometimes she makes me so mad, and I don't want to be around her, and other times she's hilarious, you know?"

I nod. "Friendships can be tricky."

She peers up at me over her glasses. "Hey, you're best friends with my dad. Is he tricky?"

I do know that her dad is Tate because it's on the note card in front of me, but I rub my neck because hearing it out loud makes it feel new.

She looks sheepish. "Oh, right; sorry. You know, sometimes I forget all about your sucky memory problem 'cause you're so easy to talk to and stuff."

I have to blink several times. It's such a kind thing to hear. "Thank you," I say.

She keeps talking. "And Tate is my dad, and he's been your best friend since you guys were little, kinda like"—she scrunches one side of her mouth—"me and Leonora."

It seems like she wants to talk about her friend problems. "I always thought that good friends make each other better people. Do you and Leonora do that for each other?"

Maree pushes her lips out, thinking. "Maybe. She said I was going to get fat if I kept eating cookies."

"She said that?"

"Yeah, so I guess she is a good friend, 'cause instead I gave her all my cookies and that was very nice of me." She holds up a small booklet held together by pink and green staples. "Can I read my Uki story to you now?"

I settle into the beanbag. "Of course."

She opens the book. "Once upon a time, there was a brave strong warrior girl named Uki, and she was smart and fast, and she didn't take crap from anyone."

I bite my tongue, decide to let the choice of words pass in favor of hearing her story.

"There was a boy in Uki's village who was the shortest and smallest of every kid, and he was scared of everyone. There was a troll who lived under a bridge, and he threw rocks and staples and pencils at the boy and called him lots of mean names. The boy trembled with fear."

She shows me an illustration of a big orange blob with horns—the troll, I assume—beside a small stick-figure boy with pencils sticking out of him and a tear falling to the ground.

"So Uki collected a bunch of sap and tricked the troll into drinking it. It stuck to his mouth like glue and so he couldn't talk and never said mean things to the boy ever again."

This picture is of the orange blob with horns and a tear falling off its face. She turns the page to a big pink heart.

"And the boy loved her from that day on."

She closes the book.

"I loved it. You're very creative, Maree."

"That's the last one. I'm all out of Uki stories."

"That's a shame," I say.

She shrugs. "That's life."

"Next station, please," Kiko announces, and Maree pops up from the beanbag chair like only a kid can.

"My birthday's on Saturday. Don't forget!"

I smile, hold my hands out in front of me, and say, because I think we are comfortable with each other, "Oops, I already have!"

Her face lights up, and she laughs so hard she bends in half. "Oh, Ms. Claire, you're so funny." She takes the note card from my lap, flips it over, and writes, *Dont forget again! Maree turns 10 on Saturday!*, and hands it back to me. "Now you won't forget. Bye, Ms. Claire!" She skips to the computer center and takes a seat.

I smile at the uneven scrawl across my note card, then check my schedule for today, pleased to see that I'm going to Anchorage this afternoon with Ruth. I'll pick up a present for Maree there.

~

I meet Ruth in the lobby, and when I get there, a waterfall of young voices floats from the area by the front door. A dim light, the brightest it gets in winter, stretches lazily inside, highlighting fingerprint smudges and one that looks like lips pressed into the window. Beside me, Ruth mumbles something under her breath as we make our way past the kids and toward the front doors. I don't have to understand her to know what she says, because Ruth is of the opinion that the kids shouldn't be allowed to hang out in the lobby after school. *Isn't that what the playground is for? Or their apartments?*

"Hi, Ms. H.!" says a girl with blonde hair that's shaved on both sides so that she looks like she has a long Mohawk on top. A smaller girl beside her giggles. "Maree's not here."

"Okay," I respond with a smile that I hope doesn't look as vacant as it feels.

Beside me Ruth grunts, leans toward me, and whispers, "You've been giving guitar lessons to Maree, and she's also Tate's daughter."

My hand goes to my chest.

She touches my arm, her eyes soft. "They moved here a few months ago. You know all about it, but you're still adjusting to it."

I let the news settle, give Ruth a grateful smile. "Okay, thank you."

The glass in the doors is frosted white on the edges, tiny sparkling snowflakes frozen into the corners. When I push against the door, it resists, the wind outside slipping between cracks, howling to come inside, and already my nose starts to drip. Ruth and I pull our hats low, wrap our scarves extra tight, and step outside into the bitter cold.

The ice on Ruth's windshield is thin but stubborn. I've built up a sweat trying to scrape it off, but when I finish, Ruth's old Jeep is warmed up enough to drive, and I slide into the passenger seat, my cheeks tingling from the hot air that blasts through the vents. Ruth pats the dashboard. "Old girl still gets hot."

I laugh and shake my head, pull my notebook out of my bag, locate the pages for today, February 20. *Errands in Anchorage, Ruth will drive*—and then a note that lifts my eyebrows. *Tate's daughter, Maree, is turning 10 on February 23. You will bake a cake. Get her a present in Anchorage, something to do with Audrey Hepburn. Ask Ruth for help.*

"So," I begin, "I'd like to get Maree a birthday gift."

"That's nice."

"She loves old movies and Audrey Hepburn," I say. "Maybe we can find like an old movie-poster print somewhere."

"That's a great idea."

We approach the tunnel; Ruth idles the Jeep, waiting for the light to turn. We've made it in time, before the tunnel shifts direction to allow cars from the Bear Valley side to travel through to Whittier. Ruth gives a happy thump on the steering wheel. She loves it when things are well timed. Her hat is pulled to just above her gray eyebrows, mouth set in a firm line as she eyes the camera mounted on the light post. "Unnecessary," she mumbles. "Intrusive."

I try to hide my smile. Ruth's a private person who believes that it's best to leave folks to their own business. For the most part, that's how she's lived her life. Except when it comes to me. Ruth's always made sure I was taken care of, made sure I never felt alone, and thinking about all she's done for me warms me more than the Jeep's unfailing heat. "Do you remember that time you told Mom off?"

"Sure do."

It was a few weeks before Mom abandoned us and a particularly low moment, when Dad had been on the road for a while and Mom hadn't left the apartment in nearly a month. When I came home from school that day, I gagged at the stagnant air in the apartment infused by the sour smell of liquor oozing through her pores. I found her on the couch, passed out and splayed across the faded flower-patterned cushions. She had been beautiful once. But there wasn't much of that left anymore except for her hair, which flowed down her shoulders, shiny and brown and perfect. I stood there staring at her, listening to her ragged breathing, an empty hole gnawing at my chest and my fingernails digging into the soft skin of my palms until I felt pricks of pain run up my arms. I turned and sprinted from the apartment, found myself banging on Ruth's door.

Why can't I be enough for her? I didn't know I was crying, but Ruth's face softened and she reached out a hand, touched my wet cheek. *Can I stay here tonight?*

Of course. She stepped to the side to allow me to pass first, then slipped out into the hallway. *Be right back.* She walked to my apartment, arms stiff by her sides, her chin lifted in a determined way.

No, Ruth, please.

She turned, pinned me with her gray stare. *Some people are worth fighting for, Claire. You'll always be worth it.*

I didn't follow but I heard her well enough. Ruth wasn't a loud person, but when she spoke to my mom, her voice carried a fierce admonition. *Alice? Wake up. Wake up!*

What the hell, Ruth? My mom's voice sounded groggy and slurred.

Even with all this, I still think of you as my friend. And good friends look out for each other, take care of each other. But I can't make you sober, and the only way I know to do right by you is to take care of that beautiful girl of yours. And if she can't make you turn your life around, then nothing here will.

Ruth. Mom's voice was plaintive, sad. *I love her; you know that.*

Then do one good thing for her.

What?

Get sober. And if you can't do that here, then leave.

I'd scuttled inside Ruth's apartment, flopped on the couch, and tried to pretend that I hadn't heard a word.

I look down at my lap, and I'm thankful for the dark tunnel that surrounds the Jeep and hides my face. I think of the words I shouted at Mom outside BTI. *Why can't you stop? I hate you so much!* "You stood up for me, Ruth," I say. "You've always stood up for me." The lights flick past, golden spots that dance across our skin. "Do you think she would have left if you hadn't said anything?" I don't mean to ask, don't want

Ruth to think it's her fault. Except for a tightness around her mouth, she doesn't answer right away, and I wonder whether I've asked this before. My cheeks warm. Maybe I've asked this a hundred times.

Wind whips against the side of the Jeep when we emerge from the tunnel, rocking the vehicle with its force. Ruth grips the steering wheel hard, and her eyes don't leave the road when she speaks. "I don't know. Maybe. Or maybe it was something she'd been planning for a while. Seemed that way to me. I mean, you can't just up and leave without a plan for when you get through the tunnel." Ruth glances quickly in my direction. "She needed help, Claire, and she wasn't getting it here. And to see her now—healthy, sober, and doing everything she can to be your mom again—then I'm glad I said something. Are you?" Her chin trembles the tiniest bit. I'd miss it on anyone else, but on Ruth, who doesn't let her emotions ever get the best of her—well, this is an emotional display that hits me square in the chest.

My answer comes automatically. "I think that leaving was the best thing she could have done for me." Her head jerks in my direction, and it's not hard for me to guess that this isn't an answer I've given before. "You did the right thing, Ruth."

I stare out the windshield, take in the stretch of glacier-blue water that runs alongside the road, breathe in a lightness that spreads across my shoulders.

"And she's doing better. You have that in your notes, right?"

My answer slides out almost on its own. "Yes." I study her profile, suddenly overwhelmed with a need to give her something. "You know I've always thought of you as my mom, too, Ruth."

Ruth blinks fast but her mouth stays in a firm line, her eyes keep their tightness, and she doesn't respond except for a soft *harrumph* that makes me smile.

~

When we return, it's dark out and my phone buzzes with a reminder that makes me adjust the clip in my hair. "I'm having dinner with Tate tonight," I tell Ruth as we carefully pick our way through the ice on our way from her Jeep to the building. "He's coming over to watch a movie."

Ruth hits a slippery patch and starts to slide, but I stabilize my boot on the pavement and grab her arm to keep her upright. "Thanks," she says, regaining her footing. "Have fun. He's a good man, Claire, and he loves you, and you deserve to be loved, do you hear me? Write that down."

My face turns hot. "Okay."

She grunts. "Good."

~

I look through the peephole before I open the door, and seeing him sends a jittery rush through my leg muscles. His hair is pushed up and out of his face, and even through the distortion of the peephole, I can see his clean-shaven face, his luminous green eyes. I touch my hair and lean into the door, breathing through a desire to yank it open and pull him into me.

He knocks and I step back and open the door. "Hi, Tate," I say, trying not to act like the nervous teenage girl I feel like inside. He's the man I remember but also different—older, broader, handsomer, if that's even possible.

He smiles, hands me a bouquet of sunflowers and a note card. "You look beautiful."

I look down to hide the blush spreading up my cheeks and read the card.

I live in Whittier with my daughter, Maree. You teach her guitar and she adores you. I know about the baby and I'm not married anymore. I love you, Claire.

The number four is written on the other side, so large it takes up the entire card. "Four?"

He runs a hand through his hair and I watch, desperately wishing it were my own fingers. "It's our fourth date." Then he leans in and brushes his lips against my cheek. I inhale oak and musk. It makes my legs go weak. "I love you, Claire," he says and his voice is deep, smooth. "And I'm not g . . . g-oing anywhere, so you might as well get used to it."

A giddy happiness explodes into a smile. "You're already dropping the *L* word on the fourth date? Don't you think that's a bit fast?"

He laughs. "I've loved you my whole life, Claire, so no, not t . . . t-oo fast at all."

I touch the wall to remind myself to stand, smile, and hope he can't tell how his words disarm me.

"Can I come in?" Our eyes lock and I'm transported back in time to our first kiss, feel my gaze lower to his lips, and my thoughts quickly turn to the memory of his skin against mine and—

"Claire?"

"Huh?"

He's smiling. "Can I come in?"

"Oh, yes, um, of course." I cringe at the way I stumble over my words like an adolescent girl.

Tate makes himself comfortable on the couch, stretching his long legs out in front of him, hands on the back of his head, grinning. "I love you," he says.

I hold up the card. "That's three times, now. Are you going for a record?"

He chuckles. "I figure if I keep saying it that one day you'll just have to accept it."

My cheek tingles where he kissed me, and I have to sit on my hand to keep from touching it. It makes me wonder whether I feel like this every time I see him.

He's looking at me, a smile playing around the corners of his mouth. "You do."

"What?"

"You're w . . . w-ondering if you act like this every time I come around." My mouth drops open and he holds his hand up. "No, I'm not psychic, it's something you've asked before. And just so you know"—he leans forward, and the way he fills the space between us turns my stomach into knots—"I love it. What man wouldn't w . . . w-ant constant adoration from the woman he loves?" He winks, leans back, and crosses his arms, looking every bit a Cheshire cat.

He hasn't changed. It's the Tate I remember, all right, still with that gleam in his eyes, the one who says, *Let's skip school and smoke a joint.* The one who is trouble and fun and kind and caring all at the same time. The one who held my hand when Mom left. Except he's different now—grown up, I suppose. Just like me. I drop my gaze, see the card in my hand. He's a father and I'm Claire, the woman with no memory. How can I be anything more than that to him?

He reaches out and stops my writing hand. "Cross that out."

"What?"

"All of it. You keep telling yourself that you don't deserve to be happy w . . . w-ith me."

My shoulders drop and my mind spins backward to when I was pregnant, how my body grew in strange ways, the heartburn that snaked up from my gut and into my ears, the constant ache in my lower back and the fear that kept me awake at night. *What kind of mother would I be? How was I going to do it alone?* The waves of loneliness and hormones that spurred thoughts of Tate, happy in his new life with Maria.

My stomach clenches. "What happened to your wife?"

Tate adjusts on the couch, looking suddenly uncomfortable. "She didn't stay around long enough to learn her name. But it w . . . w-as for the best." He works his jaw.

I think of his daughter, her fate so similar to my own, and feel my heart ache for this girl whose face I can't remember.

"Is Maria like my mom, Tate?"

Tate's face hardens. "She's n . . . n-othing like Alice, Claire."

I'm nodding. "I know; Mom's sober now, right?" I tap my pocket. "And she's here now."

A slow smile spreads across his face. "That's right, Claire, she is. We all are."

His words add warmth to the room, and I join him on the couch, sitting close enough that our shoulders touch.

"What are we watching?" I say.

"*Breakfast at Tiffany's.*"

My head cocks back. I know I've seen the movie at some point, because it feels familiar, even if I can't recall the details.

"Do you . . . remember Jeanine?" he says.

My eyebrows meet. I do; she was one of a line of his father's live-in girlfriends. She'd had platinum-blonde hair and had loved bright-red lipstick, but she'd been around for only a few months when we were nine. "She was the one you really liked, right?"

"She w . . . w-as the only one I liked." He lightly hits the side of his head, and his smile diffuses the sad truth of his words. "I think I even called her Mom."

I feel a twinge thinking about him back then—skinny, ill dressed, more alone than me—and I move closer to him on the couch, take his hand in mine, and squeeze.

He squeezes back. "Anyway, she loved this movie and let me watch it with her." He laughs. "We must have watched it a hundred times."

"I don't think I've seen it," I say.

"Good, then it will be like the first time for me too." He pushes play and Audrey Hepburn lights up the screen, timelessly elegant in all black, hair perfectly coiffed in a beautiful beehive.

CHAPTER
TWENTY-EIGHT

Thursday, February 21

The silence around my kitchen table is good, punctured only by the clink of forks and knives on plates. I'm hosting dinner tonight, and it's a perfect evening to be inside with friends and my mom, who joined us because she lives in Whittier now. I am surprised to find that her presence feels natural and easy, and I bask in a welcome sensation that she is back in my life. Outside, a winter storm batters the coastline, and the snow is falling thick and fast.

Sefina sits back, pats her stomach. "I've got to save room for dessert. That was delicious, Claire." She's older than when we first met—I can tell from the shallow lines that spider out from her eyes—but always beautiful, still exuding a contentment that she didn't have when she first got here. A contentment she credits to my dad for making sure her abusive ex-husband left Whittier for good.

Harriet barks a laugh that is laced with a roughness that comes from years of smoking. "Best chicken parm I've had in ages, and that includes the one I had in a trattoria in Manarola when Pete and I backpacked through Italy years ago."

Ruth groans and keeps eating, and I just smile while I scan my talking points. There aren't many on the page, as though I was too busy to prepare, but I don't feel panicked by it, at least not in their company. "Ruth tells me that some of the townspeople aren't too happy with all the proposed development at the harbor."

Mom laughs and I'm struck by how alive she looks—so different from the woman who left. "That towns*person* happens to be Ruth herself. She goes to every single council meeting to voice her opposition."

"Last time she had protest signs," Sefina adds. "It's a wonder Tate's even speaking to you, Ruth."

Ruth raises her eyebrows, sniffs, and eats the last bite of her chicken. "Must be my sparkling personality."

I smile, look at Ruth, who is as sturdy and dependable as a lighthouse in a storm. She's been alone since her husband left, I think, and suddenly, I can't bear the idea of her without someone to care about her for once. "When are you going to share that sparkling personality with someone, Ruth?"

Her mouth hangs open, and the lines in her forehead deepen with surprise.

Harriet points a pasta-laden fork at Ruth. "See, we all know about it, Ruth. Even Claire." She smiles at me. "No offense." Ruth presses her lips together, her cheeks colored pink, and gives Harriet a look.

"You and Hank are terrible at hiding your feelings anyway," Sefina adds.

I gasp. "You're with Hank? What? How long? Why hasn't anyone told me?" They all turn to stare at me, and I can't speak, my body so light I think I'm hovering above the seat, overcome with happiness. "Oh, have you? Sorry." I'm combing through my notebook, but the lines blur together from my smile, and I look up, not needing to read about it, wanting to enjoy the moment with them. "That's so great, Ruth." I was only seven when her husband left, but I can still remember the sadness reflected in her eyes for months afterward.

Ruth's face softens and she gives a relaxed smile that makes her instantly younger. "I have you to thank, Claire."

"Me?"

She nods and I think her eyes are wet. "I've watched you living your life no matter what was in your path, making the best out of every single lemon life gave you. One day I just decided it was time to stop feeling sorry for myself and get on with it." She shrugs. "And Hank was right there, so."

This I do write down, in detail, because I never want to forget the happiness that smooths her skin, illuminates her eyes.

Mom's phone rings. "Hi, Tate. Oh no . . . yes." She visibly softens. "I'm sure she'd love that. Okay, send her up." She presses end, meets my eyes. "Tate is in Anchorage and is going to miss the tunnel. His daughter, Maree, is at a friend's house, but she doesn't want to spend the night there. She asked if she could stay here."

My mind spins. Tate. His daughter. I wait for the information to settle. "With me?"

"Yes, Tate's daughter, Maree, the girl you teach guitar and volunteer with at school."

My shoulders lift with a sudden rush of excitement. "I'd love that . . . oh"—a sudden wave of insecurity hits me—"do you think I can do it?"

A knock at the door, and Sefina rises. "No time like the present to find out, hey, Claire?" She opens the door to a little girl, who immediately hops into the room, shouldering a full backpack, a white teddy bear squeezed between her arms. She's wearing pajamas with little rabbits bouncing from the sleeves to the legs. A silver name tag is affixed to the front pocket of her jammie shirt. *Maree.*

"Hi, everybody. Hi, Ms. Claire."

I get her a chair and sit her right beside me. "Hi, Maree. I'm glad you're here."

Mom brings over a spongy brown cake; rings of pineapple glisten yellow across the top.

"Oh, yum. What's that?" Maree asks.

"A pineapple upside-down cake. Have you had one before?" Mom says.

Maree shakes her head. "I'd remember a cake like that."

"Who wants coffee?" Harriet asks.

While Harriet makes coffee, I am furiously creating a plan for my surprise guest. I tug at the ends of my hair, trying to pretend that I'm not as nervous as I feel inside. I don't want to screw this up.

Sefina leans over, taps my notebook. "Claire?"

I look up; everyone is drinking coffee, and most of their plates are nearly empty. "Oh, sorry. I just wanted to make sure I was organized for tonight."

The little girl chews her last bite and looks at me thoughtfully. "We've spent tons of time together, Ms. Claire, and I'm really good at helping you remember. Dad says it's because I talk so much. So you don't have to worry. I'll help you."

"Thank you, Maree." I am overwhelmed but somehow not surprised. The girl seems comfortable with me, as though we are old friends, and it warms me from the inside out. I set my pen down. "I'd better not miss out on this cake."

Harriet slides a piece onto my plate, and the cake is spongy and sweet, and the baked pineapples pair perfectly with the bursting accompaniment of plump cherries and the earthiness of the coffee.

"Do you know that this is Dad's favorite cake?" I say. Ruth nods; her eyes shift and I see her looking at my note card. I tap it. *Dad died from a heart attack on September 21.* My throat tightens and I add another hash mark to the card. "Mom made it for his birthday every year." I look at Maree. "One year he took the pineapples and stuck them to his face like glasses." Maree giggles. "And I laughed so hard that milk came out my nose."

Mom laughs now and it's the same beautiful, melodic sound that I never got tired of hearing. *Oh, Vance,* she'd said to my dad and gently took off the pineapples; then she'd cupped the side of his face. They'd locked eyes, smiling at each other in a way that made my seven-year-old heart burst like the cherries in the cake. Then he'd pulled her into his lap and kissed her, and I remember scrunching my nose. *Ewww!* What I really thought was that they were like a knight and a princess, and our lives were a perfect fairy tale.

Sefina pipes up. "Claire, did you hear about the people who got caught camping inside the Buckner last week?"

I shake my head, not surprised because the Buckner attracts everything from ghost hunters to adventure seekers to people fascinated with history and abandoned buildings.

Harriet's hoarse laugh settles over us like a rough blanket. "Started a fire and everything, like they were outside under the stars. Ridiculous!"

"They were filming a video," Sefina says. "Young guy was skiing down the stairwell and crashed. Broke his hand, I think." Sefina's eyes are big, bright. News in Whittier is limited, so I'm sure this has made the circuit a number of times, perhaps with a few refinements along the way.

"That's right," Ruth adds. "He said he saw a ghost."

Maree's eyes get wide. They are a beautiful deep blue, ringed in green. "Ghosts?"

Harriet laughs so hard she wheezes. "No, Maree, not ghosts. Just a bunch of kids who think skiing inside an old building is adventure. Hah! I'll give them real adventure. Try summiting Annapurna or living for a year with Buddhists who've taken a vow of silence."

Ruth groans and Harriet grins—amused, I know, to have irritated Ruth with her larger-than-life and very likely made-up adventures. This is a game the two of them have played for years.

We finish dessert and everyone cleans up together in a companionable silence, even Maree, who scrapes plates into the trash bin.

Afterward, we play Pictionary, and Maree quickly teams up with Ruth and Sefina against Harriet, Mom, and me.

"No offense," Maree says to me. "But I think this team might remember more stuff."

I can't help but laugh. I enjoy a little bit of smack talk. "None taken, kiddo. But you should know, I haven't forgotten my competitiveness." I wink. "I still like to win."

When the game wraps up, I tell Maree to brush her teeth while Mom helps me make up a bed on the couch. Mom's the last to leave. She hesitates at the door, and we both look at Maree, who is curled up on the couch, her feet tucked under her, a book spread open on her lap. Her eyes droop as she reads. Outside, the snow obliterates any light from the harbor, making it appear as though BTI is a ship out at sea. The windows creak from the wind.

"I'm nervous," I say. "What if I forget? What if it scares her?"

Mom's face softens. "You'll be fine. Besides, she looks pretty comfortable here. But if you need anything, you know where to find Ruth, and I'm just two floors away."

I smile and nod, comforted to know she's near, surprised I feel this way. When she's gone, I sit on the couch across from the girl and notice that she's wearing cat-eye glasses that are taped in the middle. "What happened to your glasses?" I ask.

The girl looks up from her book, crosses her eyes to see the glasses on her face. "Oh, well, you broke them."

"I did?"

"Yeah. Hey, I added more pictures to the photo album I made for you. Want to look through it later?"

"Sure, but I'm sorry I broke your glasses."

"Yeah, it happened a long time ago, and you were just upset because of your dad and everything. Here." She hands me a note card with her handwriting. *I'm Maree and your best friend Tate is my dad and your mom lives here and your dad died. Im sorry.*

I swallow hard, notice that there are note cards like this all over my apartment, on the refrigerator, scattered across the kitchen counter, on the end tables, taped to the front door.

"Ms. Claire?"

"Mhmmm?"

"So you know how we are the same 'cause both our moms left us?"

I did not know that. "Okay," I say instead.

"Well, my mom is still gone, but yours is here." She points to a card, this one with my handwriting, that tells me her mother is not in the picture.

"Okay." I wonder where she's going with this, worry it might be a conversation that's too big for me.

"Well, if my mom lived here, I'd be hugging her all the time. But you never hug your mom."

"Is that so?" So the girl knows my mom?

"Yeah." She scoots over, settles herself so close to me that our arms touch, lays her head against my shoulder and yawns. "And she's a really nice lady too. She makes me think of you, even."

A memory of a night similar to this one rises up. It was a couple of days before my thirteenth birthday, and I was sick with a fever, huddled under blankets on the couch while snow hit the window, fluffy and wet. Mom had made me chicken noodle soup and then afterward sat next to me and pulled my head into her lap, ran her fingers absently through my hair. I lay very still, scared that if I moved she'd remember that her drink was on the counter just out of reach. She was soberish, I recall, and her attention was a soft, golden light that surrounded me like a spotlight, leaving all the bad in the shadows beyond the light. She was beautiful again, even if her stomach poofed over the tops of her jeans now and even if her skin was mottled and pale. In that moment I felt closer to her than I had for a while, pierced with longing and a childish belief that she could stop drinking and be my mom again. Foolishly, I thought I could be honest, speak what was in my heart.

You're more sick than I am, Mom.

My words erased her smile, dimmed her eyes, and plunged the space around us into a cold blue light. Her hand had trembled, shaking the mug of tea violently until she set it on the table.

Why can't you get better? I spoke in a stream that ended with a stifled sob. And when she looked at me, her face was red, as though my words had been a slap.

I don't know, honey. I've tried—

I scuttled away from her and to the other side of the couch, knees drawn to my chest. *Tried?* My head hurt, but I was shouting anyway, a heated eruption of doubt and a fear that she was slipping away. *All you've done is give up!* I liked how my words seemed to make her shrink, grow so small that I could pretend I didn't care anymore. She hadn't fought back or left the room, just sat on the couch with her hands limp in her lap, absorbing my anger like a punching bag until I was empty and crying. She left two days later.

"Ms. Claire?"

The girl is looking at me, and I take in a ragged breath.

"I'm Maree," she says softly. "And I'm spending the night 'cause my dad, who's your best friend, Tate, missed the tunnel, and I didn't want to stay with Leonora 'cause I'm mad at her."

"Who's Leonora?"

"My best friend." She bites on a nail, looks up at me. "Do you want to know why I didn't want to spend the night with Leonora?"

I nod.

"It's 'cause she says she hates my stories about Uki. She says they're fake 'cause nobody has a mom like that, and also, didn't I know that Santa was a big fake too."

I can see tears brimming in her eyes; she wipes them away with the back of her hand, but her bottom lip trembles. Instinctively, I put an arm around her. Her hair smells like soap. She snuggles closer against my side, and her nearness touches on a yearning I try to keep stuffed inside.

She continues but this time in a whisper, "I know Uki's not real. Don't tell Dad, okay? But I know my real mom wouldn't leave me if she didn't have to." Her hands are squeezed into small fists and her body tenses. "She'll come home as soon as she can." Tears are running down her face now. "But I didn't know about Santa!"

I squeeze her gently and we sit like that for a while, listening to the storm rage outside, warm and cozy in here. *Maree is spending the night,* I repeat to myself because I don't want to move; I want to sit here like a normal person and comfort her. So I lean my head back and keep the mantra on a repeating loop. *Maree is spending the night. Maree is spending the night.*

Her breathing deepens, so I slide out and cover her with a blanket. Her eyes flutter open. "How will you remember me in the morning?" she asks.

"I'll write it on my whiteboard so I'll see it when I wake up first thing. Is that okay?"

She nods, points to a photo album on the coffee table. "And keep my pictures by your bed so you recognize me." She yawns with a wide-open mouth, eyes squeezed shut. "Do you want to come with me to make doughnuts? It's tomorrow morning before school."

I write it down and add it to my phone. "I'd love that."

"Good night, Ms. Claire." She smiles at me above a wool blanket she's pulled to her shoulders. It's a sweet smile that deepens a dimple in her chin. I reach down, tuck a piece of hair behind her ear, touch the dimple lightly.

"Good night, Maree. I'm glad you're here."

CHAPTER TWENTY-NINE

Friday, February 22

The next morning, I find a pan of cinnamon rolls outside my door along with a note. *This was our favorite weekend treat. Do you remember how it filled our entire apartment with the smell of sugar and dough? Dad said it smelled like family. I love you, Claire, and I hope this batch tastes as good as you remember. Love, Mom (I live in Whittier and I'm sober.)*

I bring the rolls inside, stick her note to the refrigerator, which is covered with note cards similar to this one, from her and—my face warms—Tate Dunn. I do remember her cinnamon rolls. The scent would pull me out of bed on the coldest and darkest of mornings, and we'd sit around the table, my parents with mugs of strong black coffee, me with a glass of milk.

Maree and I eat the rolls, which are as good as I remember, and she entertains me with her near-constant stream of chatter. I love it. She's in the bathroom taking a shower when there's a knock at my door.

I open it to a handsome dark-haired and older version of Tate. My knees go weak, and I touch my hair, wondering whether I've bothered to pull a comb through it yet.

He's smiling. "How did Maree do?"

I tilt my head, try to come up with an answer.

"My daughter, Maree, stayed the n . . . n-ight with you because I missed the tunnel. Oh, here." He hands me a note card, which I read, feeling the blush spread up my cheeks, before I attach it to the fridge with all the others.

But my apartment is empty, and just as a panic starts to spread, I hear a whooshing sound from the bathroom pipes and smile. "She's in the shower."

"Perfect." Tate takes my hand, pulls me toward him, and the contact startles me even if it feels familiar and comfortable. He's everything I remember, except different and more, his chest hard and solid, arms firm around me, and then he kisses me like it's the most natural thing in the world, pressing his lips into mine, hands spanning my hips.

I kiss him back, delight in the leathery smell of his aftershave, the warmth of his body. I feel normal. I feel like the Claire I remember, unbounded by lost minutes and scattered thoughts. I feel—

"Ho-ly cow! What are you doing to her, Daddy!"

Tate groans and pulls away from me but doesn't seem embarrassed or upset. "Hi, peanut." He crosses the room, kisses the top of her head.

"Daddy," she says with a stomp of her foot.

"I was kissing her," he says with a chuckle.

"Well, did she want you to do that? 'Cause it looked messy."

I start laughing, first behind my hand because I don't want the girl to think I'm laughing at her, but when Tate starts, I can't help it, and soon all three of us are laughing, and the sound mingles with the lingering smell of cinnamon rolls.

My phone buzzes. **Doughnut day with Maree at school.** I hold it up. "Should we go?"

"Yes!"

The three of us take the elevator to the basement, then use the tunnel to get to the school. Inside, a surprising number of kids and adults are spread out in the small cafeteria. Maree sprints to the kitchen, throws her arms around a woman who is surrounded by mixing bowls, wooden spoons, and measuring cups. My breath catches because the woman is my mother, and she couldn't look more in her element than at this moment. She wears a black-and-white-printed apron, and her dark hair is pulled into a loose bun. Kids flank her on either side, elbows on the counter, eyes trained on the dough she spins in a mixer. I'm rooted to the floor when she looks up, catches me staring at her, and a smile lights up her face, illuminates her eyes. I smile back.

"Today we're making glazed doughnuts," she tells the kids.

A tiny girl with a pink headband in her silky black hair says, "Can I put chocolate on mine?"

"Yes, of course, but first we have to make them. Who wants to help?"

Every kid raises a hand. While they work, Tate snaps pictures and records short videos with his phone. He promises to put everything in a memory catalog he's making for me.

While the kids are eating the finished doughnuts, Mom comes over, wiping her hands on her apron. "Hi, Claire. This is a surprise."

Maree's chest puffs up. "I invited her."

"That was a great idea, Maree. Thank you."

A woman approaches with two little kids, no more than five and seven, trailing her, doughnuts in hand. The woman's hair is greasy, pulled back into a lank ponytail, and I notice her eyes—red rimmed, tired—a small tremble in her hands. I push down a lump; my eyes go to the kids.

"They loved it. Thanks for inviting us, Alice."

My mother touches her shoulder. "Anytime, Jory. Call me if you need me, okay?"

The woman nods and walks away, eyes lowered, her back bent like she's already given up on the day.

"Who is that?" I say.

Mom leans close, lowers her voice. "Jory is a recovering alcoholic." Mom seems to reconsider her words. "She's trying, at least. It's been hard for her." Her voice is gentle, soft, full of empathy.

It loosens something in my chest. "You're helping her?"

"I'm trying."

I hug her, clumsy, holding on like she might melt away, and beside me I hear the click of a camera taking pictures. Then I release her, and I sit down to write and write and write across a fresh page of my notebook because this I want to get down and make sure that I never, ever forget. *Mom is sober. Mom is sober.*

CHAPTER THIRTY

Saturday, February 23

Today is Maree's tenth birthday. I know this because I've written it down so many times I think I might actually remember it. Hah. That's a laugh. A buzz from my phone. Birthday party for Maree at 3 p.m. Hang decorations. Today is her 10th birthday. You have cake and a present.

Outside, a deep-blue sky shimmers above a fresh layer of snow blanketing the entire town. I love walking in powdery new snow; maybe I'll go for a walk later.

Someone knocks on my door. My mother. At first I can't move, but she smiles at me and she looks normal and sober and suddenly I'm smiling back, happy to see her. She hands me a note card, which I read before putting it on the refrigerator with several others.

She sets a covered cake pan on the counter. "Ruth said you planned on baking a cake for Maree but that you may have forgotten to do that."

I chew my bottom lip, scan the kitchen, don't see anything. She uncovers the cake. Chocolate frosting with flowers and candy letters that spell out HAPPY 10TH BIRTHDAY, MAREE!

My chest tightens. "Thanks, Mom." A buzz from my phone. Decorate for Maree's birthday. On my desk are decorations, still packaged, that I obviously intend to hang.

"Can I help?" Mom asks.

There isn't much, just a few metallic streamers and a banner and a few balloons. "Here." She hands me one end of the banner, and together we hang it across the kitchen cabinets. We work in a comfortable silence. When we're done, we both step back to survey our work. Mom touches my arm and I lean into her. "That looks nice, Claire. She'll love it."

"Do you want to stay?" I ask.

Mom tilts her head, looks surprised. "Yes, but not today. I'd love to come over another time, if you'd like?"

"How about tomorrow?"

Her eyes are bright and she nods, lips pressed together. "Yes, yes, that sounds lovely."

My phone buzzes—Birthday party for Maree at 3 p.m. Today is her 10th birthday—just as the door opens and a little girl walks in. Mom winks at me, then touches the little girl on the head, says, "Happy birthday, Maree," and leaves.

"Bye, Ms. Alice." Maree stands awkwardly in the middle of the living room, arms wrapped around her stomach like she feels sick.

"Sweetheart, are you okay?" I say.

"Yeah." Her eyes trail around the apartment, seem to take in the shiny streamers fluttering from the ceiling. "Did you do this all for me?"

"Of course."

"That's so nice." I think her voice breaks, but she's turned away from me to stand by the table, stares at the cake and presents. I pick up a wrapped gift, hand it to her. "Happy birthday, Maree. I hope you like it." She makes no move to open it. "Go ahead, open it."

She does, stops halfway, looks up at me. "Do you remember what it is?"

I shake my head. "Nope, but I'm excited to see what I got."

This gets a small smile out of her, and she tears off the rest of the paper, lifts out a pair of cat-eye glasses that don't look like the prescription kind, more like dress-up. I clap my hands, delighted to see that she wears a similar pair that have been broken at some point and taped back together. "To replace your broken ones!" I say. "And it looks like the new ones might fit your face better. They're a bit smaller."

"Oh, that's so nice, Ms. Claire." Her voice cracks on my name. "You're so nice. I love them. Thank you." She throws her arms around my neck and hugs me tight.

"You're welcome," I say into her hair.

She takes off the old ones, but when she slides the new pair on, I pull back, hand to chest. Tears spill down her face. Her bottom lip trembles. A deep sadness comes off her in waves, and I can't connect the dots, can't figure out why, and my mind scrambles to find an answer.

"What's wrong, Maree?"

"I asked Leonora to help me find my mom." Her voice is raw, face wet. "So Leonora searched on the internet 'cause she's always on the computer and knows how to do stuff."

I'm writing and writing, wanting to listen but needing to make sure I get it down because I have to tell someone; I can't be the only one with this information.

She pulls the sleeve of her shirt over her hand, wipes it across her eyes. "And she's not a hero. She's in jail and she does bad things for drugs, and she could call me 'cause I could love her even if she is bad, but she never, ever has."

I want to hold her, rock her, something to ease her pain, but I can't stop writing, because this little girl needs someone better than me to help her.

"Maree," I say. "I'm going to call Ruth, and we are going to get some help, okay?"

Her nostrils flare and she stares at the notebook in my hands; then she grabs it from me, and I'm so surprised that I don't react quickly enough when she runs to the door.

"I'm sorry, Ms. Claire. I'm so sorry. But I don't want to remember this either. I want to forget like you."

Then she is gone, and I am standing in my apartment staring at a HAPPY BIRTHDAY banner above my sink and an uneaten cake on the counter and wrapping paper on the floor. My phone is in my hand with a reminder on the screen. **Birthday party for Maree at 3 p.m.** I sit down, breathe in, breathe out, heart racing, and try to let the facts accumulate.

The present is open, which means that Maree was here. The cake has not been eaten, but maybe she didn't feel like cake. My hands clench into fists, run up and down my thighs, anxious. I feel very anxious. Why? I sit down at my desk, check the calendar.

Today is Saturday, February 23, and this morning I went to the gardens and then this afternoon I had a birthday party for Maree. I check the time. 3:30. I guess it was a short party. I sit back in the chair, my hands shaking from an uneasiness that I can't explain, and look out the window to a clear blue sky. Maybe a walk will help me work out this excess energy. I grab my coat and gloves and head outside.

CHAPTER THIRTY-ONE

It's colder than it looks outside. As soon as the icy air hits my skin, I pull up my gaiter and breathe in and out, waiting as my body adjusts to the drop in temperature. A feeling clings to my skin, spreads through my body in pins and pricks. I am scared or sad or nervous or all three, and I don't understand why. I walk at a slow, lumbering pace, my legs heavy, shoulders curved like I'm carrying a backpack full of rocks.

I take my regular path, down Glacier Avenue through the pedestrian tunnel toward the harbor and back again. The streets are empty, businesses shuttered for the winter. I stop at the boardwalk. It's quiet, the harbor deserted at this time of year, only the boats bobbing up and down in the waves. I inhale fish and salt, exhale a sob.

What is wrong with me? A strong desire turns me around. I need to see Ruth or Sefina or . . . someone because I don't want to be alone right now. I reach for my notebook, but my bag is empty and it makes my heart beat faster. Why don't I have it? I hurry back through the tunnel and down Whittier Street toward the Buckner Building, but today I don't want to stand in front of that sad place. So I cut through the parking lot by the city offices and head back to BTI. Just as I'm rounding the corner, something catches my eye, and when I turn I see the backside hump of a bear running past the Buckner and into the trees. My eyebrows meet. Food must be scarce if the bears are coming out to eat. Then I see something that stops me. A small figure—a little kid, I'm pretty sure—disappearing behind the building. I hurry up the road. Kids should not go inside that building. It's dangerous. I should know. Especially now, when the mountain obscures whatever light is offered by the winter sun.

I set a reminder on my phone. Kid in Buckner Building. Tell them to come out. I notice that my battery is low and hurry up the hill, where I stand at the base of the building.

I look up. The building has been dying for decades: rotted flooring, ceilings splayed open like festering wounds. It looms above me, all hollow eyes and mold growing in black strands down the sides. "Hello!" I call.

No answer. My phone buzzes. Kid in Buckner Building. Tell them to come out. "Hey, kid, you can't be in there. It's dangerous!" No answer, and I feel a twisting in my gut.

The windows give away nothing but an opaque blackness that hides whatever is inside, and it occurs to me that I have no flashlight except for the one on my phone. My leg muscles tingle, and I feel the emptiness of my hands, my entire being bound to the fickleness of time and memory. From deep inside I hear what I think is a scream, and my heart races. The Buckner was once called the *city under one roof*. A city. And a kid is somewhere inside amid half-rotted floors and mold and God knows what else.

Another cry, I'm sure of it. My body jerks ahead of my brain, and before I know it I'm climbing through a side door by the freight elevator, where the fence pulls away enough to slip through. Once inside I'm met with an iron coldness that spreads across my back, coats my tongue. Panic races a loop inside me. What am I thinking? I send Ruth a quick text. Followed kid into Buckner. Might need help.

Another buzz from my phone. **Kid in Buckner Building.** I try to slow my racing pulse. My phone will remind me what I'm doing. I'll be okay. I won't forget.

Another cry, high-pitched and terrified, comes from somewhere in this massive building, and I lurch forward, repeating a mantra, *Kid inside, kid inside, kid inside.*

The flashlight on my phone spreads a cone of light that catches on a concrete wall, drags across the walls behind it. In the dark, the building is otherworldly, and the near-constant drip of water echoing inside gives the sensation that it breathes.

Cans and other trash crunch underfoot, and my breath is smoke in the cold air. I move deeper into the building. *Kid inside, kid inside, kid inside.* Snow piles up against the windows of a room to my right, leaving the middle empty and vast, littered with insulation, rusted pieces of metal, and large chunks of drywall. *Kid inside, kid inside, kid inside.* Where am I? *I'm in the Buckner, Buckner, Buckner.* I swing my phone flashlight around, and a chill runs down my spine. I think of the night Mom left. How did I ever spend a night alone in here? And what am I doing in here now?

The phone reminds me. **Kid in Buckner Building.** The battery is on red. My stomach drops. With a sense of urgency, I swing the light, picking my way through what looks to be one of the long hallways. "Hello!" The idea that my phone could die and I'll be left in here without a flashlight, without a way to remind myself, makes the hair on my arms stand on end. *Kid inside, kid inside, kid inside.* I clench my hands into fists and keep moving.

"Hello?" I call, quietly, as though I'm afraid to wake something up that I shouldn't. My heart beats wildly. "Do you need help?" The building takes my voice, turns it thin. I move down the hallway. "It's dangerous in here," I say, stronger this time. *Kid inside, kid inside, kid inside.*

From within the bowels of the building, I hear a voice echoing down the long hallway. The building is huge, and panic swells, sets my pulse racing. Did I call someone else to help me search for her? I don't have time to look for the answer, and I need to stay focused. *Kid inside, kid inside, kid inside.* I call out, "Hello? Where are you?" Silence.

Now I'm in a hallway that extends in long, dark fingers on either side of me. I keep walking, tripping over blocks of wood, metal, and beer cans that hide in the shadows. The walls are littered in graffiti, some funny and cute, others dark and malevolent. *Kid inside, kid inside, kid inside.* When I get to a stairwell, it is covered in snow that piles high, making the steps disappear under a giant white slide. Except for the beam of my flashlight, the blue darkness coils around me, leaves me disoriented, like the space inside this building is infinite and I am small and finite. I keep going, armed with my own voice and the reminder that I say out loud. I'm drawn forward like a magnet.

I try to climb up the stairs, but my feet keep sliding on the snow. I have no traction. *Kid inside, kid inside, kid inside.* The futility of trying to find a kid in all this darkness curls around me, and I have to breathe deep to press down a rising panic. The kid could be anywhere. I swing my flashlight around, see nothing. "Hello!" I call and am met with a soft whimper. "Hello!"

With much difficulty, I climb the snow-covered stairs, past a gaping hole to my right. I swing my flashlight inside. An elevator shaft. Direct the beam down, holding my breath. Empty. Keep climbing to the next level, where I stand at the end of another long hallway, dark rooms on either side, the floor wet, filled with jagged pieces of building material, moss, and mold.

And then, from somewhere down the massive second-floor hall, I hear a girl. She's crying and the sound splinters my heart. I keep walking; blood pounds against my skull, and combined with my repeated mantra, my head aches with effort. I ignore the pain and keep moving because I will not leave this building without her.

Inside a cavernous room, the flashlight sweeps across hanging wires, splintered floors. "Hello?" I call.

"Ms. Claire?"

Relief that she knows me. "Yes, that's me."

"It's me, Maree." She sobs with what I'm sure is relief. "I'm so scared, Ms. Claire. I dropped my phone, and it cracked and broke, and I can't see anything." Her words end in quiet sniffles.

I walk toward the voice, careful to step around holes in the floor, until I find her huddled in a small ball with her back to the wall, shivering in the darkness. "What in the world are you doing here?"

Her face is small, heart shaped, and wet from her tears, her nose running. "I-I'm sorry I stole your memory. I'm so sorry." She cries so hard she's gulping.

My chest tightens and I bend my legs, sit beside her on the wet and cold floor, shine the flashlight up so we have light between us. She's shivering so hard I think I hear her teeth chatter, so I slide my hat over her head, put an arm around her.

She looks up at me. "Oh," she chatters. "I'm M-M-Maree and you're Ms. Claire, and you teach me guitar lessons and give me birthday presents, and I stole your memory." More gulping.

I don't try to guess at what she's talking about because all I know is that we need to leave. "Sh-sh-sh. It's okay. We can talk later because we need to get out of here. It's dark and very cold, and it's not a place for little kids. Okay?"

Without warning, the flashlight on my phone is extinguished, plunging the two of us into complete darkness. I flinch, my ears loud with the thump of my heart. It's so dark I can't see in front of my nose. In the blackness, my fear is a slithering thing that coils around my head, squeezes my thoughts until they make no sense. Where am I?

Someone grabs my hands, squeezes so tight I think the bones might break. "Ms. Claire?" A little girl's voice, and hearing it calms me. I am a teacher and I can be strong for this girl.

"Yes?" In the dark my mind wanders.

"Can we leave now?"

"Well, no, I don't think that's a good idea." I smell damp earth.

A little body nestles close to me. "We're in the Buckner Building, and your light went out, and I'm Maree and you're Ms. Claire."

"Thank you, Maree," I say, and my voice trembles. "Listen, Maree, it's very hard for me to remember why I'm here. Can you keep talking to me?"

I feel her lay her head against my shoulder. "You want me to be your memory?" she whispers.

"Exactly."

"I'm good at that."

"Perfect."

"Can you tell me a story, Ms. Claire? I'm scared and I keep seeing things in the dark, so I just want to close my eyes, but I promise I won't fall asleep, okay?"

I try to get a deep breath to calm the tremors that rack my body. "Sure, I'll try." I search my mind, and the one that comes easy to me is about Dad. So I tell her about the bear that broke into BTI when I was seven.

She laughs. "I love that story," she says. "Can you tell me ones about you and my dad? He's Tate, and you're best friends."

I am dizzy trying to connect the dots, but in the dark, I could be twelve or twenty-five or fifty. I am unbounded by time, floating, and what she says doesn't make sense, but my childhood memories come to me in the black night—rich in detail, vivid in color—and I latch on to them and talk. I tell her about Tate's dad. How he was a mean giant and that I had to throw a rock at his head to stop him from being cruel to a little boy. I told her about the bully I glued to his seat. She laughs so hard I feel her body shake in my arms, and in the darkness I remember that I am a teacher. "Wait, how old are you?"

"Ten."

"Don't throw rocks and don't glue people to their seats; get an adult to help you instead." Giving advice, this little bit of normalcy in the terrifying blackness that surrounds us, helps me to breathe a little easier. "Okay?"

"Okay." Her voice is small and I hug her close, grateful for the contact. "You sound like Uki," she says.

"Who?"

"Uki. My dad tells me stories about her at bedtime." I hear her sniffle. "I thought he was telling me stories about my mom, but I was wrong because Uki is brave and strong, and the boy loves her. She sounds like you."

A man's voice booms from somewhere below us, shouting, calling, tinged with a desperation that makes his words stutter and stop. And my pulse races because I know that voice. "C . . . C-laire! Are you . . . h . . . h-ere? M . . . M-aree!"

"It's Daddy!" She squeezes my hand. "It's Tate, your best friend! He lives in Whittier, and he kissed you once. I saw him!"

I gasp but my chattering teeth make it a vibrating sound.

He calls again. "Maree! Claire!"

"Here, we're here!" I scream until my voice is hoarse. My head pounds, chest hurts, but despite the darkness and the hollow feeling that I've forgotten everything important and the girl in the dark who feels like she's always belonged with me, I smile. Tate, the skinny boy with the thick black hair and the glacier-green eyes who held my hand when my mom left, is here.

CHAPTER THIRTY-TWO

We stand in the lobby of BTI, the girl, Tate, and me. She holds on to his legs, sobbing, and he rubs circles on her back. Then she turns from him to me, and when I kneel down, she wraps her arms around me and squeezes. "Thank you," she whispers.

I touch the back of her head, run my hand down her length of soft brown hair, and feel my heart expand when I breathe in, because the moment feels exactly as it should.

The elevator doors slide open to Ruth and—my eyes widen—Mom. I choke back a sob, try to understand why the sight of her eases the tension that needles my back.

Tate clears his throat. "I need to take Maree home." His eyes darken. "Ruth, Alice, I'll be up as soon as I can."

When he and the girl leave, I feel their absence in the tears that well in my eyes. "Mom?" I say. "Ruth?" My muscles shake, threaten to take me down like a tree. They lead me upstairs to my apartment and sit on either side of me on the couch.

"What happened?" I ask, my teeth still chattering from a cold that lingers beneath my skin. I must have been outside. From the kitchen comes the whistle of a kettle. Ruth rises from the couch, comes back with a mug of tea. I sip it, grateful for the warmth it spreads.

"Maree is Tate's daughter," Ruth says. "They both live in Whittier, and you are very close to them."

The information is new, yet I don't feel totally surprised by it. "Okay."

"Maree thought she found out some upsetting information about her mother and ran away."

My brain connects two dots. "Maria?"

Mom squeezes my hand. "Yes, but Maree doesn't know, and she got it all wrong."

Ruth takes the mug of tea from my hands and sets it on the table. It feels like a protective gesture, and I can't meet her eyes because I think they are about to tell me something, and I'm suddenly nervous. What doesn't the girl know? I wrap my arms across myself. "What did she get wrong?"

Ruth and Mom exchange looks, and then Ruth inhales. "Maree is your daughter, Claire."

At first I don't respond, can't respond, because my face has hardened to stone, and what she says doesn't connect any dots that make sense. I ball my hands into fists. "Why would you say that, Ruth?" My voice is high-pitched, strained. "My baby died. You know that."

Mom touches my arm, squeezes gently. "No, honey. Your baby lived, and she's Maree."

I yank my arm away, push to my feet, and nearly stumble into Ruth. They're wrong because this is something I *know*, something I *remember*, and for some reason they are lying. When I woke up that night, I couldn't see from the fireworks of pain exploding across my head, and then Dad was there and we were in his truck and then . . . nothing. But she died. I *know* it because if she had lived, how could I have ever forgotten her? I cover my face with my hands. Why would they lie about this? It's so cruel. Even now I feel the way her tiny foot pushed against me, straining my skin until I could see the faint shape of a heel sliding underneath. It was otherworldly. It was magical. I pound my palm flat against my head, as if I can shake memories out like coins from a piggy bank. It's useless. I never got to see her face, hear her cries, cradle her tiny body, or smell her fresh, new skin. I never got the chance to say goodbye. And if I did, those memories drifted away from me and into the vast and empty ocean of all the things I lose, and the only answer that makes sense is that she's gone.

"My baby died," I say through my teeth.

Mom lowers her eyes, hands clasped in her lap, face twisted at my pain, I think, and suddenly an angry swell rises up from my toes, and I am reminded of the woman she was—broken, weak, and able to walk away from her own daughter. Something I would never do if I had the choice. I can't look at her anymore.

Ruth stands, moves into my line of sight. "Listen to me, Claire. Mirabelle lived. That's Maree's full name." Her eyes are wet and I hear a tremble in her voice. It stops me. Ruth is as strong as they come, and I don't think I've ever seen her cry. "We thought we were going to lose you both, but once they delivered her, your seizure stopped. That little girl is a fighter just like you. She lived, Claire. Mirabelle lived."

The room spins and I want to lie down, but I can't, not yet, because Ruth is lying, and I need her to stop. "How can that be?" I whisper. "What kind of mother forgets her own child?" I scratch at my arms, the person I truly am exposed, vulnerable, pathetic.

"You couldn't remember anything after your seizure, sweetheart," Ruth says. "You assumed that you had lost her."

I stand in the middle of the room with my hands held out in front of me as though I can swat her words away. My mother sits on the couch, face streaked in tears, watching but letting Ruth talk.

"That first year was so terrible for you. We tried to help you remember; we thought that with time, you'd grow used to seeing her. But it only upset you to realize that you couldn't remember her. Then you started to leave yourself notes that Mirabelle deserved better, that she belonged with a mother who could love her, not one who couldn't remember she existed, that she belonged with her father. Eventually, you refused to see her anymore, and that's when you called Tate."

Mom looks at me, her eyes reflecting a mixture of sadness and longing. I ask even though I already know, but I think I want to hurt her. "Where were you then, Mom?"

She meets my stare and doesn't look away. "That was before I was sober, Claire. I'm so sorry, honey."

My legs betray me and I grab for a chair, sit down. My skin is a weighted blanket, and a deep ache settles behind my eyes, around my temples, shoots down my neck and back. I can't think, my thoughts muddled with images of a baby I never knew existed, of what I have lost, and my hands are fists, pounding into my thighs.

Ruth approaches, hands out like she wants to stop me. "Claire—"

"Please leave," I say.

"But Claire—" Ruth says.

"Leave!" My vision dims and I move slowly to my bed, where I see my journal on the pillow. I grab a sticky note, press it onto the cover, and scribble the only words that easily come to mind before I slip under the covers fully clothed, and close my eyes. *Mirabelle lived. Mirabelle lived.* The truth blooms inside me, blotting out the person I thought I was, replacing it with the one I am. The mother who walked away. I try to hold on to everything because I want to remember even if it hurts so bad I can't breathe. I don't want to forget, except I do, bit by bit, until I'm breathing normally and sleep takes the rest.

~

I wake up and reach for my journal, but it's not there. My face is dry and hot, eyes gritty, and my whole body hurts. I sit up, panicked, searching the room for something to help me understand the sob lodged in my chest. My journal is half-open on the floor and I breathe out, relieved. It must have fallen during the night. I pick it up, hoping it will explain this prickling sensation that makes my hands shake when I press them into my stomach. Already I see a line in my journal that resonates somewhere deep inside me. *You lost the baby.* I close the journal, squeeze my eyes shut. I remember this. Don't I? In the tunnel, when the headache was so bad I couldn't see, even then I knew I was going to lose her. When I open my eyes, I see a sticky note on the cover of the journal. My heart beats painfully because the writing is mine but jagged, with lines pressed deep into the paper. And the words make my eyes blur. *Mirabelle lived. Mirabelle lived.* The journal falls from my hands, and when I look up, I see my whiteboard is filled with my mother's handwriting.

> *Your father (who died last year) wanted us to all be together. He was tired of waiting for you to be ready. I live here and I'm sober. Tate and his daughter, Maree, live here too. Maree is your daughter, Claire. She is Mirabelle and Mirabelle lived but you couldn't remember.*

It's so much information at once. My father is dead. I pull my knees up to my chest, wrap my arms around my shins, and rock, trying to connect the dots, resisting a strong desire to pull the covers over my head and go back to sleep. My mother is sober. Tate lives here. And my daughter, Tate's daughter, Mirabelle, is alive. A fluttering deep inside me gives rise to a surge of hope. My heart aches for it to be true at the same time that I want to pick up the eraser and wipe the board clean. She lived?

> *There's a photo album beside your bed. Look at the pictures and come out when you're ready. You can do this, Claire. You're stronger than you know. Love, Mom*

The first picture is one of me, facing to the side, rounded belly protruding away from my body. In my father's handwriting, the caption reads, *Claire, 8 months pregnant.* My eyes prick with tears because this I do remember, and my hand involuntarily rubs what is now flat and empty. There's another picture of me and Sefina, standing on what I think is Shotgun Cove Road in snowshoes, my belly straining against my winter coat, and a caption: *Claire, still on her snowshoes, 9 months pregnant.* I almost smile. It was a cold day, and I was so out of breath and heavy with the baby that I couldn't go very fast, and Sefina made a big deal about beating me to the end of the trail. There are a few more pictures of me pregnant, and then come ones that are from after, ones of me with a baby. I can't feel my hands and my face is frozen, but I keep flipping the pages and my heart presses against my ribs. *Claire and Mirabelle at the hospital.* I lay on a hospital bed, tiny baby resting in a bassinet beside the bed, her brown hair clinging to her tiny head in gentle curls, thumb stuck securely in her small mouth. A baby, Mirabelle. It's not possible. I glance at my journal, flip to a page worn thin from time and use. I had a seizure. My baby died. I press my arms into my stomach, try to ignore the way I hurt from wanting it to all be true.

Tears slip from my eyes, burn my cheeks. I turn the page to find another photo of Tate holding the baby in a front carrier out by the water. I'm in a chair, mouth twisted as if I'm in pain, Dad beside me with a fishing pole. The sky is a perfect blue, and the water reflects its entire canvas. I cover my mouth, shocked at the listless expression on my face, my empty stare at the camera. My hands shake when I turn the page to find another picture of Mirabelle lying across Tate's chest, asleep, and the camera captures only the side of his face because he's staring down at her. I swallow hard, touch the picture. I start flipping the pages faster. Find another one of me kissing her chubby, perfect cheek while she stares at the camera with her big dark-blue eyes. There are more pictures, mostly of Tate and the baby, who grows into a beautiful little, brown-haired girl. The photos make it real and a fairy tale at the same time. And it hurts so damn bad. A thousand bee stings. What happened? I hit the bed with one fist. I want to remember. I want to remember. I want to remember.

There's a sticky note on the last page of the album with my mother's handwriting. *Your baby lived, Claire. You asked Tate to raise her away from you. Her name is Maree and she lives in Whittier with Tate. She doesn't know that you're her mother yet, but she already adores you. Look through the other photo album. Maree made it.*

I open it to pictures of me and a little girl in cat-eye glasses too big for her small heart-shaped face. I touch her face in the picture, longing to remember, and notice a strong resemblance to my mom: dark-blue eyes, wavy hair, a little dimple in her chin just like Dad's. Nose like Tate's. Sorrow sticks to my insides, regret clamps on to my heart, making the air in my bedroom stuffy, claustrophobic.

A sticky note on the last page of the album. *When you're ready, we're waiting for you in the living room. Love, Mom*

I hold the albums to my chest, breathe in, and open the bedroom door. Ruth is at my table. Tate and Mom are on the kitchen stools. Ruth starts to speak. "Alice and Tate both live here—"

I hold up a hand to stop her, look at Tate—tall, handsome. My Tate. "My baby lived?"

He nods.

The strength leaves my legs, and I sink into the couch to keep from falling. I open the album and point to a picture of me and a baby. "What happened?" I croak.

They let Ruth answer. "Mirabelle lived, Claire. They were able to save her, but you couldn't remember her. It upset you every time to learn that, and eventually you asked Tate to raise her without you." Ruth looks at me, and it's in that strong way of hers. The kind that is a beacon of light in the middle of a raging storm. "We tried to convince you otherwise, but it was your decision. You loved her so much. You did what you thought was right for her."

The room spins. I point to the album that Maree made for me. "But she's here now and I know her." I have to swallow because suddenly I've lost my voice, and in a hoarse whisper I add, "And she knows me?"

Tate kneels in front of me, takes my hands in his own, and he is the Tate I remember—older, but with the same kindness that deepens his green eyes. "She doesn't know who you are, Claire, but she's g . . . g-rown to love you anyway. As the person you are right n . . . n-ow, memory loss and all."

"She doesn't know I'm her mother?"

Mom takes a seat on one side of me, Ruth on the other, and Tate kneeling in front of me. "Not yet," he says. "I w . . . w-anted to . . ." His mouth forms an O and I wait. Finally, he says, "I hoped to find the right time." He smiles. "But Maree got to you first."

I flip through the albums again and again, over and over, wishing I could burn the images into my mind, knowing it's a futile wish. My heart grows, pushes against my chest until it fills me with a paralyzing longing for what I can never get back. I stare at a picture of Maree and me by the reindeer. She tilts her head into mine, big grin on her face. My smile is wide and real, and I can see the happy moment reflected in our eyes. "You were everything I wanted," I whisper to the girl in the photo. "Why would I have ever given you up?"

Mom brings my face up with her finger until our eyes lock. Her gaze is steady. "You did it because you love her, Claire. But you're ready to be her mother. It's time. Your father knew it, I know it; Tate, Ruth, even sweet Maree knows it on some level. Now you have to believe it."

"How?" I cry. "How can I be a good mother like this? How can I be anything more than I am now?"

"That's the thing, honey," Mom says. "You don't need to be more. You just need to be you."

I notice Tate has pulled out a tablet and is typing away, Ruth is writing on note cards—*Maree is your daughter. Maree is your daughter.* She scatters them around the apartment like a flower girl.

Their efforts start a tingling in my body and my heart thumps faster. "But how will I remember her, Mom?"

Her face softens and she takes my hands into her own. They are soft and warm, and I am six years old and she is the mom I always wanted. "You'll remember with our help, Claire. We can all be your memory."

CHAPTER THIRTY-THREE

Claire, July, one year later

Summer arrives quietly to Whittier, in bits and pieces—a budding leaf here, a wildflower there—until it's an explosion of new life. The harbor is bustling with activity today. Cruise ships and fishing boats crowd the water while people mill around town, overrun the parking lots. The port is busy with tourists who come to stare at our odd little town and wonder how anyone would ever want to live in one building in the middle of nowhere.

I smile and turn from the window, allowing my attention to drift to the buzzing phone. *Time to wake up your daughter, Maree.*

I stare at the screen, a hand to my cheek, breathing in this knowledge that I have a daughter. It drifts inside me like a feather, tickles my brain, until it lands in a pile of similar feathers, and I am left feeling that this information is not new, even if my heart nearly explodes at the idea of it.

But that's okay. I could read this kind of news for the first time every single day of my life.

I feel a hand on my shoulder and look up, nearly falling out of my chair at the man who smiles down at me. Tate. His black hair is short, with fine bits of gray winding around his temples, and his eyes are that same deep green that makes me weak in the knees.

"G . . . g-ood morning, beautiful," he says and sets a steaming cup of coffee on the tiled coaster on my desk.

"Hi, Tate," I say. A blush heats the tips of my ears. I nervously touch my hair. Have I showered today? I look down to find I'm still wearing pajamas, wish I'd thought to put something nice on, and squirm in my seat, embarrassed by a sudden rush of teenage-like hormones.

"Relax," he says, and leans down, kisses me on the lips, and while it feels new and exhilarating, he kisses me with a comfortableness that must mean he does this quite often. He breaks away but keeps his face close to mine. He smells like pine trees and coffee beans. "We got married this past winter. It was a perfect Alaskan day, gray and foggy, with so much snow we couldn't make it to the reception, so we held it here. You were stunning and our daughter spilled all the flower petals before she made it down the aisle. It was perfect." He hands me a tablet and it's scrolling through pictures that I can guess are from our wedding. Me in a long white dress standing next to a dark-haired girl who looks like a combination of my mother and Tate. He kisses me once more before going into the kitchen, and I hear the sizzle of eggs frying, smell bacon in the air. I press a hand to my cheek, feel my stomach doing cartwheels. I'm married to Tate.

More pictures slide by, and I sip my coffee and watch. There are pictures of me with Mom on a boat with a caption that reads, *Claire and Alice on a fishing expedition.* I smile. She's sober now. Another of me and Tate and Maree standing at the top of Portage Pass Trail. The pictures scroll on and I watch, enjoying every one that shows a full life. Even if I can't recall the details, I think I feel them in the warmth that radiates through my body.

A hand touches my shoulder, squeezes gently. I look up, smile. It's Tate from the pictures. My husband. He hands me a note card. "Maree likes for you to wake her up every morning." The handwriting on the card is even but slightly messy in that familiar kid kind of way. *Hi Mom, please wake me up. This is Maree your daughter I love you.* I stand in front of a closed bedroom door, with the card pressed against my chest, and I smile and breathe in this new life of mine.

I knock and, with my heart in my throat, push open the door.

ACKNOWLEDGMENTS

A few years ago, I watched a documentary on the town of Whittier, and I was struck not by the remoteness of its location, or the harsh weather, or the oddness of a town under one roof, but by a comment from a community member: "We don't always love each other, we don't always get along, but when something awful happens, everyone is going to be there to help you." I thought that was such a poignant reminder that beauty and kindness are found everywhere, even and especially in unlikely places and people.

I couldn't wait to set a story in a town like Whittier.

But this story of love and loss, addiction and recovery, failure and forgiveness would not have happened without the insight of the many people who took the time to speak with me, answer my questions, or be my own personal tour guide. And it is to them and to so many others who are integral parts of the book-writing process that I want to extend my sincere thanks.

To the people of Whittier, especially Anna and Dave, who opened their home, invited me to meals and morning hikes, and made sure I was introduced to everything Whittier, including a late night at the Anchor. Thanks to Theresa for being the first to welcome me to town before I drove through the tunnel for my first time, and Victor, Millie, Becca, and Mathias for your willingness to share your experiences. And thank you to Beverly for singing my favorite song, and to June for a lovely stay at your bed-and-breakfast, where I was treated to stunning views. I tried to maintain as much accuracy as I could in regard to location, weather, environment, and historical data regarding Whittier, but I have taken artistic license in creating a select few fictional locations. I hope you all enjoy the view of Whittier through the eyes of my characters and the lens of this story.

To Dr. Melissa Duff, associate professor in the Department for Hearing and Speech Sciences at Vanderbilt University Medical Center, and to Dr. Nicole Licking and Dr. Veena Mathad for taking the time to answer my questions regarding Claire both over email and phone. It was very important to me that Claire's experience with the world of memory and memory loss was as authentic as possible for someone with anterograde amnesia. Thank you, Dr. Duff, for your work with people who experience this kind of challenge and for the empathy you made sure I brought in developing Claire's character. I hope I got the job done.

To my editor, Chris Werner, who saw what was special about Claire from the very first draft and believed her story was worth telling, even if I still had a few rounds to get there. And to my agent, Jessica Faust, for your optimism, expertise, and honesty and, as always, for your support of writers at all stages of the craft. To the deeply talented Tiffany Yates Martin for yet again walking beside me on the editing journey and deftly guiding this story to levels beyond my expectations. And to Gabe Dumpit, Laura Barrett, Rachel Norfleet, Kellie Osborne, and the entire Lake Union team for shepherding this book to publication. You make it look so easy.

And to all my early readers and critique partners, who see my writing and storytelling at its absolute ugliest, but whose honesty I depend on to create a better story: Sara Miller, Mary Johnson and Elizabeth Richards, Christi Moffat, Nicole Hackett, Taryn Young, Matt Adams, Mindy Pellegrino, Sarah Chase, and Denise Boeding. And to Emery Archer for sharing your love of music and guitar know-how with me.

And to the people who let me live in a made-up world, obsess over characters, travel to far-flung destinations, and love and support me every step of the way—my family. Mom and Dad, for making me believe I could do whatever I set my mind to. Ella, Keira, and Sawyer: my life is infinitely richer because of you. And finally, to Sean, my heart, my best friend, the man who makes me coffee every morning: you are the perfect partner to this wild adventure.

ABOUT THE AUTHOR

Photo © 2018 Eric Weber Studios

Melissa Payne is the bestselling author of *The Secrets of Lost Stones*. For as long as she can remember, Melissa has been telling stories in one form or another—from high school newspaper articles to a graduate thesis to blogging about marriage and motherhood. But she first learned the real importance of storytelling when she worked for a residential and day treatment center for abused and neglected children. There she wrote speeches and letters to raise funds for the children. The truth in those stories was piercing and painful and written to invoke in the reader a call to action: to give, to help, to make a difference. Melissa's love of writing and sharing stories in all forms has endured. She lives in the foothills of the Rocky Mountains with her husband and three children, a friendly mutt, a very loud cat, and the occasional bear. For more information, visit www.melissapayneauthor.com.